The Rosewood Guitar

Jon's Story

Other Books by the Author

Stone Trilogy
The Distant Shore
Under the Same Sun
Song of the Storm
Prequels
Waiting for a Song, Naomi's Story
The Rosewood Guitar: Jon's Story

Coming Soon

Stone Series
Sound of Falling Snow, A Carlsson Christmas, Winter 2015

Sunset Bay Series
written with CW Morgan
The Nobody Girl, Fall 2015

The Rosewood Guitar

Jon's Story

Mariam Kobras

Buddhapuss Ink LLC ❖ Edison NJ

Cover Art *Carried Away* ©2008 Eric G. Thompson
Author Photo by Sarah Fulford
Cover and Book Layout/Design by The Book Team
Editor, MaryChris Bradley
Copyeditor, Andrea H. Curley
Library of Congress Control Number: 2014959321
ISBN 978-1-941523-03-2 (Paperback Original)
First Printing February 2015

To contact the artist Eric G. Thompson or learn more about his works, go to:
www.ericgthompson.com

Buddhapuss Ink LLC and our logos are trademarks of Buddhapuss Ink LLC.
www.buddhapussink.com

For Sarah Fulford and Patsy Boros,
my music people.

Chapter One

THE WORDS WOULDN'T come.

Jon sat staring at the blank sheet of paper on the desk as if he could make them appear magically. Each time he put the pencil to the paper, his mind went empty as if the words, seeing him start to write, would scamper away. He imagined them just outside the window screen, dancing in tune with the raindrops pelting against it, mocking him, mocking his attempt to capture them.

His section of the store was nearly empty. There was one woman standing next to the table of used poetry books, a battered edition of *The Complete Works of Edgar Allan Poe* in her gloved hand. Her coat exuded the musty smell of wet wool; her boots left dirty puddles that carefully avoided the bag standing beside her on the old hardwood floor.

From where Jon sat, he could see Steve guiding another customer toward the cookbook section. Jenny, a pen between her fingers, was watching the traffic jam outside from her position behind the counter. The lamp above her threw golden highlights on her strawberry-blond hair, and that made Jon smile. She was like a bright-yellow flower in the dark melancholy of a November afternoon.

His eyes drifted back to the empty piece of paper.

"The River," he wrote at the top. He wrote it carefully, in slow, neat letters, in his best handwriting, the beautiful, old-fashioned copperplate his father had taught him. The melody was right there. He'd been humming it on his way to work, first while walking to the subway station and then on the train while he watched the lights in the tunnel flit by, and then again on his short walk from the Union Square stop to the bookstore. Two blocks in the bitter November rain, his collar turned up and his hands deep in the pockets of his coat, he walked quickly, the wordless song running through his brain.

Mr. Brown had glanced up and given him a sharp look when

1

he walked in, mumbling that he was late again and to please take an earlier train next time, but Jon had ignored him. Falling asleep last night, on that threshold between being awake and drifting off into dreams, he'd found the perfect words. He remembered feeling elated, knowing they were perfect, and he'd tried to get up and write them down; but even while he was thinking that, he'd fallen asleep. In the morning they'd been gone, no more than a memory, like an echo in a hallway.

Shaving, he'd racked his brain, trying to catch them; but all he could recall was the word *along* because it rhymed so nicely with *song*. The rest was gone.

Now, sitting at his help desk in the store, watching the woman with the Poe book, he wondered if he'd ever make it, if he'd ever be a good enough songwriter for the big stage when he couldn't even remember his own lyrics.

Jenny was looking his way. She'd put down the pencil and was gesturing at him furtively, rolling her eyes. He knew what that meant. Quickly he pushed the sheet under a couple of store fliers and sat up straight.

"Well, Jon," Mr. Brown said from behind him, "don't you think you should go over and ask the lady if she needs help?"

"I've been watching her," Jon replied. "She's been holding that book for ten minutes. Maybe she just wants to find a passage or something."

Bending down so he could whisper, Mr. Brown offered, "And since when are we a library, Mr. Stone? If she wants to read that book she should buy it, shouldn't she?"

Jon rose from his seat. "Yes, sir."

"You were daydreaming again, I'm guessing."

Jon felt the prickle of sweat on his back. "Not really, sir. But it's a very quiet day."

Mr. Brown turned to look toward the windows and the shop entrance. "Yes, that's true. A miserable, dreary day. Nobody wants to be outside, not even in New York." He raised his finger with a glare at Jon. "But mark my words, Jon. It's only one week until Thanksgiving. Even if today is slow, things will change soon! The holiday season is almost here!"

"Yes, sir," Jon repeated. He could see it already: shoppers laden with bags and parcels pushing through the narrow aisles of the store, upsetting Mr. Brown's careful piles of books; and he would have to clamber after them to pick up the fallen copies, climb up ladders to fetch desired titles, and carry baskets back to the counter, smiling all the while.

"I need to leave a little early tonight," he said just as Mr. Brown was about to walk away. "I have an appointment."

"And what might that be, young Mr. Stone?" Mr. Brown straightened the red bow tie he was wearing. It clashed with his greenish tweed jacket; but over the past months Jon had discovered that his boss had a set schedule for his bow ties, and this week was red. While Jon was still wondering if it was because Christmas was approaching, Mr. Brown asked, "Has it anything to do with that guitar lying on top of your locker?"

Jon's blood rushed straight to his ears. "Yes, sir." He didn't know how to say it. "I'm playing tonight. I have a gig." Spoken out loud, it sounded preposterous.

"A gig?" Mr. Brown's brows vanished under the unruly hair hanging down over his forehead. "You mean you're giving a concert!"

Jon pulled up his shoulders. "Not quite, Mr. Brown. It's just me, and my guitar, and a few of my songs. 'Concert' sounds a bit grand."

"Well."

The woman with the Poe book was coming toward them, leaving a trail of heart-shaped footprints. "Excuse me," she said, "I wonder if there's an illustrated complete Poe edition?"

Mr. Brown gestured to Jon, and Jon sighed. "Follow me, please," he said.

> *Take me down to the river, let me listen to its song.*
> *Can't you hear the river's heartbeat,*
> *It's the place where I belong."*

"And the other one, right next to it?" The woman pointed, and Jon reached up to get the book she meant. Once in his hand, he realized it was a beautiful edition, the violet linen cover a bit faded but the gold letters on it still intact.

"I don't think it has illustrations." He handed it to her and climbed down the ladder.

They were in one of the musty aisles between high book shelves, barely wide enough to hold two people.

"The writing on the cover is nice." Jon pointed at the golden letters. "Art Deco, very pretty."

Again the words ran through his head, making him forget his customer for a moment. He could almost hear the drums: heavy, insistent, like a beating heart.

"… And that Julia Child cookbook."

Perplexed, Jon looked at her. "Do you know a word that rhymes with *heartbeat*?"

The woman blinked. "*Neat? Fleet?*" She tilted her head, intrigued. "*Greet* or *meet? Feet?*"

"*Feet*," Jon repeated slowly. "Yes, *feet*. Thank you."

"Are you a poet then? Seems fitting, since you work in the poetry department." She clamped the book under her arm and followed when he pointed toward the cookbook section.

"Suzanne will help you with the Julia Child. She knows everything about cookbooks."

Mr. Brown was nowhere in sight, so Jon returned to his desk and pulled out the sheet of paper again to write down the words that had popped into his mind.

"*Feet*," he mumbled to himself. "Meet my feet. Meet and greet my feet." Again the rhyme eluded him, despite the help he'd gotten. He could see the image he wanted to paint, could almost hear the song dancing around him; and then it was gone again, like a wisp of fog.

> *All my life I have been waiting for this moment to appear.*
> *River's heartbeat, river calling, that is all I came to hear.*

There it was, and with it the insistent tap of the snare, a slap bass, and the bass drum like the pulse of the song.

Jon's hand trembled a bit as he wrote down the first verse, then the second, and then the chorus. Humming it under his breath, he felt for flaws in the rhythm; but there weren't any really bad kinks, nothing he wouldn't be able to cheat away when he sang it.

"The River." Jon tasted the title on his lips. It pleased him, made him smile, and made him want to perform it. He glanced at his watch. It was nearly seven, almost time to leave. He'd have to walk all the way to Bleecker Street. It wasn't that far, no worse than the stretch he walked each day from home to the subway station; but it was still drizzling, and he was worried about his guitar.

With one last look in Jenny's direction, he got up and made his way back to the locker room. His old, battered leather jacket hung near the heater where he had put it to dry when he came in. The guitar case was still on top of his locker.

Jon brought it down and opened it. The instrument inside was simple, a well-used, basic pinewood guitar, its surface black lacquer, its belt a colorful band that his parents had brought back for him from a vacation in Mexico. It was quite frayed, and he had asked his mother a number of times to stitch it back together. She'd done it, complaining about the chore, but Jon refused to replace it. It was his good luck charm, and he wanted to feel it on his shoulder when he played, as if it was his mother's hand, his father's smile of approval, something that would keep him grounded, feeling loved.

His mother, Helen, had promised to come to his gig tonight even though she hated clubs and their strict drinking rules. She could never, she kept telling him, deal with two drinks, and she hated the waste of having to pay for them and not drink them.

Jon had offered to pay for her; but she had scoffed at him, saying he could hardly afford the subway, and where, please, was he going to come up with the money for two cocktails?

And as she said it, she had fished a fifty-dollar bill out of her wallet and pressed it into his hand.

"You need to go back and finish college, Jon," she had told him. "Go get your degree, and a good job. You know you could have a decent place by now and be making a good income. You're wasting your life away working part-time at that bookstore and trying to become a star."

"I don't want to be a star, Mother," he'd replied, the money burning in his palm. "All I want is to perform my music and earn enough to make a living doing it. I don't need the Hollywood, or fame." It was a lie, and she knew it.

"Yes, you do, Jon. You want it so badly, it's like a tattoo on your forehead." Helen had looked at him with sad eyes, and it had nearly broken his heart. "So many want to make that dream come true. And so few succeed. I just wish you weren't one of them! Look at you! Twenty-four years old and not a penny to your name!"

JON looked in the mirror inside his locker.

His hair needed to be cut badly. He was wearing it like all other young men, longish, nearly touching his shoulders; but it looked straggly and unkempt now. The plain, white cotton shirt he was wearing was his best, but it was just that: a white shirt. He looked like a member of a church choir and not at all like an up-and-coming rock star.

Just as he was zipping up his jacket, Jenny came in. She stopped in the doorway, scrutinizing him. "You're going onstage in your best shirt? You'll ruin it!"

"Yeah." Just what he needed, another woman telling him how to lead his life. A deep crease appeared between his eyes, and he pulled up his eyebrows to make it go away. "Don't have another one now; it'll have to be this one."

He tried to walk past her, the guitar case slung over his back, but Jenny stepped in his way. Rising onto her toes, holding on to the lapels of his jacket, she planted a kiss on his lips. "Good luck, Jon. I wish I could come along, but my shift isn't over until ten. Will you come straight home? Promise?"

Her hopeful tone made Jon sigh. "Not right away but pretty soon," he replied, and tried to make it sound gentle enough. "My mom will be there, and I'll have to escort her home first. But then I'll come home. I promise."

She took it very well. There was only a tiny tightening of her lips,

6

but her eyes smiled at him in blue brightness. "Well then! I'll stay up for you! Sing your heart out, Mr. Stone!"

Jon left the bookstore and stood on the corner of Broadway and Twelfth, breathing in the cold, wet air of a late fall evening.

He could hear the hum of the city, hear it intermingle with the music running in his head, whispering words to him and wrapping its love around him as he turned south toward Bleecker Street.

Chapter Two

HE'D BEEN TOLD to use the back entrance, so Jon made his way through the alley at the side of the building. Plastic bags filled with garbage had been dumped there; he had to tread around them and their spilled contents carefully. Every step he made brought forth an ominous scrabbling and squeaking, and a couple of times the flitting shadow of a small animal. It stank. The rain itself seemed to smell of waste and refuse, of rotten food and other, even viler stuff, every single raindrop its own flacon of stench.

Jon stopped outside the metal door with the single, dim light over it and tried to shake off the smell before he pulled it open.

A new mixture of aromas greeted him: cigarette smoke; stale beer; the bitter, stony smell of toilets that weren't often cleaned; and underlying it all, the sickly sweet fume of weed. Someone had used this dingy corridor for a time-out.

Music and bar noises filled the space: someone was playing the piano, fast, jazzy melodies, creating a rhythm without any percussion at all, fingers dancing over the keys in a way that made Jon's want to dance and his feet tap. He recognized the style, and it made him grin. Sean, that was Sean making that piano sing and laugh. No one played like Sean; no one else could make it sound so effortless.

Another door opened, and the manager of the club appeared. The fat cigar clamped between his lips added to the miasma of odors, making Jon feel queasy and slightly dizzy. The man was dressed in an abysmally tasteless shirt, the orange and blue stripes accentuating his rotund belly and highlighting the curls of black hair on his chest, visible above the three top buttons he'd left open.

"Oh, there you are," he said in place of a greeting. "We've been waiting for you. You'll have to play the whole evening; are you up to that? The other act called in sick, and we don't have anyone else to replace her. So tell me now: Do you have enough songs under your belt to perform for two hours?"

Blood rushed into Jon's ears, making him feel faint. Incongruously, his first thought was the white shirt and what it would look like after two hours of playing, and then he remembered his mother, whom he'd promised that it was only a brief stint, no more than five songs at the most, and yes, she'd be home in plenty of time to get enough sleep.

"Easily," Jon replied, shifting his guitar from his back into his hands. "No problem. Thanks for the opportunity, Bob."

Bob pushed the cigar from one corner of his mouth to the other. "Yeah." He didn't sound convinced. "Are you sure? Because I really don't want to be stranded without music. You don't look like you could hold anyone's attention for more than ten seconds."

Jon grinned. "Don't worry. If I run out of songs I can always do some Beach Boys hits. Or Elvis."

"And no frigging ballads, you understand? This isn't a romantic dinner place. People who come here want to hear rock." Pointing toward a door with a faded peace sign on it, Bob added, "There's the dressing room. Well, you know your way around, don't you? You'll have to share it with the pianist and the guy who just came off the stage. He's in there right now, nursing his battered ego. People were throwing their pretzels at him. Hope they won't throw their beer at *you* tonight, my boy." Muttering evil words about kids who lacked talent or guts, he wandered away toward the noise and light, leaving Jon to find his own way.

THE so-called dressing room was nothing more than a storage room with two chairs, a dirty mirror, and a rickety table with a half-empty bottle of Coke on it. There was no window, no room to store his guitar case, and no heater to dry his soaked jacket.

A man was stretched out on one of the chairs, his legs crossed, and a beer held between his hands, resting on his stomach.

"Hey," Jon said, and received a nod in return.

The stranger watched silently as Jon brought out his instrument and began tuning it, how he sorted his music, and played a few bars to loosen the stiff, cold muscles in his fingers, then sang a couple of verses to warm up his voice. Irritated by the stoic scrutiny, Jon started the hard, fast, opening lines of "The River," and promptly dropped his pick into the resonance hole of the guitar. Furious at himself, he started searching for another one even though he was quite sure he hadn't brought any.

"Here." The stranger was holding out a pick to him. It wasn't just a plain plastic one like his either but was made from wood, and it fit between his fingers like a fingerprint.

"Rosewood," the man said, and a crooked grin made his face turn handsome. "I always use rosewood picks."

He reached behind him to his guitar case and brought out his own instrument. It shone even in the dull light, its wood as warm and rich as beaten copper, as beautiful as a red-haired girl. "My lover. Koa wood, custom-made." His blue eyes sparkled at Jon. "I used to be a Wall Street banker; made a mint. But it didn't fill the heart, if you know what I mean. The name is Jones." He held out his hand, and Jon took it. "Pleased to meet you."

"Bob said it didn't go too well for you?" Jon let the pick glide over the strings. It made a totally different sound: more mellow, gentler than his old one.

Jones shrugged. "I'm not a singer. They wanted someone to sing to them. I only play the guitar. Got too boring for them, I guess. There's a really good piano player out there though. Never got a chance to talk to him; a pity." He took another swig of his beer. "Yeah, well, tonight didn't go so well. What I need is a band. Won't get anywhere on my own, I'm afraid. Or I need to find a job as a studio musician. Guess I'll move to LA soon. That's where the music is created these days."

A tiny something blossomed in Jon. It was as if magic words had been spoken, as if a window in his soul had just cracked open, letting in a sliver of bright light; and the echo of that magic word was still humming in him.

"LA?" he repeated softly. "You want to go to LA? Leave everything behind and take such a daring step?"

Again Jones grinned. "Hell, yeah! You either do it or you don't. If you want to get somewhere you have to commit, isn't that right, or you'll stay a dreamer with a temp job your whole life and end up playing under a tree in Union Square. I want a better life than that, and with the music, please. You can't make a career in music in New York right now. The labels are all out in California these days."

"And what if you don't make it?" Jon's heart filled with fear, but also with an exhilaration he hadn't felt in a long time.

With a twitch of his shoulders, Jones packed up his guitar. "The weather is better in LA. That's one thing that will always be true. I'd rather wait tables in the sun than freeze my ass off in a New York winter." Rising, he picked up a ragged coat and his guitar case. "See ya, kiddo. Break a leg out there." And vanished through the doorway like a desperado going on his last ride.

Jon stood up and gathered his music. He took a deep breath and let it flow out slowly, let it resonate in his chest and expand his lungs, let it pass his vocal cords like a gentle massage and his lips like a breeze. His eyes closed, he took another one and exhaled through his nose, humming all the while. The one thing he really wanted was a cigarette, but he had learned by now that smoking just before singing would only cost him at least two songs until his voice was clear again.

A girl appeared in the door. "Two minutes," she announced, and vanished.

It was time. Jon followed her out into the bar.

The room was nearly dark, with three stark-white beams pointed at the small, wooden stage. There was a microphone in a stand, a stool, and that was it. They hadn't even provided a glass of water or a towel, nothing. On the floor just below the stage Jon could see the piano pushed up against the wall and Sean sitting on the bench in front of it. A cigarette was hanging from his lips, and his longish, curly hair was hanging to his thin shoulders. He was in a faded t-shirt that left his thin arms bare, showing a tattoo of a wilted rose.

"Hey, Jon," he mumbled when Jon walked past him, and nodded, giving him a friendly, encouraging smile. Jon returned it, but his mind was already away, already tuning in on his music, his hands twitching with the tune he would be strumming soon. The guitar hanging on its strap, the rosewood pick securely between his fingers, he adjusted the microphone, blinked into the glare of the stage lights, and said, "Ladies and gentlemen, I am Jon Stone."

He began to play. His eyes closed, he let the music take him, ignoring the sound of voices and clinking glasses, of laughter and scraping chairs.

Clear and strong the lyrics flew from his lips; he sang them fearlessly, riding the wind of his creation with joy and conviction.

The applause when he finished his first song was good, enthusiastic, and he launched into the next one without even waiting for them to stop. The stool pushed out of his way, Jon stood and moved with the rhythm of the music.

It didn't take long. One verse and half-way into the chorus they were clapping along; the room was on its feet.

He tried not to smile and to concentrate, but Jon knew he had them on his side now, had them captured; and for a heartbeat it made him wonder how he did it, how it could happen that these strangers resonated with his compositions and enjoyed them instantly.

He'd seen it happen before, even when he played on the streets on a Saturday afternoon. For him they would stop and listen, and even throw money into his open guitar case.

AFTER three songs he needed a break for a sip of water. His mouth was dry, his tongue sticking to his teeth.

"I need a drink," Jon said into the microphone. "So you're getting a potty break. Don't go too far; I'll be back in ten seconds. Then we'll rock this place!" He paused for the length of a breath and then added, delivering it in his best stage voice, letting it go gravelly and dark, "I have a couple of ballads in my stash. If you want your ladies to swoon a bit, this is your chance, guys!" It earned him cheers and laughter.

The man at the piano turned when Jon got back from the bar. Too hyped, too thirsty, Jon took three big gulps of the icy water before he greeted him properly.

"Hey, Sean," he said, trying to keep his voice down to soothe it a bit. "Good to see you."

Sean's lips twitched. "Any new songs?"

"Yeah. One. But it's not finished; it's not… the lyrics. The lyrics are a bitch." He sighed. "Maybe I should stop trying for the lyrics. Maybe I should just compose, write movie sound tracks, whatever." He pulled the sheets from his pocket and handed them over.

"Nah, you're doing fine." Sean slapped his shoulder after reading the words, humming the tune. "You're lazy, that's all. You don't want to bother your head with the lyrics. But you're good at them, you know. Not everything can be as easy as writing music, my friend."

They'd played together, Jon and Sean. They knew they were good together: easy, friendly. They understood each other. For Jon's taste, Sean understood him too well.

Back on the stage, Jon picked up his guitar. One string was slightly out of tune, and he adjusted it. He reached for the new pick and held it between his thumb and index finger, gently rubbing the smooth surface. It seemed as if the moment this little sliver of wood had come to him his luck had woken, raised its head, and looked around curiously.

Sean was watching him, waiting for his cue, and Jon nodded, offering him the intro.

It was "The River."

Surprise washed over Jon. He fumbled for the words, trying to remember them, panicking for a second. Sean was smiling, and Jon, throwing all caution to the wind, sang.

Chapter Three

"YOU NEED A band," Bob told him when Jon left the stage after a third encore, by now without Sean playing along. They had exhausted all the sheet music, and still the audience had called for more. Even now, after he'd told them he was out of songs and breath, they didn't leave and ordered more drinks as if hoping he'd change his mind.

Bob was counting out Jon's money. When he reached the amount promised earlier, he hesitated a moment, then added another fifty dollars.

"I have a feeling I won't see you here much anymore, Jon. When you first showed up, I never thought you'd have the stamina to keep going. You seemed like such a bookish, shy kid. And look at you now, two years later. You're still up there, and hungrier than ever."

"Yeah." Jon reached for another bottle of water and wiped his brow with the back of his hand. He wished he'd thought to bring a sweater. His shirt was soaked, and he was freezing in the draft from the entrance. Sean was still sitting at the piano, playing soft melodies, more to himself than to any listeners.

"I can see you signing a record deal soon." Bob's words, those magic words he wanted to hear more than anything else, found their way to Jon's exhausted brain. "Someday soon you'll play in a club, and the right people will be there, and you'll be lost to us."

"Nah, I won't be lost." His voice was rough from singing. "I promise, Bob. Even if that happens, even if I do make it, I promise I'll come back for a gig or two."

Bob's loud laugh made some of the guests turn in their direction. "Like hell you will. You'll live in a Malibu mansion and own a penthouse on Fifth, drive a Jag, and have the prettiest girl in Hollywood as your lover. Your shows at the Greek Theatre will be sold out, and you'll forget there ever was a club on Bleecker Street."

A wave of dizziness washed over Jon at those words, a yearning so strong that he had to grip the edge of the counter.

He could see it, could paint the picture in his mind: walks along a beach in the bronze light of a California sunset, and beside him, walking with him, a girl with flowing black hair, and in her hands she was holding seashells that she had gathered from the surf; a house by the sea, a big house with a big yard, really more a park than a garden, with trees and hidden nooks where he could sit and write; and in the garage, a black Porsche, a classy, elegant car. Nothing showy and flimsy like a Ferrari—he wanted class.

"I don't know," he said out loud. "Lately I've been thinking that I'm getting too old to be dreaming of success. Maybe my mother is right, and I should go back to school and finish my degree." It was just like always. The moment the glow of the performance faded he felt lonelier, emptier than before, as if he was alive only when he was playing and singing to an audience and the rest of his life was a dream. He needed the reassurance, the magic words.

"That would be an incredible waste of outstanding talent, Jon," Bob replied while he stuffed the rest of the bills back into his pocket. "You shouldn't even think of giving up." He picked up the grubby calendar from where he kept it next to the whiskey bottles. "Tell you what; I have a late-night slot open for next Friday. How do you feel about playing from midnight till two in the morning? Are you up to that?"

"Yeah!" The offer made Jon feel better instantly. "But only if Sean is free and can come too." He looked around, trying to find him. Sean was talking to someone who was leaning on the piano, a man his own age in an ill-fitting gray suit. The curls on his round head seemed to stand up in every direction and swayed gently every time he moved.

"I'll just go over and talk to him." Jon pointed in their direction. "I really liked what he did tonight."

"So did I," Bob agreed. "But you still need a band. You need proper backing, Jon." He held on to Jon's sleeve. "Just you and your guitar, that's not your style. You need a band, and a big one. And backup singers. Your songs are crying for more music."

Jon choked a little on the bitter taste in his throat. "I know. When I write them, I always hear an orchestra playing. Maybe someday."

BEFORE he could even open his mouth to ask Sean, the stranger stretched out his hand. "My name is Sal. I'd like to manage you."

Jon gazed down at the hand. "I can't afford a manager."

"You don't pay your manager, Jon." Sal showed his teeth in a grin that resembled a shark. "A manager sells you and gets his percentages from that."

That made Jon laugh. "I was just going to share tonight's pay with Sean. There won't be anything left over for you, manager or not." Handing Sean the fifty-dollar bill, he added thoughtfully, "And there isn't anything to manage. I don't have anything. No record deal, no scheduled performances, not even a band. Thanks for the offer though."

"You have a pianist," Sean threw in with a smile. "That's a start, isn't it?"

"I do." Again Jon felt dizzy. He'd left work and walked through the New York streets in the rainy darkness, and while he'd trudged along he'd let his mind wander and dream; and it had presented a scenario much like this one: someday, some night after a gig, someone would walk up to him and offer him a record deal. Out of the blue, when he least expected it, this miracle would happen, and everything would change. Everything.

And here he was now, with Sean and this funny stranger, both looking at him expectantly.

"I can't pay you!" Jon repeated, only this time directed at Sean. "I don't even make enough to feed my own sorry face."

"You need a record deal." The magic words, dropped so casually by Sal, still leaning on the piano but now with a bowl of peanuts in one hand, tossing one nut after the other into his mouth without dropping them and talking at the same time. "You need a record deal, and you need to move to LA. No decent record deals in New York."

Those words reminded him of the guitar player, Jones, who'd said much the same thing to him earlier. The guitar pick was in his jeans pocket. Miraculously, he hadn't dropped it during his entire performance, not once, and that was saying something. Jon wished he'd asked Jones for a phone number, address, anything. But he'd been like a person in a fairy tale, there at the right moment and long gone when the hero of the story noticed the impact of his brief appearance.

"Yes," Jon said. There was little else to say. Sal was right.

"So… let me work for you." Sal set down the bowl and stopped chewing, as if it had been no more than an act to show how relaxed and easy he was about this harebrained scheme, and produced a business card from an inside pocket of his jacket. "Sal. My name is Sal Rosenberg. I'm not from New York, if you care to know. I'm Las Vegas born and bred, and that should tell you something. I'm not scared of a risky gamble. But I don't think you're one."

From where he was standing, Jon could see his mother, patiently waiting for him to finish, an empty wine glass on the table before her. She had come alone, again. The rest of his family didn't want anything to do with his folly. They were realistic people, doctors and teachers, and had little time for the grandeur of his dreams.

"Why ever not." The words were out of his mouth before he could even think them. "What the hell, why ever not. If you feel you want to manage me, whatever that means, go right ahead and manage. It's not as if I have anything to lose. It's not as if somewhere in the whole wide world someone is waving a contract at me and I only need to notice."

"That came out a little bitter," Sal commented, and returned to his peanuts. "I sincerely hope that's not the way you really feel, because it would be an incredible waste of energy. You know you have a long road ahead of you, don't you. A long road to becoming an icon in the rock music world. You will have your star on the Hollywood Walk of Fame, and you will stand on the stage at the Grammy Awards and hold your trophy. Only it may take a few years to get there." He wiped his hand on his trousers before he clapped Jon on the shoulder. "And your journey begins today. Today everything changes, young Master Stone. Today you've jumped on the wagon that will take you to fame!"

This speech made Jon think of the Wizard of Oz. He could see this man, Sal, hiding away in the ugly castle and speaking through amplifiers, showing his face only through projectors and mirrors, and all because he was a master dazzler.

"I'm going to take my mother home now." The card was in his hands. It had Sal's name on it, an LA address, and a phone number. Jon had no idea what to do with it.

"Meet me for lunch tomorrow," Sal said. "We need to talk. You, and Sean too, if he's a member of your band now. Are you?" With the speed of a bird, Sal turned to Sean. "Are you a member of Mr. Stone's band? Or let's say, the kernel of his band?"

Again Sean smiled that smile that was as fine and gentle as a hand-drawn treble clef. "If he wants me, I'm in. That future you're envisioning, Sal. I can see that too. His music is outstanding. Where do you want to meet for lunch?"

Sal sank his fists into his trouser pockets. "Well, we aren't rich enough for the Russian Tea Room yet. Let's meet at my favorite pizza place in Little Italy for now. Lunch is on me. Once you've made us wealthy and famous, Jon, you can take us to other places." He named a restaurant that Jon knew quite well. Nodding a farewell to them, he returned to Bob.

"That guitar player who had the slot before me, Bob," he said.

Bob nodded. "Yeah. What about him?"

"Do you have his phone number?"

"Turns out I do." Bob narrowed his eyes at Jon. "Why are you asking?"

"Nothing. I have something that belongs to him, and I want to return it. He loaned me a guitar pick." To prove his point, Jon brought it out and held it up. "It's a special pick. It's magical. And I think he might need it back."

"And did the magic work for you?" Bob asked, scribbling a phone number on a scrap of paper and handing it to Jon.

"It might have." His glance wandered back to where Sean and Sal were still talking to each other. Sean, with a laugh, turned back to the piano and began to play, his narrow shoulders moving in the rhythm of the music.

Again it was "The River," and Sean was whipping it through a hard, rocking version, a version that made Jon think of a steamy jungle in the middle of the night and the river a wide band of molasses under mysterious, silver moonlight. His fingers itched; sweat gathered in his palms. He wanted the feel of the microphone in his hand, the weight of the guitar around his neck, the vibration of the stage floor as the bass drum rolled out the beat.

He wanted to feel the music stream through him more than anything else, more than hearing it played, more than breathing, more than living itself.

Chapter Four

JENNY HAD FALLEN asleep on the couch. Curled up under the quilt, just a few strands of hair and the tip of her nose were visible, she reminded him of a kitten. She had been reading; a book lay on the floor where she had dropped it, a couple of pages crumpled, the dust cover flipped off. It was a cookbook by a famous TV cook Jon knew she adored. The price sticker from the store was still on it, which made him wonder if she had borrowed it. Returning it would be hard now with the damaged pages.

Carefully Jon put down his guitar. He removed the money from his pocket and put it on the table, pleased that all of it was still there, that he hadn't given in to the temptation of a burger and fries before coming home. His mother had treated them to a cab, all the way from the club to her home, even offered to pay the driver to take him to his apartment; but there his pride had reared its head, and he had gracefully refused.

A walk, he said, would do him good after hours of singing and playing in a room full of smoke and stale air, and it wasn't even a complete lie.

He'd trudged through the drizzle, along the silent streets, until he reached Atlantic Avenue and the building where he and Jenny lived above her father's store. Up three flights, down a narrow hallway, and he was home. It had cost his pride a lot to accept the offer of this studio apartment when he and Jenny had decided to move in together.

He'd hesitated before opening the door, shaking off the elation of the evening, the glimmer of a breakthrough, the ghost of hope. It was too early. Nothing was settled yet. He didn't even know if this guy Sal would show up the next day, if all this had just been a joke or a figment of his overheated imagination.

Silently, in his stocking feet, Jon went into the kitchen niche to fill the kettle. While the water heated, he stood, gazing out the window. If he opened it and reached out, he'd be able to touch the wall of the neighboring building. Only the fire ladder separated them. No sun ever lit this spot of the little studio. Jenny had given up on growing herbs or flowers on the windowsill. One last, withered cactus remained, defying the dimness.

Jon opened the fridge. There wasn't a lot inside: a few slices of bologna and a corner of cheese, some carrots, three eggs, and a nearly empty carton of milk. A bag of bread sat on the counter, next to it a butter dish with a tiny morsel left inside. His stomach rumbled. Eggs, bologna, and butter…everything he needed for a decent omelet; but that would leave them without anything for breakfast.

"You're home!"

He hadn't heard her. She looked so cute wrapped in the quilt, her hair a mess, and the thick woolen socks slipping down on her ankles. His mother had made them for him, but Jenny had stolen them the moment he'd brought them home, saying they were perfect for snuggly evenings on the couch, and he wouldn't wear them anyway. Which was true. Jon couldn't imagine a time or place where he wanted to be caught in hand-knit socks.

"Yeah, just got here." There was no coffee left, so he opted for tea.

With a yawn, Jenny came over and sat on the small table, her feet on the only chair. "So how did it go?" She picked up a flier from a new pizza joint and studied it.

"It went really well! Bob was so pleased he paid me an extra fifty bucks." The water was boiling. Jon poured it into their mugs, right onto the tea bags inside them, watching how it spread over the thin paper in an amorphous pattern.

"Really?" That news made her sit up straight. "That's great, Jon! That means we can actually pay my dad some rent!"

"Nah." He handed her one of the mugs. "I gave it to Sean. You know, the piano player. God, that man is good! I hope I can get him to play in my band." The look on her face stopped him. "The rest is on the table."

"You gave your money away? You gave it away, Jon, when we could have shown Dad that we're at last able to afford to pay him some rent?" Her hands shook, making her spill some of the tea on the quilt.

Jon raised his brows at her. "Yes, I gave it away. He accompanied me all evening long, and he was damn good at it too. He deserved to be paid."

"But did you ask him to? Did you ask him to play for you, Jon?" She put down the tea to wipe her hand on her pajama pants. "We can't afford to give money away!"

"I didn't ask; he offered. And I took the offer. And paid him. That's the decent thing to do, Jenny. It was a great night, and I was glad Sean was there."

"Sean." The way she said it, it sounded like a curse, like something she had to spit out to clear her chest. "Sean. Is he another dreamer like you, another man who spends his life running after a useless dream?"

There it was again, the ugly beast of her discontent.

Jon turned his back on her. "I can't understand why you won't see this, Jen. It's only a matter of time until I get my chance. I have to keep going, have to take my music out there and knock on as many doors as I can, but eventually I will be a success. I know I'm good enough to make a career of it, dammit. Why can't you have some faith?"

"Because, Jon, I live in the real world. I don't dream of being a rock star, or a writer, or a famous singer, or whatever. My dreams are realistic, and in the here and now. I want my own house, a family, children. A husband who can support us, someone with a regular job and a decent income."

Jon could hear her slipping off the table, but he managed not to steal a glance at her legs.

"Jon." Her voice was right behind him, right behind his back. "Jon, please. We're not high school kids anymore. We're twenty-four! We should start leading a normal life! Can't you go back to school and finish your degree? You did so well there. You could go into real estate, or work for an insurance company, and we'd be well off! We could have kids. A car. And go on vacations. Please?"

In a moment she would slide her arms around him and lay her

head on his shoulder; he knew it. Her warmth would wrap around him, and he would melt and turn into her embrace. He'd say something comforting, promise to think about it, tell her to be patient for just a bit longer and if it didn't work out by spring…

"I met a manager today," Jon said instead. "A real manager. And I'm going to see him for lunch tomorrow. He thinks I should move to LA. He believes I have the potential to make it."

"Make it." Coming from her lips, spoken with that inflection, it sounded like a mocking echo. "Make what, Jon? Do you really think you'll be a superstar someday? Some sort of musical demigod featured on the title page of *Rolling Stone*? Do you know what it takes to get there? Do you realize how lucky you must be?"

"I know what it takes to get there, believe me." He could feel it. He could feel all the labor and doubt, the fear and despair, and the moments of exhilaration, feel the entire bouquet of emotions wrapped in a tight wreath around his heart. "I know what it takes, and I have it. I have the guts, the patience and the stamina. I will get there, Jenny. I know I will because it's the only thing that makes sense to me. It's where I belong."

"Oh, look at you." Bitterness crept into her voice. "All right then, Jon Stone, rock star. You do that. You follow that path. But I warn you; it will be a long, lonely road." Jenny let go of him and, gathering the quilt around her like a regal cape, returned to the couch. Her eyes came to rest on the crumpled bills Jon had dropped on the table. "That and what I'm making won't even buy us enough food to last till the end of the month. Look at us, Jon! We have nothing! We live in a furnished studio on a noisy street in Brooklyn, and we can only do that because the building belongs to my family. The only decent window faces out on the street, which means we can't open it because of the noise; and it never gets really warm up here in winter either. How much longer do you want to live like this?"

Jon brought her the discarded mug, but she shook her head and hid her hands under the quilt.

"I'm telling you," he repeated gently, "I'm meeting Sal and Sean for lunch tomorrow. Let's see what Sal has to say about moving to

LA. Wouldn't you like that, baby? Wouldn't you like to live in California, in the sun? Or... or... we could find a decent place right here, and I'll just go to Los Angeles when I have to." He tried to sound encouraging, bring some spark back into her lovely blue eyes, only Jenny wouldn't even look at him; and to be honest, he'd been ready to slap his own wayward mouth for making that suggestion. No, there would be no Brooklyn home for them. He wanted Los Angeles, he wanted the California sun, he wanted to wake up to the sound of surf and whispering palm trees. He wanted out so badly that his heart hurt at the thought.

"Mr. Brown offered me a promotion today," she said. "He wants me to work in management. He wants me to go back to school part-time and get my degree, and then work in management. And I want to do it." Her head came up. "I'm going to do this, Jon. This is something tangible, something with a certain future. If I work hard and get my degree, I might end up owning a bookstore some-day. Or at least running one. That is a realistic dream, not like your music thing."

Very slowly, very softly, anger was forming in Jon's chest. It was like a swirl of mist, starting very diffuse and feathery, and getting denser with every breath he took.

"Ever since I was a kid," Jon replied, his voice calm and collected, "I've had this one dream: One day I'll stand on the stage of the Greek Theatre, a custom rosewood guitar in my hands, my band playing behind me, and I'll sing my own songs to an audience of thousands. They'd come from all over to see me, to hear my music, and every single one of them would know my name. They'd know me so well that they would sing along with me, hum my melodies, wait for a special song they liked best."

Jenny laughed, which made him nod and go on. "And yes, they'd know my face because it was on the cover of *Rolling Stone*." His finger came up, pointing at the guitar case in the corner of the room. "If every single year just one songwriter in the whole wide world can do this, then why shouldn't it be me? If only one single singer makes it to fame in any given year, why not me? Who says this lottery will pass me by? I'm not going to take the risk of not trying, Jenny. I will try. And I'm willing to work until I bleed. So why should I give this up? Because you want a house and a car?"

"Well, yes, because I want a house and a car." The words came out in a brittle, shivering tone. Jon knew she was holding back the tears, but he couldn't make himself care. "Because I want a stable life, with you in it, as my husband, as the father of my children. Look at me! I'm twenty-four, and I have nothing!"

The tea was getting cold. Jon drank it in one big gulp and set down the mug.

"You have everything, Jenny," he answered sadly. "You have me. And if you loved me, you'd believe in me. You know I do make things happen."

"Well, for a start you could make the full fridge happen," was her bitter reply, "because I really could do with some decent food, and I'm out of excuses to go eat with my parents."

Chapter Five

SHE DIDN'T WANT to make love.

Once they were in bed, Jenny turned her back on him and pulled up the covers. When he reached out to her, she mumbled something about a headache and not being in the mood, so Jon drew back and left her alone.

Lying there in the dark, waiting for the lights of a passing car to illuminate the room briefly, he let his thoughts wander back to those exhilarating moments when the audience had stood and cheered, when he'd felt that elusive connection to their hearts and souls.

That, and nothing else. Those moments meant everything. Jon couldn't imagine that any amount of money, or anything that money could buy, would make him feel more glorious than that instant of being one with his music and his audience.

It had almost felt like a sudden silence, as if he had created a silent, white bubble inside the music where all their minds met, where everything could be understood, and where there was nothing but joy, acceptance, love.

He closed his eyes, wondering if he could make the words he'd spoken to Jenny in the kitchen come true.

That bowl in the Hollywood Hills surrounded by forest, those rows of seats up the slope, the shell of the stage, the one place in the world where he wanted to perform, and he wondered if he could create that moment of white light there too.

What an amazing experience that would be. Thousands of fans swaying to his music under the open, star-scattered sky, and his band would fill the night with songs while he sang.

A band.

How he wanted that, a real band and not just the bare bones; but at least two guitars beside his own, a percussionist, a bassist, a drummer, and a second piano. Or better, a keyboard and a piano. Oh, and background singers, hell yeah, and maybe even some strings. A full sound, a sound that would satisfy the ear and not be like the scratching of a hungry cat locked in the garage. He wanted real music.

Excitement made Jon sit up.

They would go on tour; they'd tour the United States and then hop across the Atlantic to win Europe. There would be a private plane for all of them, and hotels where they'd be comfortable; and they would fill huge venues, would play in football arenas. And driving from the airports through the towns, he'd see his face on posters and a sticker across it saying "sold out." And outside their hotel would be hordes of fans waiting for them to get off the bus, begging for autographs, hoping for a smile; beautiful girls humming his songs, knowing them by heart.

The urge to jump out of bed and go find Sal right now was so strong that Jon had to force himself to lie down again.

Jenny was asleep. He could hear her soft, regular breathing. Careful not to wake her, Jon moved closer and wrapped his arm around her waist. She did not react, so he laid his face against her shoulder and closed his eyes. The words of "The River" running through his head, he finally fell asleep.

In the light of the early morning, with tepid tea for breakfast instead of coffee and a bologna sandwich instead of an omelet, the world didn't look quite that friendly anymore. Jenny seemed exhausted. The tender skin under her eyes looked bruised, and her lips had the tired attitude of wilted rose petals. Dressed in her bathrobe and with her hair piled into a knot on top of her head, she seemed like a dispirited, older version of herself.

"I'm going to work today," she said after she'd refilled his cup, "even though it's my day off. I want to talk to Mr. Brown about his offer, and then I'll go up to Columbia and see about some courses. Maybe even enroll for next term if they'll let me."

He didn't have to ask. Her father would be only too glad to pay her tuition; he might even encourage her to give up her job completely and go back to school to earn what he called a "real degree"—law or medicine—and move back in with them, back into her old room, and forget the attic studio, and Jon.

"I love you," she said. It came out angrily, as if she had surprised herself with it. "I've always loved you, Jon, ever since you helped me pick up the books I'd dropped in that puddle. You picked them up and wiped them on your sweater before handing them back, and that was the nicest thing anyone had ever done for me."

"For God's sake, Jen, we were in sixth grade!" The memory made him smile. She'd been wearing blue tights that made her legs look sleek and lovely. Her hair had been even longer than it was now, and she'd always worn it loose, as if to show it off. She'd been very proud of it.

"Yes, sixth grade, just after spring break. I felt as klutzy as a cow; but there you were, the shy, cute boy from the last row, and you helped me without making any scathing remarks like the others would have." Her hand let go of her mug to touch his briefly. "That was the moment I knew I wanted to be your girlfriend, and some-day, your wife."

Only a few weeks earlier Jon would have said that she was that, all of that, and in a while they'd get married, just wait and see. He wondered if she knew about the ring he'd bought for her? But now he couldn't say anything at all. His head bowed, his eyes on his uneaten sandwich, he listened.

"I have my wedding dress picked out; did you know that? I know what kind of flowers I want and what kind of veil. Only you haven't asked; and even if you did, I'm not sure I'd say yes anymore." She fell silent, as if waiting for him to reply, to make things right and assure her that of course everything would change and what was she thinking; she was his one and only.

Jon felt a calm sadness sink into his heart, a still, accepting sadness that settled into each nook and waited, sighing softly.

"You could at least lie to me." Jenny's voice took on that brittle quality again. It made him think of tears strung like pearls on a necklace, and every time she spoke they shivered, rainbows vibrating in them from the resonance. "You could lie and tell me you love me."

That one was easy, and it wasn't even a lie. "I do love you, Jenny." He did, but not in the way she needed.

29

"But you love your music more." There it was, the whole truth, and she knew. "You love nothing, and no one, as much as you love your music. I'll always have only second place in your heart." She was nodding to herself as she said it.

"Yes." It really was as simple as that. "That's true. My music is my greatest and first love, and that will never change. And I won't ever give it up. I'm sorry."

Her bread uneaten, Jenny pushed the plate aside and rose from her chair. "I'm going to take a shower, and then I'm off to the bookstore. Don't bother about dinner tonight; I'll be at my parents' house."

"I'm going to lunch with Sean and Sal, so I won't need dinner anyway." He realized he sounded like an obstinate kid, but he didn't mind.

"Right." Her hair came down in a tumble when she pulled out the pin. Jon had always loved the reddish cascade, loved how it shone like a mix of gold and copper when sunlight struck it; but now, in the gray light of another rainy November morning, it looked more like dull brass.

"I guess I should wish you luck," she said, standing in the bathroom door. "I guess if this is your great chance, then I should wish you luck."

Jon's patience snapped. Three big steps and he gripped her arm to turn her around. "Why in the world do you act as if it doesn't concern you, Jenny? Are you breaking up with me? Because I sure don't mean to break up with you. All I'm trying to do is achieve what you want: success, and enough money to give us a decent life. So why, the moment I come home and tell you that I've finally met someone interested in my music, why do you turn on me at that exact moment? That's what I'd like to know."

Her lips moved, but she didn't speak.

"There's only one possible explanation, and it's so dire that I don't even want to think about it." Letting go of her, Jon took a step back. "You never wanted me to succeed as a songwriter. Your hope was that I'd sort of outgrow the music thing. You hoped I'd wake up one morning and throw out the guitar and proclaim my music

30

a folly, and useless. That's why you kept quiet about it all the time. You hoped I'd change."

He knew he was right by the way she looked away from him.

"Well, I'm not changing, Jenny. I'm not going to give this up. I'm not going to become a different man for your sake. I'm not going to be the family man and provider who would make you and your father happy. I'm a musician! That is my chosen career!"

She'd gone into the bathroom by now and was busy squeezing the last bits of toothpaste out of the tube.

"Jenny."

There was no response.

"Jenny, please listen to me. Things are going to change, I promise. Last night was… fantastic! There's no other way to put it. The audience was so receptive; and there was this moment, this one moment, when it felt as if everything became one: me, the music, the instruments, the people. It felt like one living, breathing entity. And that was the moment when I realized that I can do this. I have what it takes to reach people! I don't know what it is, but it's there. My songs touch other people's hearts. I know I can be a success!"

Jenny, her eyes blazing with tears, threw her toothbrush at him. "Would you listen to yourself, Jon? It's always about you! You and your music, you and your audience, you and your guitar. As if you're the center of the world, and everyone and everything has to revolve around you. But you're nothing, Jon. Nothing. You're only a dreamer who's wasting away his life like a Don Quixote fighting imaginary giants. There are no giants! You will never be a rock star! It doesn't happen that way!"

"Who said that? Who said it can't happen this way?" Furious now, Jon didn't pick up the toothbrush that had landed right in front of his feet but gave it a good kick, only to make it vanish under the bathtub. "Everything is possible! Everything can happen, and why not today? And yeah, the world revolves around me all right! It does that with anyone who manages to be true to their dreams and who works to achieve them."

"Oh, spare me the philosophical crap! You know that was invented by losers to comfort other losers and nothing more." She went down on her knees to retrieve her toothbrush. It was filthy, covered in cobwebs and dust, and totally useless. With a disgusted sigh, she threw it in the wastebasket.

"So that's how you see me." Another step away from her, and one more, and it seemed as if the distance between them was so much more than the few yards of their apartment. Even standing in the middle of the room watching her, the abyss widened with every heartbeat. "That's how you see me," Jon repeated softly. "You see me as a loser, a hopeless dreamer. One of those men who grow old clinging to their dreams, neither realizing them nor finding an alternative but lost in the seediness of their homemade poverty. Well."

His jacket was still hanging by the heater; his guitar stood in the corner. It took him no more than three seconds to get dressed and grab his instrument, and the shopping bag with his demo tapes.

"This dreamer," Jon said, opening the apartment door, "is off now. Good-bye, Jenny."

This time he didn't wait for a response.

Chapter Six

HE FELT STUPID walking into the restaurant with his guitar on his back, but neither Sal nor Sean even glanced at it as he leaned it against the wall behind his chair.

"So," Sal said when Jon sat down, "let's talk business." In the bright daylight he looked different: There was little left of the impishness and studied coolness; he was all brisk and focused. "Let's make this clear right from the start. You know what they say about overnight success, right? It takes a long time. So don't get impatient if your first album doesn't make gold or platinum. It may take a couple of years. But we'll do it together, and with hard work and some good connections, we'll get there." And LA, he went on, Jon would have to move to LA so he could meet the right people, attend the right parties, get some studio time with the important record companies.

"And you're going to see to that?" Jon had no idea how these things were done, but he would bite off his tongue before he let Sal know that.

Their pizza arrived. The scent almost made Jon drool; there had been no dinner for him, and a bitter discussion with Jenny instead of breakfast.

"I'm going to see to that," Sal assured him. "Or at least I'll do my best to see to it." He launched into a recitation of things they would have to do: find Jon a place to live, find him a job in LA that would support him as well as leave him enough time to compose and record.

"Studio time," he finished, "we'll have to get studio time for you, and find musicians. You have Sean, for now. But that's not enough. You need a band. Maybe we can hire some musicians."

There wasn't a crumb left on Jon's plate. Rather regretfully, he peered at Sean's half-eaten pizza, but his good manners kept him from asking if he was finished.

"If you get all that stuff done," he said to Sal after a moment's

33

thought, "if you really can do all that you're offering, then I'll pay you eighteen percent."

Surprised, Sal leaned back in his chair. "I was going to ask for fifteen. That's the going rate for managers and agents these days."

Jon grinned. "I know. That's why I'm offering eighteen. Of course, right now it's eighteen percent of nothing. But it's your job now to turn it into eighteen percent of millions. So do it. Also, I don't want you seeking too many other clients. If you're going to work for me, I'd appreciate it if you'd put some effort into it. Are you going to draw up the contract?"

Sal cleared his throat. "Uh...yes, I will. I'm a bit overwhelmed by your...let's call it drive. I haven't met many songwriters who can, or even want to, deal with numbers."

"Yeah." Jon wondered if he could order a dessert without looking too greedy. So he said, "I wouldn't mind some coffee. And yes, I do like numbers. Business school, Columbia. If not for the music, I'd have been a banker or something. Maybe real estate."

Their coffee was served, and with it big pieces of cheesecake.

"There's just one thing though." Licking the cream off his fork, Jon looked sharply at Sal. "One thing bothers me about this whole thing. You see me perform last night, and *wham*, you offer to be my agent deal? No demo tapes, nothing? Just like that, on good faith?"

The shark's grin appeared again on Sal's face. "Hell, no. It's not that easy. I've been watching you for a while now. Mind you, not personally. But I do have my spies, always on the lookout for promising young artists. The time seemed right to come over and see you myself." Carefully he spooned sugar into the espresso. "It was now or never. I'm betting that someone would have snapped you up within the next two months, and I wanted to make sure it was me." Forgetting the coffee, ignoring the cake, Sal put his elbows on the table. "What you did last night, Jon. I don't know if you realize it, but you created that magic moment when everything flows together: the music, the singer, the audience. And that's what I'm looking for, someone who can do that. Someone who can draw in his listeners and create that space within the music where they forget everything else. You're one of the best I've seen. If you keep going, Jon, if you don't quit halfway up the slope, then I can promise you that you'll be a star among stars. You'll be among the very best. And I want to be there when that happens. I want to be part of it."

With a deep sigh he dug out a pack of cigarettes. "Right, gentlemen. I need a brandy. Anyone else need a brandy?"

HE was going back to California soon, Sean informed him, to visit his family, and he wasn't sure he would return to New York since it looked as if Jon was coming out to join them in LA pretty soon. Together they watched Sal walk away, his hands in his pockets, whistling a merry tune to himself, well pleased with the world and the way things were going.

"Call me" had been Sal's parting words. "Anytime, all the time, whenever you think you need me, for anything at all. If anyone approaches you about anything music related, make sure and call me. Tell them to contact me. I'll be seeing you in LA in January." With that he pressed a small pack of business cards into Jon's hand.

Snow had begun to fall. The flakes were tiny; they looked like confectioner's sugar drifting on the air, doing intricate dances over the subway grates, gathering in corners and nooks instead of covering surfaces. Jon noted how people looked skyward before turning up the collars of their coats, most of them with smiles on their faces. It made them look young, surprised, as if they were children again.

"I'd really like to keep playing with you," Sean said. "I like your music. So where and when do I have to apply for the job?"

"I can't pay you! I'm telling you; I have nothing." The entire thing was so ludicrous, he didn't even know what to say. Jon felt like laughing and crying at the same time; he had to resist the strong urge to pinch his own arm or slap his own cheek. Dreams, and how they suddenly came true. It was too much to digest. "I don't even know how to get to LA."

"That's easy." Sean grinned. "Hitch a ride. Take your time crossing the US. Have you ever done that? It's fun!"

"No." He didn't feel like admitting that he'd never been farther than Jersey City. But the idea appealed to him. He'd approach California the slow way, traveling across the country as the settlers had done.

"When you get there, let me know. I can put you up for a while." Sean tossed the butt of his cigarette into the gutter.

"I may need a place sooner than that." Jenny. He couldn't even imagine how she would react to this.

"The girlfriend?"

"Yeah. She's not too happy with me right now. Wants me to find a regular job and stuff." Somehow it didn't feel embarrassing at all to talk to Sean about this.

"Surely she'll be happy once you're well-known and making a lot of money. Once you're cruising through Hollywood in your Porsche, she'll love it. Is she the one and only?"

Surprised, Jon gazed at Sean. He was such a quiet, calm, and friendly person; yet he had this habit of cutting right to the heart of the matter with his questions. Jon liked it.

"You know," he said softly, "now that you ask, I'm not sure. You know when you get together in high school and then sort of just drift into a relationship because you're used to it, because everyone expects it? When you don't even think about what you really want? That's how it was with Jenny and me."

He'd said *was* without realizing it, and it hurt. Sean was nodding, not looking at him but down the street to where cabs and cars were blocking the intersection.

"I figure if this hadn't happened, we'd have gotten married some-time next year and been miserable with each other. Me because I wouldn't be leading the life I wanted to, Jenny because she would know that she's the reason for that. And eventually we'd have gotten a divorce. We'd have ended as a disillusioned, middle-aged couple with nothing to say to each other."

"Like so many others." Again said in that gentle, quiet voice and with that fine smile. Jon was beginning to like Sean quite a bit.

"So maybe it's better to have a clean break, sad as it may be." Sean picked up the thought for him. "Will your heart break leaving her?"

"No." Jon had to think about it. "Yeah. A bit. I hate breaking promises, and I sort of promised her all would be well. But it won't. Or at least not for the two of us. And I guess I've known that for a long time. We just hung on to what we had for loyalty's sake. But I can't. Not anymore."

They'd been standing near the entrance of the restaurant, under the red awning, to stay out of the snow. Dusk was falling already, even though it was still the middle of the afternoon. The high-rise buildings of Manhattan vanished into the clouds and swirls of snow like fairy castles, blinking with a million lights. All along the street, every shop, every restaurant, was decorated for the season. Even some of the passing cabs had wreaths and bows in their rear windows.

"You have to do what your heart tells you, Jon," Sean was saying. "You have to be true to yourself. You have this enormous gift; you're a composer. Right now you're only writing songs. But I can see you, years from now, when the songwriting will be too small for you and you'll try your hand at bigger things, like movie sound tracks, and who knows, maybe even a musical or two. Yes, I can see that. Your compositions are so much larger than songs should be. You can't let anyone, anyone at all, hold you back. I'm really glad we met." That small smile, and belief in his eyes. Sean clapped his shoulder. "It's my privilege, and if you take me on, I'll always be there for you."

"It's a miracle." Jon sighed. "There's no other explanation for it. Of course I'll take you on, Sean. The way you played "The River" last night, I thought I was going to die. You turned the song into what it should be, and you did it with just a piano. It was fantastic!"

"Yeah, well. It's what I heard in it when you sang." Suddenly serious, Sean offered him another cigarette. "It should go like this, Jon. You open a show with a couple, maybe three, fast numbers, then two ballads to bring them down again, and then, and then we do "The River," and we go full tilt. We make it as hot, as steamy, as sexy as we can. We'll make them sweat and moan with the drumbeat, and the bass, and your voice. The rest of the concert will be a breeze after that."

He was on the verge of moving away but stopped and gazed at Jon thoughtfully.

"Hey, if you need a place to sleep, you can come over to my apartment. I have a couch. You've got my number."

It seemed to Jon as if a huge load dropped off his shoulders.

"Thank you, Sean," he replied. "I may just take you up on that."

With a wave, Sean crossed the street and vanished into the rush-hour traffic.

SEAN'S words echoed in Jon's head as he sat in the subway train heading back home a short while later.

He could see it; he could feel it: a big venue, a huge open-air arena, a humid summer night, and "The River" rolling up the rows of seats, expanding all the way to the sky, making the air throb with its heartbeat, and he at the center of it all, making it all happen. And behind him, at the piano, understanding his music so well, would be Sean.

Across the aisle sat a woman about his age, maybe a little older, a couple of shopping bags at her feet. She was wrapped in a gray winter coat, a red scarf tucked into her collar. Her hair was the color of a hungry mouse, her skin pale and tired. But she was watching him, and in her eyes was the light of a smile, a hint of yearning, as if she was waiting for him to do something, say a word, sing a few bars.

Jon winked at her. The smile wandered from her eyes to her mouth.

Chapter Seven

HELEN WAS ALWAYS in a fierce mood just before Thanksgiving.

Jon remembered only too well how he and his siblings had known to stay out of her way so she would not put them to work, and how she had found them anyway and loaded them with chores that absolutely needed to be done, according to her. Useless, tedious chores such as cleaning windows and hanging freshly washed curtains. No Christmas decorations, Helen would tell them, not a single sprig of greenery, would be put up until the house was sparkling clean.

"Your sister," she said to Jon instead of a greeting, "has chosen to go away for the weekend, allegedly to a teachers' vocational training class. I don't believe a word of it. I'm convinced she's nicely settled in at a friend's house in Vermont and will only return in time for Thanksgiving dinner. Your brother has informed me that he has to study for his exams right up to Thursday. So I'm glad you're here, Jon. Would you mind going out and buying a Christmas tree?"

He found he didn't mind at all. In fact, he loved the idea of going out into the snow and the stillness it created, walking the short stretch to the Promenade, buying some roasted chestnuts from the vendor on the way, having a chat with the guy who sold the trees. Here, his elation stopped. For a moment he had forgotten that it would most probably be Jenny's brother.

The snowflakes had grown in size since he'd gotten off the subway, and now they were staying put where they fell. The small street where his family lived was covered in white. Jon, standing on the sidewalk and looking up his parents' street, noted how the snow clung to every iron fence, settled on the trellises. Cars passed, but they went slowly, silently, as if floating on a cotton candy carpet. Magical, it was magical how the world changed with the first snow.

His jacket tightly buttoned up, Jon slowly walked down to the Promenade. Despite the falling snow he could see the lights of Manhattan blinking across the river and make out the shape of the shining buildings. He loved coming here for a stroll and watch as the sunlight played over the façades of Manhattan.

There was one house on the Promenade, a huge, old, white one with a garden surrounding it that always drew his attention. Every time he came here he'd stop and stare, wonder who lived there, who could possibly afford that kind of house and grounds in the heart of Brooklyn Heights. He'd dreamed of living there, of calling this house his own.

The bag of hot chestnuts in his hands, he once again stood and looked up at the big bay windows on the ground floor and the grand balcony above them. That room, the one with the balcony— that would be his studio. He'd have a Steinway grand, brand-new, custom-made, his alone, and no one else would ever play it.

Except maybe Sean, Jon corrected his dream; he would let Sean play it while he was on the guitar.

That thought made him smile, but just as he was about to turn away and find the stand with the Christmas trees, something else crept into his mind—a shadowy picture, a surprising image—and he stopped in his tracks.

A baby's chubby, sticky fingers, and they were hitting the keys of his precious Steinway with the abandoned glee of innocence while he was watching, smiling, encouraging, even holding the child in his lap. The funny thing was, he couldn't find any impatience or anger in his heart; there was something else altogether: a bright gladness, and a yearning so strong that it hurt.

Jon took another step away from the house, his eyes still fixed on it, still seeing that picture, still hearing the wild tinkling of the piano and the child's excited giggling. A sudden sadness clasped his heart when it faded away, a feeling of mourning for something that he had never possessed, and he had to swallow it away. He popped another chestnut into his mouth to make the bitter taste of loss vanish, but the echo lingered like the memory of a song heard on the radio.

BRAD threw him a black look, so Jon ignored him and wandered around the trees instead. Not too big, Helen had said, and not too small either. Just the right kind of tree for her living room, and he'd known what to buy.

Jon wanted one that smelled of tree. He wanted the real deal, the resin and pine scent, the needles pointy and sharp, and the tree itself, the perfect cone shape. He wasn't the only one shopping for a tree, but he was the only one who wasn't offered mulled punch. Brad ignored him as long as he could, in fact until Jon went right up to him and tapped his shoulder.

"Are you going to sell me this damn tree now or what?" he asked.

"Jenny came home last night." Brad didn't move from his spot by the heater. "She locked herself up with our parents, and I could hear her crying. What's going on?"

"Nothing that you should worry about. Sell me the frigging tree already." Impatiently Jon pointed at the one he had selected. "Let's get on with it."

"Are you breaking up with my sister?"

Jon wanted to smack him in the face. He'd never cared for Brad. What looked lovely and elegant on Jenny—the white skin and red hair—made Brad look weak and soppy.

"I'm not breaking up with her. She's breaking up with me. I want to move to LA; she wants to keep her job at the bookstore. Different plans, different lives." There. He had said it, and it hadn't even hurt, not one bit. If he was quite honest, it was a relief.

"LA, huh." Brad pulled the work gloves from his pocket and slowly moved toward Jon's tree. "So, instead of making my sister happy, you're going to LA to be a superstar, eh? Did you know she had her wedding dress picked out? She was just waiting for you to get your head on straight and start acting like a real man."

Jon wanted a cigarette, and a cup of hot coffee. The shoes he was wearing weren't meant for snow. His feet felt like clumps of ice.

"Are you happy, Brad?" he asked.

That made Brad stop wrapping string around the tree and stand up. "Happy? Yeah, I'm happy. I've sold more trees than expected; it was a good day! And when I get home, there'll be beef stew and noodles for dinner, and that makes me pretty happy too."

"Not that kind of happy. I meant happy in a big way, with your life, with what you're doing with your life. What are your plans for your future? Are you doing what you always dreamed you'd do? Come on, Brad. Those moments when you weren't really paying attention, when you let your mind wander. What did you dream of doing after you finished school?"

The snow was falling on Brad's red hair, and on him it looked almost like a halo, and very pretty. For a second he wasn't the pallid male version of his sister but something beautiful, something nearly otherworldly.

"Well, I always knew I'd join Dad in the flower shop," he replied slowly. "And that I'd take it over someday. Guess I had my future cut out for me, eh."

"But what did you *want* to do?" Jon pushed. His heart was singing. He'd never before said it this clearly to himself or tried to explain to anyone else why he was so driven by the music, why he couldn't give it up, no matter the cost. "What did your soul tell you to do? Wasn't there anything that you wanted to do so badly that the thought of it alone nearly made you weep with longing? What's your impossible dream, Brad? And why are you here, selling Christmas trees on a cold New York afternoon instead of making that dream come true?"

Embarrassed, Brad slapped his gloved hand against his jeans. "I don't know. Those are teenage dreams and have nothing to do with real life, Jon. Not everyone is like you, ruthless enough to follow them at the cost of hurting other people." He shrugged. "I wanted to be a trucker. I dreamed of owning a huge, blue Mack truck and driving all over the country, maybe even up to Canada and Alaska. I wanted a life on the road."

A barge came down the river; it was just passing under the bridge. Colorful strings of lights shone in the windows of its cabin; an illuminated Santa sat on its roof. The sight made Jon smile. Warmth and happiness flooded him, a gratefulness he hadn't felt in a long time. It was as if he was standing at the center of all things, as if everything around him was falling into its designated place and the world was finally the way it was supposed to be.

"I think we should all strive to live the life we were meant to live and not settle for something that's tossed our way by chance. That's cheating life, Brad. I think life is meant to be more than just existing and working, and not where in bed at night is the only place where we live our dreams." The old, familiar ache gripped his heart, and to ease it he balled his hands into fists. "We are given the chance to fly. We are meant to be so much more than just these crawling creatures who live without imagination, without loving themselves for what they can do. Why aren't you a trucker? You're twenty-seven, aren't you? Why aren't you a trucker, Brad?"

"How the hell am I supposed to know." Brad shouldered the trussed-up tree and carried it to the tent where the punch was bubbling away. The small heater in the corner made it warmer inside. "I'm not a trucker because somehow there never was an opportunity. It just didn't happen, and I knew Dad needed me. So I'm here."

With a nod of thanks Jon accepted a cup of the punch. It smelled of cinnamon, cloves, and cherry; and it brought back memories of evenings just like this one when he'd gone with his father to buy a tree. His father, who was still working, even at this time of the day; and Jon wondered what he would say to him, seeing him break up with his girl, and their family, to move to the other side of the continent.

"I'm not breaking up with Jenny," he said again. "I wish she'd come with me. But she is afraid of the uncertainty. She wants the safety of a job, of her family, of a regular life. I understand that. But it's not for me."

"Well, you picked a frigging stupid time for that decision, Jon, just before the holidays." Brad's voice didn't sound quite that angry anymore. "So when are you leaving?"

"Right after the holidays." He hadn't even thought about it, but saying it now, the thing began to take on life. "I'm going to hitch a ride the day after Christmas."

"Hitch a ride?" A light shone in Brad's eyes at those words. "You're going to hitchhike across America? Seriously, Jon?"

"Yeah. I'll see where I end up. Hope it's Santa Monica beach." Grinning, Jon added, "Now, if you were a trucker and had a big, blue Mack truck, I'd see if I could get a ride with you, Brad."

"Yeah."

Jon hoisted the tree onto his shoulder. "My mom is waiting. She wants me to put it up tonight. She gets all frantic and antsy before the holidays. The older we get, the more she thinks she has to make it nice for us." He walked away, humming to himself, and he was nearly home before he realized it was a Christmas carol.

Chapter Eight

"I NEED TO borrow some money."

The sentence hung in the room like the ornaments hung on the boughs of the tree, still shivering, gleaming from the dusting Helen had given them, uncertain yet of their impact.

His mother was on the ladder, the angel that went on the top of the tree in one hand while she tried to stabilize herself with the other.

Jon went over and steadied the rickety ladder. "I promise to pay it back, Mom, but I need a little help to survive in LA until I have a job. And then, of course, I hope to secure a record deal in the near future." Said like that, it sounded like a teenage dream again and made him feel foolish.

"How much?" She didn't look at him but carefully fastened the angel in place.

"Heck, I have no idea." Sweat was gathering on his neck. "A couple hundred? I'll make do, somehow."

He held out his hand to her as she climbed down. Helen brushed her fingers on her jeans, nodding thoughtfully, and indicated for him to remove the ladder. They were done decorating, and she seemed pleased enough. Putting on the angel last was almost a ritual, and done in defiance of common sense. His father had been after her every single year for doing it this way, but she insisted on it, saying it was the crowning moment, the last touch to make the house festive and bring in the Christmas mood. So far she'd never knocked off any of the other ornaments, and, Jon thought, she was right. There was something deeply symbolic about crowning the tree last.

"I'll help you, Jon," Helen said into his thoughts, "and I'll give you the money. I'll give you one thousand, and it will be my Christmas gift to you. Only there are two conditions."

"Yes?"

Her blue eyes came to rest on him. There was a trace of sadness

45

in them but also, incredibly, pride. "Don't tell your father about the money. He thinks you're old enough to look after yourself. I disagree. Well, at least to some extent. He also has enough on his plate with his work and doesn't need another worry. And I want you to call me once a week. I want a call from you every Sunday, every single Sunday, for as long as you're farther away from home than Broadway. I want updates on what you're doing and how you're faring. And, Jon." The last word, his name, came out sharply, just the way she had always said it when he brought home another middling report card. "No drugs. No slipping into a useless hippie life. You're going to LA to make a career. I expect you to do that. Do we have an agreement?"

"Yes! Of course we do!" There was little sense in telling her how his heart burned for that same thing, that career, that success. She knew.

"Good. And how are you going to get to LA? It just occurred to me—you don't have a car, and you don't have the money for a plane ticket. Is that new manager guy going to send you one?"

This was the hard part. She'd not like the idea. "I'm going to hitchhike. It will be a great adventure, and I'll see the country."

To his surprise, Helen nodded. "Just take care, Jon, will you? I'm worried about you. But then again, there's nothing I can say to stop you, I guess." On the point of returning to the kitchen, she added, "I'll drive you as far as the New Jersey Turnpike. You should be able to find someone going west from there. We can have lunch at a rest stop, and I can see you off just as if you were hopping on a plane."

And just like that it was settled.

His fingers tingled. He wanted to rush back to the apartment and start packing right away and walk until he found a highway and could stop a truck, and vanish into the night. Four weeks—he'd have to face Jenny, clean his stuff out of their apartment, call Sean and tell him he was moving in, maybe even help Jenny move back to her parents' house.

"And Jenny?" Helen called from the kitchen. As if she could read his mind, as if she knew where the feelings of guilt were roiling.

"Yeah, tomorrow," Jon shouted back.

"Go now." She reappeared, a dishcloth in her hands. "Don't make that girl more unhappy than necessary, Jon. It's bad enough for her as it is. Don't be cruel." Waving at the kitchen, Helen added, "Just tell her that you're going, Jon; don't leave her hanging."

"Mom, I'd love for her to go with me; I really would!" Jon began to say, but Helen shook her head.

"You don't, Jon. You're fooling yourself, and I love you for that. But you're not being honest with yourself. You don't need anyone like Jenny with you on this. She'd be a burden you couldn't shoulder. You need to be free for this. You don't need a wife right now." As if caught in an act of unnecessary honesty, she pulled up her shoulder. "I hope you find someone in good time, someone who takes you the way you are, music and all. Someone who shares that dream. But it won't be Jenny. She deserves better, and worse. She'll be happy marrying a local boy and spending her life right here in Brooklyn. Her dreams aren't very big."

Jon looked around the room. He didn't want to leave the festive, cozy house, walk all the way to Atlantic just to find an angry, sad, and accusing Jenny; his mother was right. He knew she was right, and sighing, he again put on his jacket and left.

IN the end, it wasn't as hard as he had expected.

Jenny was curled up in her corner of the couch, as always, the quilt over her legs, a mug of tea between her hands. It was warm in the apartment; there was a new, electric heater glowing happily. It was surely a gift from Daddy to his darling girl. He hated it, and he hated himself, but it lasted for only a moment.

She had packed his bags. They were sitting in the middle of the small room, silent, waiting, accusing.

"I packed for you," Jenny said with a little wave of her hand. "I thought it would be easier for both of us."

Jon sat down at the other end of the couch, careful not to touch her. "Jenny, listen to me. It doesn't have to be this way. Why don't you come with me? Let's go to California together, you and me. Let's see what life is like there. I'm sure we'll make it. Please?"

47

It was very quiet. Jenny had never cared very much for music or the radio running in the background; she preferred silence. She preferred sitting in silence when she read a book, and that made Jon realize how often she must have been at the end of her endurance when she was trying to read and he had been strumming away on the guitar, composing.

And that couldn't even be called music. It was just that, searching for new melodies.

"I'm not coming." Her voice shook him out of his dark thoughts. "I've talked to my parents. I'm moving home and going back to college full-time. I've also talked to Mr. Brown. He promised to hire me again once I have my degree. I'm all set, Jon. All I need is for you to take your stuff and leave."

She had been crying. He could see that now, see the crumpled tissue in her hand and the dark shadows under her eyes.

"Tell me you don't love me," he demanded. "Tell me to my face. Tell me you want me to go away and never see you again! I want to hear it from you! You're breaking my heart, Jenny."

A small, sad smile appeared on her lips. "You and your drama. I wonder what you'd say if I wanted to go with you. Seriously, I'd like to see your face if I did that. You'd flip, Jon. You don't want me there any more than I want to go. We're at the end of our road."

"Yes." There was something else, though, that bothered him. "You said you can't see me making a success with my music. Why did you say that, Jenny?"

"Oh, Jon." She put down the mug with a sigh. "The question should be, why do *you* think you can? Look at us: We're just Brooklyn kids with a middling family background, nothing important about us! We grew up here, we have all our connections here, and you think you can just up and go and be a Hollywood star! I love you for your romantic ideas, but this is taking it too far. Do you really think you can just waltz into LA and take it over?" Her face softened, and she reached out to him. "I just wish you could be a little more realistic. It's okay for a kid to cling to his dreams, but you're no kid anymore. You have to grow up now, or you'll end up waiting tables in some California restaurant wasting your life."

Jon took her hands in his. They were cold, ringless, and cold. He knew she had wanted one thing from him for a long time, a ring, and he hadn't given her one yet. "That's not how it's going to be, Jen. I'm not the kind of guy who fritters his life away on useless dreams. I'm sorry that you can't believe a little more in me. I really am. I'd have loved to have you by my side on this adventure."

She pulled back from him, her fingers slipping from his like the last speck of hope, the final spark of love.

His bags weren't half as heavy as he had expected. They contained everything he'd brought into their life together. It wasn't much.

"Good-bye, Jenny," Jon said. She nodded but did not respond. "I wish you luck," he went on, his voice cracking a bit on the last word, sadness sweeping over him. "I wish you a happy life, sweetheart."

The door closed behind him, and he stood and listened, waiting for her to call him back, waiting for a sign or sound; there was nothing.

A subway track ran past Sean's living-room window.

It seemed to Jon as if a train raced past every two minutes, rattling the building, shaking the couch, throwing a yellow strobe pulse across the shabby carpet.

He wondered where the people in those trains were going: home, work, to meet someone, or leave someone.

Leaving. What a harsh concept that was, now that he was on the path.

Somewhere in the building a child was crying; a man's voice answered in loud, harsh tones; a door slammed. The room smelled musty, of old water damage and wet mortar, and other, less definable things.

But Sean had welcomed him as if he was an old friend returning from a very long voyage, or his beloved brother. Jon was welcome to stay, he said, until he left for LA just before Christmas. He waved at the dismal furniture.

"It's not mine. I'm giving the place up when I leave. I have a feeling that whatever happens, I won't be returning here."

They'd spent a couple of delightful hours working on his songs, drinking beer, chatting about life in New York and life in general, and Jon had gone to bed with his heart light, a lot lighter than it had been when he'd left Jenny.

Crossing his arms under his head, he watched another train hurtle past and wished it was a plane, a starship, anything, and he could board it and be in California when he woke up.

IT was still snowing. The old brownstones on the quiet streets seemed like well-fed cats, like fat, content cats resting on white pillows, watching the world through the windows lit with Christmas decorations. Jon imaged them watching him as he walked past, their steady gaze following his steps, resenting him disturbing their fluffy snow beds. Shifting the weight of his luggage, he turned onto the street where his family lived. It seemed fitting somehow to spend his last days in New York with his family, to leave on his big adventure from the home where he'd grown up.

His sister, Valerie, opened the door. "If it isn't the lost son," she greeted him, and popped a cookie into her mouth. Jon snatched the one she was still holding from her hand.

"I'm not lost," he replied, "or if I was, I didn't know it. But now it's time to move on."

"You're not really going off to LA, are you, Jon? You're kidding, right? Mom said you're going to California after the holidays."

"Yeah, I am." He hung his jacket over the banister. "Right after Christmas. Until then, you'll have to bear having me around."

Val, looking him up and down, shrugged. "I guess I can. Especially since I think I won't be seeing you again once you leave. You won't come back, the way I know you. You don't give a crap about us."

It was more than he could take. "Of course, Val. As soon as I get to LA I'll be an overnight sensation, make millions, buy a house on the beach with a high wall, and hire a bodyguard. And no one will be able to get to me without my consent. That's exactly how it will be." On the point of going into the kitchen, he stopped and added, "And I'll own a frigging Porsche. Or a Jaguar. Just watch me. I'll do all that in three months, make no mistake. I'm sick and tired of you saying I can't do it. I will be a success if only to prove you and Jenny wrong." The scent of roast and potatoes made his stomach rumble, and he remembered that he hadn't eaten in quite a while. "Three years from now I'll *own* Hollywood. Just watch me."

Val's laughter followed him as he went to kiss his mother's cheek as he stole a slice of the roast she was cutting.

Chapter Nine

SAL CALLED ON Christmas Eve to ask if Jon was still alive, and planning on coming to California, and when to expect him.

"I need a date," he said. "There are some people who want to meet you. Nothing big, just a couple of music producers. They were quite impressed by your demo tapes. So how soon can you get here?" He laughed when Jon told him his plan to hitchhike across the United States.

"You're such a romantic, Jon. All right then, I'll tell them you'll be here by the middle of January. Just, you know, don't get lost in Oklahoma or something."

Oklahoma. It sounded so far away, as if it was a different continent. For the first time, Jon realized that he wasn't going to be able to bend the universe and get from New York to LA by spending a few hours in a car or truck. It would take him a week or more.

He was packing when Helen came to tell him that dinner was ready. He'd brought his things over from Sean's place and was stowing them in his old childhood room before he left for LA.

She stood in the doorway, watching him for a few moments before she offered, "Do you need some help?"

Jon shook his head. His bag was full. He had everything he needed. He was traveling light: jeans, t-shirts, underwear, a toothbrush, some toiletries, and a guitar. Looking down into the open bag, he imagined himself in tattered clothes, barefoot, playing his songs somewhere along a beach in LA, and for an instant panic gripped his throat, made him want to turn to his mother and say it was all a joke; he didn't really mean it, and he'd go back to school and Jenny right after the holidays.

But all he said was "Thanks, I'm all packed. Don't think I'll need a lot for California. It's warm there, isn't it?"

"Jon, I don't want you sleeping on the beach."

That made him smile, and it made him feel good too, like a kid waiting impatiently for his mom to wrap a scarf around him before letting him play in the snow.

"I won't," he promised. "I have a friend in LA who said he could put me up until I have a place of my own."

She was a small woman, his mother, with bones like a bird. When he embraced her, she hardly reached his shoulder; he could easily rest his cheek on the top of her head. "Don't worry about me, Mom," Jon said gently. "I'll be careful. Nothing will happen to me." That made him laugh. "Well, nothing bad. I do hope something else happens though." He felt the sigh going through her body and released her. "It's what I have to do. At least I have to try. I don't want to be a sad, middle-aged man someday mourning my lost dreams. I want to try and live those dreams. If it doesn't work out, there's still time to do something else."

"You'll come back home?" His mother's hands gripped his tightly. "You promise to come back?"

"Heck, Mom."

She nodded quickly, biting her lips. "Yes, yes, I'm sorry. You're old enough to know what you want. It's just hard to see you go so far away. It's my prerogative to worry."

"That's playing the ultimate mom-card."

Her laughter didn't sound quite sincere, and it made Jon feel bad. This time though he didn't react and went back to his bag to rearrange some things.

"It's more than a dream," he said. "If it was only a dream I could keep it locked away in a nook of my brain and lead what Jenny calls a normal life. I wouldn't mind that if it didn't feel like more, like a possibility, like something that I *have* to do. I can visualize it, Mom. I can see myself filling football stadiums, and playing to an audience of thousands. And I think if you can dream something, you should try and do it."

"Well." Helen stepped up to him and gazed down into his bag, then rolled up her sleeves. "If that is true, then I should be a chef at the Waldorf-Astoria. I've always dreamed of reinventing their salad. Here." She plucked his socks from the bag. "Stuff these into the spaces between the jeans; that will leave room for a sweater. You should take at least one sweater."

CHRISTMAS dinner with his family passed by like a dream, as if this reality was traveling away from him before he had even left. His mind was racing ahead, thinking about the rest stop he had picked where he wanted Helen to drop him off. It was in New Jersey, just on the other side of Newark, on the interstate. She had made sure there was at least a fast-food joint there. She had the notion that they would sit together until he found a ride, chatting, drinking coffee, eating fries. Jon was sure it wasn't going to be that way at all. He was certain he'd have to approach drivers at the gas station, stand out in the cold, beg and grovel, until he found someone who took him on.

He was hardly listening to his brother, Kevin, talking about his latest adventures at the hospital, how he had saved a young woman from certain death by resuscitating her before the ER doctor showed up and how he had been praised for his fast action. His young wife, Sarah, was sitting beside him, her eyes big and blue and admiring. Val, as always, was eating her roast duck with the heartiness of a lumberjack, her glance darting from one to the other, irony gleaming in them.

"Maybe we should all go and see Jon off," she said, and then, to him, "I'm still not getting why you won't go on a plane. It's insane, tramping across the continent. What if you end up in Alaska?"

"Leave Jon alone," his father mumbled, reaching for the platter of duck. "Let the boy do what he must do."

Jon gave Val a grin. "That's the cool part. You just grab another truck going back south. I wouldn't mind seeing Alaska!" He realized she was just envious. They all were, with the exception of his mother, and they admired his guts, but they would rather have bitten off their tongues than admit it. In their eyes he was going off on a huge adventure.

"Like Bilbo Baggins," Jon said out loud. "'It is a dangerous business, Frodo, going out your door!'"

"I have no idea what you're talking about," Kevin mumbled around a mouthful of duck, but Val's face softened into a smile.

"Yes," she agreed. "And he's right, isn't he? Look at all the trouble poor Bilbo gets into, and even worse, Frodo!"

"But they succeed. Both of them, they succeed." Jon held out his plate to his mother for another piece of meat.

"Yeah, but they have to wade through a lot of crap first. They starve and freeze and get lost, and they nearly get killed." Val shot him a glance over the rim of her glasses that made Jon imagine her at school, giving the same withering look to an errant kid.

"I don't intend to starve, and I don't intend to get killed, if that's what's worrying you, sister dear. I may get lost a couple of times though. Maybe I should look at a map again before I leave."

She gave him a disdainful snort but didn't respond.

"You really want to do this?" It was Sarah who asked, and Jon sighed. He had stopped counting how often he'd heard that question over the past few weeks, starting with Brad.

Mr. Brown had raised his eyebrows at him and adjusted his bow tie, the same words on his lips; and from him they sounded like a final verdict. "The thing is," he'd gone on, "no one actually does it. It's a myth. Nothing more than a promotion gimmick. No one just goes off to Hollywood to be a star." He'd amended, "Well, they do. But they never succeed. It's just not done that way. You have to have connections, be born into the music business, to find your footing there."

Jon didn't want to believe it. He refused to believe it, and he had walked off, leaving Mr. Brown standing there by the counter right next to a pile of cookbooks with Christmas recipes. Jenny had been nowhere in sight. He'd caught himself looking for her, but she wasn't there. In a way it made him sad all over again. It felt like saying good-bye in pieces.

"Yeah, I want to do it," Jon said to Sarah, "and I will. It's a job, nothing else. You need a talent for every job, like Kevin needs his to be a surgeon, and Val is a great teacher. And I'll be a very good songwriter and performer. I really can't see what's so special about it."

"It may be a job once you get it," Val threw in, "but getting it, that's the hard part."

"Maybe." He was tired of all these discussions and wished with all his heart that at least one of them, one single person, could find it in their heart to believe in him. His gaze wandered over to his mother, sitting at the foot of the table, but she wasn't looking his way. Her brow crinkled with worry; she had her head turned toward the window and the gently falling snow. The food on her plate was untouched.

"It's useless to be afraid," she said softly. "It's useless to live a life in fear, a life aiming for safety. If you don't do what your heart tells you to do when you're young, you probably won't do it at all and will regret it forever." With a small smile, she looked over at Jon. "It scares me to death to let you go on this trip, and me, not able to watch over you. But I can feel what you feel, Jon, the drive, the determination to make this dream come true. And as much as I hate to say it, you're right to do it now, when you have the chance. You're not traveling into the abyss. You have a manager and a friend waiting for you, so that's a good thing."

Jon wanted to get up and hug her, and he would have if the family hadn't been there. But he knew he wouldn't be able to take another snide remark from Val without snapping back, and then there would be one of their fights, and the Christmas mood would go down the drain.

"Well." Helen put down her napkin. "Since this has been sorted out, I think we should have dessert. Who wants pumpkin pie and who wants chocolate trifle?" Again she smiled at Jon. It was a small, sad smile, but it was full of love too. "I know I don't have to ask you. How can a son of mine not like pumpkin pie?"

Chapter Ten

ALL HIS PLANS of traveling across America in a truck and being taken along routes he would never see again came to a sudden end when the phone rang late on Christmas Day and an unfamiliar voice said, "Hey, it's me, Jones. Remember me?"

Of course, Jon wanted to say, but his stomach was in a knot, and his breathing had suddenly failed.

"Just thought I'd give you a call. Bob told me you want to go to LA soon, and I was wondering if you'd care to go with me? I'm driving out in two days. We can share the gas and the motel rooms."

"How did you get my number?" Jon asked.

Jones laughed. "From Sal. Bob gave me Sean's number, Sean gave me Sal's number, and Sal gave me yours. He seemed quite relieved too, said you wanted to hitchhike to LA, and now that he knows you'll be traveling with a friend he's relieved."

Like a brick falling into place in exactly the spot where it belonged, like something that had been missing and was now there.

"Yes, I'll gladly travel with you! Of course I will!"

Helen poked her head out of the living room to see what he was up to, standing in the hallway next to the phone.

Jon gave her a brilliant smile. "Where should we meet? When do you want to leave?"

"Oh, let's meet at Bob's," Jones replied, and it sounded like song lyrics, coming from him. "Do you still have my plectrum? Did it bring you luck?"

"Hell, you have to ask? I'm going to California with you; I call that luck!" Jon's heart was singing. "Okay, let's meet at Bob's."

Helen seemed a bit disappointed. "Oh," she said, picking up her knitting again. "All right then. So I'll drive you to the club."

Jon bit his lips to hide a smile and sat down next to her, after stealing a cookie from the plate on the table. The living room was beautiful with its decorated tree, the stockings on the mantel, and the fire in the fireplace. Candles were quietly burning in the window, highlighting the snowflakes as they drifted down, casting a mellow, golden light on them as they passed by on their dance to Earth. Wonderful scents filled the warm room: pine, the sweetness of the cookies, the distinct smell of beeswax candles. It was just as it had always been his whole life.

"You're a real romantic, Mom!"

She didn't look up.

"No, really, you are." It was funny, and it made his heart overflow with love for his mother. "You had this notion of taking me to a rest stop on the highway and then telling some unfortunate truck driver they'd better watch out for your son or else. *You* wanted to pick the truck; don't tell me you didn't! You saw yourself standing there in the snow, waving after a truck as it pulls out of the parking lot, like a Russian mama, a shawl wrapped around your head, dusk falling, and your son is leaving. You to trudge back to your car and the long drive home on your own." Jon touched her arm to make her look at him. "You'd probably buy a coffee to go and a doughnut and then cry a bit when you crossed the bridge. You're so sentimental. I'm not going to China, for crying out loud! It's just California!"

Helen shrugged him off. "Nothing of the kind. Leave me alone."

"Yeah, just the kind. Mom, I love you." And he wrapped his arms around her, careful not to disturb her knitting, and kissed her temple.

THE snow had stopped. As if to send him off with the best possible memory of New York, the weather had changed, bringing a spotless blue sky, crisp air, and sunlight that sparkled and shone on the snow. Children were out with their sleighs, passing their house on the way to the Promenade. Their voices sounded like the cries of the seagulls cruising over the river, sharp and shrill in the still morning brightness.

Jon stood, looking up and down the street, wondering when he'd be back. Now that he was on the point of leaving it felt weird, scary, to go that far away from all he knew, from his family, even Val, who was standing at the top of the stairs out front, her sweater pulled tight against the cold.

"You watch your butt, brother," she said, and pushed her glasses up her nose. "You know we'll always take you back, even if you don't turn out to be the superstar they're all waiting for in LA." It was as close to a declaration of love as she could muster, and it made Jon grin at her.

"And you," he replied, "don't let those kids walk all over you. And for God's sake, Val. Get contacts, and find a man. You should be married, with kids." The words had a hard time wrapping around his tongue, but he managed anyway. "You'd be a fabulous mom. Don't stay alone."

She barked a laugh at him. "Sure. They're lined up to date me."

"If you'd be a little kinder, they just might," Helen, coming out of the house, tossed at her. "You aren't exactly inviting love."

Val turned around and went inside, slamming the door behind her.

"That girl." With a sigh, Helen offered Jon the car keys, but he shook his head. This one time he wanted to be in the passenger seat, wanted to feel pampered and spoiled. "You're not right, you know, with what you said," she went on, buckling her seat belt. "I'm glad you'll be traveling with a friend, and stopping at motels instead of sleeping in a truck."

Before breakfast she'd made sure he had everything he needed, checking his bag once more, asking if his money was safely stowed away, if he had a warm coat, and a scarf, and gloves. She waved away his argument that he was going to California, stating that until they got to Arizona it would be cold. She left him standing there in the kitchen to go upstairs and bring back a pair of leather gloves lined with lamb's wool.

"Here," she said, in an almost gruff tone, "these are your father's. I'll buy him new ones on my way back home. Take them. Use them. And take *care* of yourself!"

Now, in the car, he took those gloves from his coat pocket and put them on. They were soft and warm, just the right size. Jon imagined his father's hands in them as he walked to the subway to go to work at the hospital, or carried home a bag of groceries, or—and this was the vision he liked best—wrapped around his mother's fingers on a stroll along the Promenade on a cold and snowy winter night. Now they were his, a small part of home he would take with him across the mountains and the rivers, all the way to the other side of the continent. He brought them up to his face, hoping to catch the scent of his father, but they only smelled of leather.

"Your father hardly wears them," Helen stated when she noticed. "He always says they're way too warm for him. The silly man, he prefers the ones I knitted for him. I'm sure he'll even wear them when we go on our big trip."

Jon had to swallow against the knot in his throat. They had so many plans, his parents; they meant to travel all over the world, spend time in Italy and London, take the Trans-Siberian train all the way to Vladivostok and jump on a ferry to Hokkaido. Helen's dream was to see Japan, see those monkeys in the hot springs in winter. He wondered if they'd really go someday or if this dream would be unfulfilled.

JONES was waiting for them. He was standing beside his car, nursing a steaming cup of coffee, stamping his feet against the cold. A jaunty wool cap sat on his chestnut hair, and a red-and-black-check coat was buttoned up to his chin.

"He looks nice," Helen said, parking behind him. "A nice young man. Relaxed. And his car looks safe enough. It will take you all the way to LA without breaking down, I think."

"Yeah." Jon thought so too. Jones drove a big, hefty black thing with tinted windows, a car that meant business.

"Seems like he knows how to make money with his music." There was a question swinging in the statement.

"Nah, he used to be a Wall Street banker, Mom. He has some money tucked away." Helen gave him a scandalized look, so he shrugged and added, "He said it didn't feed the soul or something."

Jones came over and held out his hand to her when they got out. "Jones, ma'am."

"Well. I'm Jon's mother, and I expect you to drive carefully," she replied tersely, which made him smile. "And what kind of name is Jones?"

"Wilfred Jones, at your service. But no one calls me Wilfred if I can prevent it." He took the bag from Jon's hand to load it into his trunk. "I'm just Jones, the guitar player."

"Do you play with Jon, then?"

Jones squinted at her. "As a matter of fact, no. But I hope I will. Bob was full to his gills with praise. I'm curious to see what Jon can do. We'll have a few days on the road to find that out, won't we, and evenings in motel rooms where we can test each other's talent."

"Sounds good to me." His guitar case in hand, Jon stood on the sidewalk, uncertain how to tell Helen that this was it, time to say good-bye. Now that the moment was here, the fear of the unknown crawled up his back like a dark shadow.

"Did you bring your music?" Jones asked.

Jon nodded, patting his guitar case. "Never without it. Blank sheets and pencils too." They had been a Christmas gift from his sister, a big, neat block of empty sheets, and a box of his favorite black pencils. For an instant, when she'd handed them to him, he'd seen the glimmer of pride in her eyes, a fleeting, ephemeral thing but quite visible for that moment.

"Well." Jones clapped his hands and took a step toward the car. "We'd better be off then."

Jon embraced his mother. There was no need to talk, to repeat the same words over and over again, so all he did was kiss her cheek, hug her tightly, and then move away with a wave and a smile, calling, "Bye, Mom. I'll call when we get there!"

She raised her hand in farewell, silently, her face collected, in that ancient attitude of all women who watch their husbands or sons leave them to lead their own lives.

It was this image that Jon took away with him as the car pulled out and merged into traffic, then she was hidden by a bus coming up behind them; and he turned to look forward, westward, and at the road ahead of them.

Chapter Eleven

AN ADVENTURE, AN adventure, his heart kept singing as the car sped along the highway, leaving New York behind them.

They'd driven through the Holland Tunnel and into New Jersey. Jones handed him a couple of maps. A few cities were marked with a red dot, and Jon whispered their names as his finger followed the highway: Tulsa, Amarillo, Albuquerque, Flagstaff—the names seemed as exotic and far away as China.

Amarillo, and he associated that with adobe buildings lining dirt roads and men on horses carrying guns. He could hardly wrap his mind around the fact that in a few days he'd be in Texas.

Jones turned up the volume on the radio when it began playing an Albert Hammond tune. "Keeping my eyes on the road," it went, and Jones sang along, his voice warbling a bit on the higher notes.

He grinned at Jon. "Yeah, don't look at me like that! I'm not a singer like you. I just enjoy it!"

They stopped for a quick lunch somewhere near Wheeling and were back on the road with coffee mugs and doughnuts to go. Jones drove into the night, until they found a motel that had a vacancy sign blinking over its driveway outside of Columbus, Ohio. The room was clean, sterile in a modern, functional way, and had a generous bathroom with a walk-in shower stall, which was all Jon needed. When he returned from a long, hot shower, Jones was stretched out on his bed, his guitar on his knees, letting his fingers slip over the strings while watching a talk show on the TV.

"You know what gets me?" he asked, and Jon shook his head, waiting. "The news. The way they never really tell you what's going on politically. It's always about who had dinner with whom and what they had. But never down-to-earth, real politics."

Confused, Jon stopped, the towel still in his hand, and waited for him to go on; but the sudden statement had seemingly been enough for Jones.

65

"Can I have a look at your music?" he asked instead. "Do you trust me enough to let me have a look?"

Jon laughed. "Heck, we're sleeping in the same room. Guess I'll trust you, Wilf."

"Don't call me that!" Jones threw a candy bar at him, which Jon caught and ripped open. "I hate that name with a vengeance. If you love me, call me Jones."

"If you love me, call me Jones." Jon paused, grinning. "That sounds like a country western song." The music was tucked into the bottom of his guitar case, ordered and neat in a folder. "All right, I'll let you see my music. But it would be nice if you gave me a written promise that you won't use or copy them."

Jones's shout of laughter echoed through the room, and all the way out into the cold night. "I will," he replied, his voice shaking with mirth. "You sly bastard! I was wondering how trusting you'd be with your work, and I must say, I have to praise you! Good for you; keep your songs to yourself. But here…" He snatched a sheet from Jon and wrote out a few words on the blank back side. "Here's my promise. I could have told you though that I wouldn't have done anything anyway. I respect you way too much."

A couple of scrawled sentences and a signature, and yet Jon knew he was holding a contract of sorts in his hands, his first ever, and he was another tiny step along the road he wanted to travel so very much. The ground shifted a bit under his feet, or at least it seemed to, and he sat down on the edge of his bed.

Jones was bent over Jon's music, humming to himself, tuning the instrument. The first chord jumped from his fingers like a tiger: strong, confident, asserting itself, making Jon flinch. He knew that chord, knew which song started with it, and he held his breath.

"Right," Jones mumbled and launched into "The River," hard, fast, rocking, driving the melody with the rhythm.

Jon's heart shivered as he listened, hearing the song played once again in the same way Sean had performed it, a relentless, steamy invitation, primeval, steamy, stripped of all gentleness.

"Man." Jones put down the guitar and reached for his cigarettes.

That song is sex on staff lines. The ladies will wilt when you perform it onstage. It's really very good." He handed Jon one of the cans of beer they had bought on the road. "You have a manager waiting for you? Sal is going to work for you?"

"Yeah." It still sounded preposterous, like trying on a coat that was way too big for him. "Yes, that's what he said. We have a verbal agreement so far, but he's drawing up the contracts now. Sean wants to play in my band." Jon shrugged. "Well, the band I'm trying to put together. He's the first. Problem is, I can't pay anyone yet. We'll have to find other jobs for a while, or try and play a lot of gigs. Don't know how that will work." He tossed the empty can in the direction of the wastebasket and missed. It landed in the corner instead. With a curse on his lips Jon got up to retrieve it. "I'll be staying at Sean's place till I can find something of my own."

"Let's play some more," Jones said. "Go on; get your guitar."

CROSSING the Mississippi felt like leaving a part of himself behind, like dropping an old jacket and trying on new clothes, like a final frontier just before the point of no return. Jon knew it was an illusion; they hadn't even gone halfway yet, but it seemed that way to him.

Thoughts of home, even the stray guilty thought of Jenny, became fewer as the landscape changed.

It wasn't that everything seemed bigger; it was as if things moved farther away from one another: the houses, the cities, even the roads. The colors changed too. The farther west they went, the more brown and ochre they saw; and on their third day, driving toward Albuquerque, the sun overtook them and sank into a landscape bathed in copper and red.

It was nothing, Jones told him; he'd be overwhelmed by the sunsets over the Pacific, just wait and see. Grinning, he added that he would drive Jon to the beach when they got to LA, right down to the Santa Monica pier, and let him walk in the California surf and see the endless ocean, the seals and dolphins dancing in the waves.

Jon stared out the car window at the arid landscape and tried to wrap his mind around the image of dolphins playing in the sea.

Warm, Jones was saying, it would be warm enough in LA for a light sweater, or just a shirt.

"I want a place where I can see the ocean," Jon said over dinner. They'd driven to a Mexican restaurant. He ate spicy food with sauces that he couldn't identify, rice prepared in an unknown way, and he was enjoying it a great deal. The place was noisy, crowded, the tables standing close to one another so that the waiters had to wind around them, the trays balanced over their heads. Music was blaring from speakers above them, the songs sung in Spanish and accompanied by trumpets and guitars.

A waitress came over and set down tall glasses with salted rims. "Cheers," she said, and left; her short, colorful skirt swirling around her tanned thighs.

"Pretty." Jones stared at her legs as she walked away. "Do things like these inspire you to write your songs?"

"Girls?" There were small, dark-green bits in his glass. Jon fished out one of them with his finger and tasted it, not sure it belonged in his drink.

"Jalapeño." Jones grinned at him. "Hot, and delicious. But tell me. What inspires you? Where do you come up with your songs? I compose a bit, but only instrumental stuff. How do you come up with your lyrics?"

Jon still wasn't sure if he'd ever be a tequila lover, but this wasn't bad. "I don't, always," he replied. "Lyrics are tough. The tunes are all there, but the words…" He shook his head, remembering only too well how he'd battled with the lyrics for "The River." "Words often elude me. I have to wrestle with them."

Jones nodded, his eyes filled with the gleam of understanding.

"Inspiration." Glancing around the room, Jon said softly, "It comes at the strangest times, in the oddest places. You see a girl turn her head just so, or a raindrop falling on something, making the gentlest sound, the spray a cab makes driving through a puddle, the sun glinting on the river, a seagull cruising into the dusk. It feels as if the music is all around us, like invisible ribbons floating through the universe, and all one has to do is reach out and weave them together." He fell silent for a moment and picked up a tortilla chip, but it broke into crumbs between his fingers. "The words are imps dancing around my head, only seen from the corner of the eye, little, glimmering fairies having the time of their lives with my tortured mind. Every time I think I can grab them they dance away, giggling, pointing fingers at me, refusing to be caught."

"Seems you aren't that bad with the words at all." Shaking his head, Jones raised his hand to order another drink. "Seems they're right there, and maybe you're making them sound more difficult than they really are."

"Talking is easy." Jon wanted beer. He'd had quite enough of the salt and the peppers; he wanted a beer. "I'll talk you into buying a house with no roof if I have to. But finding the words to go with the music—totally different thing."

"You need a lyricist. Someone to write the words for you, someone who understands your music as well as you do, who can hear the words under your melodies." The girl brought their fresh drinks, and Jones gave her a brilliant, inviting smile that she returned with a sweet blush.

Jon watched them flirt, but his mind was wandering, was taking him through that door Jones had just opened for him.

Someone who'd understand his melodies the way he did. Someone who'd hear the words in them.

Briefly he thought of Sean, and wondered if he could possibly be the one, but then stepped away from that vision. Sean was a musician, possibly even more than Jon himself. He wouldn't bother with words when he could express all he wanted on the piano.

"I'm a hybrid," he said out loud. "I need both, music and words."

"Nah, you're not." Jones was holding a napkin with the girl's phone number scribbled on it. "You're music. Let someone else be the words. What you need is a poet."

A poet—the statement rang in his head as they left the restaurant to go to their motel for the night.

A poet—someone who would bring down the stars and turn them into words.

Chapter Twelve

HE'D NODDED OFF, the drone and monotony of the long drive through the desert taking its toll. Jones's voice seemed to come from far away, like a surgeon talking to a patient slowly waking from anesthesia, the sound of sanity breaking into troubled dreams.

"Welcome to California," he was saying when Jon forced his eyes open. "Won't be long now till we see LA."

Somehow, he was disappointed. He'd expected more drama, a grander view. He'd imagined crossing the mountains and seeing California spread out before him like a magic carpet, the land flattening out to the ocean where it dipped into the sunset. And exactly at that point, at the point where land and water met, would be the city, Los Angeles, a shimmering vista of towers and fairy bridges, shining like the inside of a seashell. They would drive down from the mountains and through that wonderland of beauty and eternal spring until they hit the beach, and there they would get out of the car and walk over the sand until their feet touched the water.

But all he saw were highways and fast-food joints, industrial areas and suburbs, much like anywhere else along the road.

"I'll take you to the beach," Jones said as if he'd read Jon's mind. "We'll take a short break at the next rest stop, and you can call Sean from there, to tell him we're here and where to meet us."

THE sun was beginning to set as they reached Santa Monica, and driving down toward the beach, Jon felt reconciled. He took off his sneakers and walked across the sand toward the water, feeling the warmth of a sunny day under his feet. The sky was immense. It seemed endlessly high and wide, painted as if God had emptied all the rainbows into it at once, streaking it with hues of blues and greens while the clouds got soaked with reds and pinks and violet. There was no limit, nothing to give the vista a definition or border—this was the world's end, the spot where the earth dropped off into the void of firmament and water. Wide, slow waves moved toward the shore, only to break in the tiniest whisper of foam at his feet. Surfers were out, dark, sleek silhouettes against the drama of the sky, their limbs graceful and slender, an extension of the ocean's eternal dance.

Jones pointed. "Dolphins."

His heart stopped. He wouldn't have noticed them, not knowing what to look for, but there they were, shadows of movement in the waves, enjoying the playtime shared with humans. As if to welcome him, as if they'd waited for him, one flipped out of the water and turned a jaunty somersault before splashing back into the sea.

"You're lucky!" Jones clapped his shoulder. "Seems like LA intends to be nice to you!"

Jon turned his back on the ocean and looked toward the city. The hills stood silent against the darkening sky, palm trees like paper cuts, and in his ears, the gentle rhythm of the surf; they seemed to look at him, watch him with knowing, waiting eyes.

"I think I'll like it here," he replied. "I think this city likes me."

Something nudged his toe, and he gazed down. It was a pebble moving with the water, a white, roundish thing, a snowball created by the tides. He bent down to pick it up and wipe it on his shirt before giving it a closer look. He was on the point of tossing it back but stopped. Something whispered to him, a voice he couldn't hear, more like an echo of a voice, like the last sentence said in a dream. As hard as he tried, he couldn't capture it; but he knew it had been a female voice, as clear as silver bells, as gentle as a brook's murmur. For a moment a yearning gripped him, a longing so strong it took his breath away even though he had no idea what it was that he wanted so badly. His fingers closed around the small stone, and he pushed it into his jeans pocket.

"There they are." The words tore him from his reverie.

Sean and Sal were coming toward them from the parking lot, waving, shouting, welcoming them to California. They were both tan, healthy looking, wearing sunglasses.

"I'm taking you out for dinner," Sal announced. "Come on, guys, follow us. You need your first dinner on the beach right now!"

Jon looked from one to the other. Like the Musketeers they seemed, the three of them, with himself cast in the role of d'Artagnan, the outsider generously admitted into their circle.

"Lead the way," he said, feeling in the mood for adventure, "and we'll follow!"

HE would need a car, Sal told him over their first glass of beer; he desperately needed a car, there was no getting anywhere in LA without a car. A friend of his, he said, owned a club, and he needed a bouncer; did Jon feel up to doing that? It was a good place, in a decent area. There wouldn't be any brawling or drug trafficking, just the occasional unwelcome person to turn away.

"Unwelcome person?" Dinner wasn't exactly what he had expected. They were sitting on picnic benches, eating food off paper plates bought from a food truck on the promenade while the Santa Monica nightlife flowed around them. The beach began right at their feet. After its furor of colors to welcome him, the sky had calmed down and donned a cloak of russets and gold, and was holding the glowing, red orb of the sun in its hands, gently and slowly letting it dip down into an ocean of molten copper. Out on the water, some distance away, a couple of ships passed by on their way south. The beach was a lot emptier now, but the dark, glossy figures of surfers and dolphins still played in the surf.

Behind them the hills rose into the inkiness of night.

"Well, yes." Sal popped another shrimp into his mouth after dousing it liberally with cocktail sauce. "The Hollywood royalty likes to play by itself." He grinned, showing bits of shrimp stuck between his teeth. "It's no different from any expensive club in New York. There is no social equality anywhere in the world."

As if he had a choice, and being offered a job like that was far easier than going around looking for one himself. "Thank you, Sal."

Pleased, Sal nodded. "It will give you ample time to compose and to work in the studio during the day. And the pay is good."

Studio.

Every worry, every mundane thought fell from Jon at the mention of that one magical word. The reason he'd come here.

"We have an appointment with a producer," Sal went on, ignoring Jon's sudden silence. "If things go well it won't take you a week to get a contract, but that would be a dream, of course. No one gets signed on the spot." He gazed at Jon, his head tilted. "You may just pull it off though. We'll see. I'm beginning to believe you have the devil's luck sticking to your fingers, on top of being as determined as a Mack truck going downhill."

"I'm coming, when you see that producer. You need backup, and I know your songs by now." Sean said it so calmly that it took a moment for Jon to understand.

"You need another guitar player?" Jones was looking from one to the other, the sparkle of excitement in his eyes. "I'm game if you want me."

As if his entire life in New York had been a dream, as if he had just woken up on this beach to begin his real life, surrounded by musicians, by people who understood and shared his ideas. Jon had to take another big drink of his beer.

"I'd love to have you there," he said, and added, like a mantra by now, "But I can't pay you. Yet."

"Thank you for adding that 'yet,'" Sal chimed in, "because that's exactly what it is: yet. And who says you have to pay your band yourself, Jon? We can always hire the musicians you need when we need them."

"No." His ideas on that were very clear. "I want my band to work for me all the time. I want to pay them a salary and have them play exclusively for me. Once we've found the right people I don't want a lot of change. A group of musicians has to grow together, like a family. Look at all the great orchestras: families. I want that too."

All three of them were watching him, smiles on their faces, their hands wrapped around beer bottles, and so Jon raised his. "To you. My manager, and the kernel of my band. And to a bright future filled with music, traveling, and a shitload of fun!"

"My, I'm starting to believe I may have bitten off more than I can chew with you!" Sal clinked his bottle against Jon's. "You really have your stuff together, don't you."

"If by that you mean I know where I want to be in ten years, then yes." He had to put some bravado into his voice to make it sound credible. "I don't want to end up playing in lousy clubs to disenchanted customers, still dreaming of a career when I'm in my forties. Tell me what I have to do to be a success, Sal, and I'll do it, starting tomorrow."

"I think," Sal replied, "you'll do just fine, my friend. Just fine."

SEAN'S place was in an apartment building near Venice Beach, a less-fashionable part of town. There was a balcony where they could catch a glimpse of the ocean, and once again, standing there, Jon marveled at the feeling of endless space the Pacific gave him. He imagined this shore going all the way up to Alaska, up to the Far North until it met the Arctic waters, and down, down, down to Cape Horn and its choppy currents. Limitless, it was as limitless as the sky. He could feel the pull on his soul, feel the gentle tugging that made him want to close his eyes and give himself up to this vast, empty ocean, float under the stars and hear the constellations sing to one another.

A melody crept into his mind, nothing more than a distant call, a slow heartbeat like the rhythm of the tide, a first ribbon of sunrise over the darkness of the hills. Jon closed his eyes to search for it, let his fingers run over the notes.

There was a piano in the room behind him, Sean's piano; and without asking, without even thinking, he lifted the lid and put his hands on the keys.

His heart opened wide as he played the first chord, allowing the rising song to flow from the universe through him and right into his fingers. Ecstatic, a starburst of music, much more than he had ever written, much more than he knew he was capable of, the orchestra of his imagination poured out what his mind had barely grasped.

Jon opened his eyes to see Sean sitting at the table behind him, staff paper spread out, writing busily, noting down what he had played.

"If I have to kill," he said in his soft voice, "if I have to bring down the Hollywood Hills to get it, I want to be your music director,

Jon. I want to be in on this creative process." Holding up what he'd written, he added, "You play a song, and I hear an orchestra. You open that mouth of yours to sing, and I see platinum on the walls of our studio. Why, why, why did it take you so long to make this step?" Rising, he put down the sheets in front of Jon. "Here, look. This isn't a rock song, Jon. This is a score, a movie sound track, a bloody symphony."

Jon rubbed his hands on his jeans. "Well, I was hearing the stars sing." He shrugged. "Stars can't be contained in three minutes of rock music. It's not my fault."

Sean laughed, but there were tears in his eyes, and a gladness Jon couldn't describe.

Chapter Thirteen

IT WASN'T REALLY his place, Sean told him over breakfast, but his uncle's—he was housesitting.

They were on the balcony, and he could hear the ocean and the sky humming their mystical song.

"I've never felt like this before," he said to Sean, who was returning from the kitchen with fresh coffee. "I've never felt this kind of music." He gestured at the sea. "It's as if I'm inside a huge glass bell, a wonderful, fragile, immense bell that resonates with the light, and the tides, and the wind. It feels as if I'm dissolving in it. I feel like seafoam." The moment he finished the sentence he wanted to blush like a girl and hide, but Sean smiled.

"You are that bell, Jon," he replied. "You're the medium where the music gathers. You have a magical talent, my friend. Someday you'll be so much more than just a singer-songwriter. You'll rise and shine in a sky far above any stage."

The coffee tasted different; even the toast tasted different here. Jon, his eyes still on the water, felt as if he'd been transplanted to a different planet altogether. These aliens spoke the same language and looked pretty familiar, but aside from that, everything felt strange, easier, brighter.

Sean was talking about how they had a meeting with Sal and a producer today, and if they got a chance they might be able to pop into the studio, and did Jon want to take on that guitarist Jones? Because he seemed like a pretty cool type. Oh, and they could check out the club where Jon would be working. Everything looked different during the day, didn't it.

"I think," Jon said when Sean fell silent, "I'll start the day with a walk on the beach. It's an incredible luxury, this beach, and I'd really like to enjoy it for a moment before all the other stuff starts. If you don't mind."

He wanted the sand under his feet and the water between his toes.

So different, so utterly different from his hometown. New York, even though it was right on the Atlantic, it seemed to recoil from the ocean, pulling its feet away from the water to sit dry and prim on the shore. But LA, it was a beast spread out in the sun, lying on the sand stretched out on its back; it was humming a cool, snazzy tune, enjoying the day.

SEAN dropped him off near the pier, promising to pick him up there in a couple of hours. He was going to see his family.

Alone, Jon wandered down to the water. Now, in broad daylight, the sea was just blue, nothing magical about it, and the surf was a lot less impressive than the night before. There were a few surfers playing among the waves, but the dolphins were gone.

Free, he felt free in a way he never had before. His soul expanded with the endless stretch of ocean, expanded until he thought he was floating away on it.

Again he heard the soft toll of the bell, as if he was standing inside it, under its huge dome, and the sound vibrating around him like mermaids whispering words of endearment to their lovers living on the wind. The ribbon of melody was almost tangible, a silver thread floating on the breeze, and all he had to do was reach out and touch it as it danced over the lacy surf.

He needed paper, he needed a piano and paper, now, before the music drifted away.

On the promenade, huddled in a niche between a record shop and a surfboard place, he found a window with guitars in it. The sign over the door said MUSIC AND STUFF. For a moment, before entering, Jon had the weird image of someone handing chunks of songs out from behind the counter like chocolate bars, like candy.

An elderly woman was inside, dusting the guitars on the wall. There was a piano and a drum set too, and racks of sheet music. In the glass-topped counter Jon could see small instruments: harmonicas, recorders, a tambourine, and drumsticks.

The woman turned toward him. "Yes?" It wasn't exactly a friendly greeting, and she didn't look at him in an inviting way either, but more as if he'd disturbed her at a very important task.

"Do you have staff paper?" he asked, ignoring her clouded brow, "and a pencil, maybe?"

"Does this look like a stationer's shop to you?" she asked back. Her voice had the dreary sound of rain drumming on an old oil barrel.

"Do you?" The music was pushing at his teeth from the inside; it was a breath that wanted to be exhaled, a song that wanted to be sung.

She dropped the cloth and climbed down from the stepladder, wiping her hands on the gray cotton skirt she was wearing. "Yeah, yeah, calm down. I have some old sheets lying around somewhere; give me a sec."

Mumbling, she vanished into a room at the back of the store to return with a faded box, which she put on the counter.

"No one asks for it these days. I don't know. Maybe composing has gone out of fashion." She plucked a pencil from the drawer under the counter and put it on top of the paper. "Here you go. Do you need a desk too, or can I return to my work now? That will be… Oh, let's see. I'll give it to you. It's been sitting on the shelf for ages. Just take it and go."

Jon glanced at the piano. "Could I…" The woman shot him a sharp look, but he went on, "Could I use your piano for a moment? I promise, it won't take long, but if I don't write this down, it will be lost."

She stared at him, her fists on her hips.

"I can help you clean the store, if you want. But please let me write down this melody. I could easily clean the top shelves." Pleading. He was pleading with a stranger, and he realized there was no piano in Sean's place. He wondered how he dealt with that.

She was still measuring him. "Oh, what the hell. Okay then. I hope your hands are clean, young man!"

Sheepishly, Jon held them up to show her his palms, and she nodded.

THE piano was dusty too but there were fingerprints on its top, and an old ring from a coffee mug. It made him smile and turn around, but the woman was back on the ladder, wiping away at shelves and the things on them.

"My name is Rose, if you must know," she said without turning, as if she had felt his scrutiny. "And I've been running this shop forever and a year. Now, what was it you wanted to write? Stop staring and get down to it, and then get out of here."

Jon opened the piano. The keys were yellowed with age, shiny from being used often. He rested his fingers on the keys, letting the music flow from where it was hiding in his heart, flow through his nerves and into the instrument.

Chord after chord—playing, writing, playing—made its way onto the piano and then onto the paper as he hastily scribbled it down. There were words floating somewhere on the melody, parts of words, snippets of rhyme; but he ignored them, concentrating on the silver ribbon of song weaving its miracle around him.

"Use a minor key for that last bar." Rose said it gruffly, as if she was talking to a shoplifter. "Make it sound a little more mellow."

It was like coming out of a trance, as if someone had pulled him back into reality by his hair. "Huh?"

She gestured at him, at the paper. "Minor key. Try it." Ponderously, she climbed down and, pushing her gray locks back, came over to Jon. "You're writing about the ocean and the sunset, aren't you? About the surf and the dolphins. It's good!"

Surprise ran down his back.

"I could hear it," she went on. "I could hear the surf and see the dolphins and the colors of the sunset. Damn, you're good. Who are you, boy?

"My name is Jon Stone, and I've come to LA to make a career in the music business." The moment he closed his mouth he realized how absurd he sounded, but Rose smiled.

"I'm sure you will," she said, a lot gentler than before. "I've seen many come here and say the same thing; but I always sent them on their way, the pitiful young dreamers, and they all ended up waiting tables or working as bouncers at those expensive nightclubs where the movie stars hang out. I wanted to tell them to go home to their families, to the people they left behind, disappointed and angry at them for following their dreams. You though…" She beckoned for him to follow, which Jon did, taking the sheet music with him. "I'll show you something."

In the dark hallway behind the shop, she half turned to him and cackled like a witch. "Come with me, come."

Jon had the crazy feeling that he'd find himself inside a cage in a moment, like Hansel from the fairy tale, and Rose would turn out to be a slave trader, or worse, she'd force-feed him and then make sausages out of him.

A door at the back of the building opened into a yard surrounded by a high wooden fence. There were flowers everywhere: in pots along the path and hanging from the fence, in beds meandering all over, separated from each other by lemon and orange trees.

Wind chimes hung from their branches, their sounds playing a dreamy tune in the slight breeze. At the other end of the garden was another building, a flat, gray thing with one window and a narrow stairway leading up to a roof garden.

"My husband." Rose pointed at the open door. "I want you to meet my husband, Roy."

"We make our living with Roy's work. If it was up to him we'd have closed the shop long ago. It doesn't bring in any money, you know. But I like to putter around there during the day, watch the people walk by, and have fun with the odd customer." Again she stopped to look at him. "And once in a while a miracle happens, and someone like you comes along and totally makes my day."

"Me?" It was indeed a different planet. Jon was surer of that with every passing minute.

"Yeah, you. An outstanding talent." Rose's smile softened, and the change made her face almost beautiful, almost young. "I've been dealing with musicians for too long now not to see real talent, the musical gift, shine through. And in you, my dear young man, it shines so brightly that it nearly blinds me."

"But all I did was write down a few chords!" It felt like cheating, and on a major scale.

"But they were beautiful, those few chords. They tell a story; they make me want to sit and listen, and ask you to play more, to tell me the words to the song. You write wonderful music!"

She pushed open the door and called, "Roy, we have a visitor!"

A man emerged from another room. He was wearing a leather apron, and his hair hung down his back in a thin, gray ponytail. On his narrow nose sat round glasses that looked at least a hundred years old. "Have you found another puppy, Rosie? What's so special about this one?"

Rose plucked the music sheet from Jon's unresisting hand and held it out. "He wrote this just now, in the shop. Walked in and asked for staff paper, and I could see his soul vibrating with the urge of it."

Roy threw a glance at the sheet and then put it down on the worktable in the center of the big room to return to where he had come from.

A moment later he came back with a guitar in his hand.

"Play it," he said. "I want to hear you play it on this guitar." He paused to carefully wipe the shiny surface of the instrument with the sleeve of his sweater. "I made it. I'm a guitar builder."

Jon took it from him. It was made of rosewood.

Chapter Fourteen

IT SEEMED AS if he'd been there for hours.

Once he had played the new melody they made him play other songs, made him sing them, and he had watched as Rose's face went soft and dreamy, and how she had clutched Roy's hand when he got to the gentle love ballads. He'd closed his eyes and let his voice go mellow, let the sudden yearning that came over him flow into it, the yearning for a kind of love he had not yet encountered.

The gentle breeze brought the scent of the ocean and the flowers into the workshop, where it mingled with the smell of wood and glue. The wind chimes rang softly, and when he listened carefully, they almost sounded like the silver laughter of a fairy, like the echo of laughter in a hidden glade.

Rose had made tea for them and brought out leftover Christmas cookies, and Roy had taken off his apron. Dust motes were dancing lazily in the sunbeams falling through the large, slightly grimy window, and from afar they could hear the bustle of the promenade.

Jon sat with the rosewood guitar on his knees, touching the smooth wood over and over, tracing the grain with the tips of his fingers. It reminded him of the surf at sunset: copper curls and whirls, golden lines woven through them. He loved the instrument. It's sound was like molten honey, sweet and soft, each tone a melodious statement. The vision of playing it on a big stage to an attentive audience, washed over him; and for an instant Jon pressed it against his body and closed his eyes, almost hearing the applause.

"What time is it? I have to go," he said suddenly. "My manager is waiting for me. He wants to introduce me to a producer."

"Come back soon." Roy took the guitar from him when he held it out. "Come back, and I may be able to teach you one or another thing about playing." Again he wiped the wood with his sleeve, removing Jon's fingerprints, and it felt to Jon as if he was wiping any memory of him from the instrument. A sudden bout of sadness washed over him, but he didn't have the guts to ask. He knew he wouldn't be able to afford it for a long time yet.

Back in the store, reality gradually returned. Life outside looked normal enough; nothing had changed there the way things were changing for him.

"I'm sort of dazed," Jon said. "All I wanted was some staff paper, and a moment at your piano. Strange things keep happening to me these days. I go to play a gig to make some money, and it was as if the stars decided to align for me, and I meet a fabulous pianist, a guitarist, and a manager in one evening; and all of them have nothing better to do than jump at the chance of working with me."

Rose was smiling, listening from behind her counter with her arms crossed and her hair pushed behind her ears.

"And you, grumpy enough to turn a braver man than me to stone, you offer me…" He had to swallow. "A sanctuary, a haven of music and understanding. It's as if, with the decision to come here, everything has changed."

"It seems like that, yes." She waved at the piano. "You have a way of compelling people to do your bidding, young man. A magical gift, a great asset in someone who wants to make his living from creativity." With an insulting flip of her wrist, she gestured at the passerby outside the store. "People think creativity is something that comes for free, a hobby, not something one makes a living at. It's not a real *job* to make music, or write books. It's not a real job to build guitars either. But that's because they have no use for them. But that's not how it really is, is it?"

Again the tolling of that huge bell, as if the universe was speaking to him through the mouths of strangers, the sound of the wind or the colors of the sunset.

"Creativity isn't a hobby; it's not something you unpack only when the so-called real world leaves you alone for long enough to use it. No. Creativity is at the bottom of everything. It's the first breath we take when we're born and the last before we die; it's in children's laughter, and the wish to drive a car a little faster. It's in the way you plant your garden or design your computer. Being creative means being human; only they don't see it that way. They admire Beethoven's music and da Vinci's art, but they don't see that in their time they were like you: fighting convention, going hungry, being lonely." Rose broke off, her brow wrinkled. "What was I going to say? Oh right, this: I believe you'll make your way, and quickly, Jon. But if you need a meal until then, feel free to come here anytime at all. Oh—and if you need a piano too. What the heck. What I'm trying to say is, do come back. I'd love for you to stay in touch."

"Of course." It seemed ridiculous that she would find it necessary to mention it at all. "Of course I'll be back." And to Rose, he could say what he hadn't dared to say to Roy: "I want that guitar. I want it very badly. I'll come back and play it so often that Roy won't be able to sell it to anyone else ever."

She tried to hide her smile and look gruff again, but Jon grinned at her until Rose yelled, "What are you waiting for? Get the hell out of here, you impudent pup!"

He threw her a kiss and left.

IN a way, the meeting with the producers was similar to what he'd experienced with Roy and Rose.

They offered him coffee, which he politely declined, asking for water instead, saying that coffee right before performing always made him nervous. It earned him a few appreciative nods.

He was asked if he was willing to play his songs for them, and so he did. Only this time it was in a well-appointed studio, and Sean and Jones were there with him, playing along. The night before, they had put together the playlist with great care, keeping in mind that there would only be just the three of them, and they wanted to created the best effect they possibly could with their meager kernel of a band.

Jon touched the microphone reverently. He had heard of the brand, heard other singers raving about it and its qualities; and now here he was, and the thing belonged to him for the moment. No one had told him how long he was expected to perform, and no one was paying attention to him now as he got ready to play his guitar and sing for them.

His throat was dry, raspy, clogged with anxiety; and he was craving a cigarette like never before.

"I want to fill the world with beauty," he said to Jones while they were tuning their guitars. "You know, I wish I could just do that, write the songs and perform them, and not have to bother about the whole business thing at all. Not worry about money and where I'll sleep that night, not have to think about how to get a car so I can move around, nothing. Just, you know, make music."

"I know," Jones replied around the pick between his lips. "Trust me. I know. But the world is a rough, wild place, and even musicians need to eat."

Sal was in the control room with the two men, and they were chatting amicably over coffee and cigarettes, their backs turned to them. The music engineer was laughing at something that had been said, his headphones dangling from his hand. No one seemed to care about him, and watching them, something like anger boiled up in Jon.

"Right." He adjusted the mic and grabbed his pick. "Let's do it, guys. I don't give a shit if they listen or not. I don't think they care one way or the other either. But it's a great studio, and a chance for a free rehearsal session."

The man standing with his back to him turned to look at Jon. "Your mike is open, you know. Nice little speech there, about beauty and stuff. Now let's hear if you're as good as Sal says."

Sean barked a laugh, but Jon was undeterred. He stood, his feet planted firmly on the floor, shoulders back, took a deep breath, and let it out again slowly before striking the first chord.

THEY let him go through four entire songs before he was interrupted with a terse "Thank you" and invited to take a break. Again they were offered coffee, and this time Jon accepted and took it with him to stand outside on the sidewalk for a cigarette and a breath of air.

His body was tingling from the elation of the music, from the fine harmony he and Sean had found without many words, and for Jones's bright alertness and his ability to improvise or just take a break when he didn't know a song that well. They were communicating through his music, and he loved it.

It was warm in the afternoon sun. Jon liked how it never seemed as seedy and dark here as it did in Manhattan, even here in midtown LA, where the high-rise buildings stood. The ocean was a constant presence, not like a border but more like a backdrop, a magnificent curtain, a huge playground. Jon was quite sure he could smell it even here in the middle of the city.

"You did very well." The man who had been introduced as Cole stepped outside, a cigar in his hand, and he was busy lighting it. "I'm quite taken with your songs. Your voice is good too, noticeable, something people will remember when they hear it on the radio." He gestured at the door behind him. "I think your manager is negotiating with my partner right now. Maybe you should be inside."

It was neither joy nor surprise that he felt. It was more shock, the same kind of shock and dread he felt when reading his bank statements: a sinking feeling somewhere in his bowels, a curdling of the coffee in his stomach.

"What?"

"Tom is making an offer. We'll see how it goes. Are you leaving everything to Sal? Do you trust him that unconditionally?"

Jon, panic rising in his throat, dropped his cigarette and returned inside.

Sal was coming toward him from the elevators. "There you are. Well, I was hoping for this outcome, and my well-laid plans have come through. If you want to, you can sign your first record deal in a few days. How do you feel about this company? It's not the biggest label, but they are decent folks, and they will help you grow and look out for you." He rubbed his hands. "Somehow I knew it would be spit-easy getting you a deal, and my instincts were right."

"It can't be this easy." Stunned, Jon leaned against the wall. "No one gets a record deal this easily. No one."

"You read too many trashy magazines, Jon." Sal nodded at Cole, who vanished into one of the elevators without stopping. "Yes, it is hard to get a record deal. Yes, it takes years of hard work, of playing on street corners and serving tables. Yes, most never succeed at all. And yes, some have to sleep with the boss's daughter. All those stories are true. But it's also true that real talent, talent like yours, gets snatched up right away. No one would be stupid enough to send you away after hearing you play, or even more, seeing you perform, Jon." Sal clapped his shoulder. "Jon, you will be a star! These men can tell! They know you will own the stage someday soon; they can *see* it. As I could. As anyone who knows even the least thing about music and the stage can." He fumbled for his cigarettes. "A lot of hard work is coming our way, but you knew that. You have to learn to deal with the dark side of the business: the PR and publicity work. You may not enjoy that. But then again, it's all part of the package."

"But Sal." Jon didn't even know how to put it. He'd only been in LA a few days. He hadn't even had a chance to settle in, and here he was: discussing contracts with a well-known music label.

"Yeah. I know. You're a true wonder boy. I want you to promise me one thing, Jon. Take me with you on your crazy ride." There was an emotion painted on Sal's face that Jon couldn't name: a kind of wistfulness, awe, and, weirdly, love.

"I need to," Jon said, and his voice sounded rough. "I need to go somewhere. There's something I have to do. I have to make sure a guitar I saw today doesn't get sold before I can buy it when my advance comes through." He paused. "There will be an advance?"

Sal laughed. "Of course, Jon. It won't be millions, but certainly enough to get you settled in. They looked at all the songs you gave me. We're talking a two-album deal here. What guitar?"

The words *two-album deal* were clanking is his head like huge, big boulders.

"One I saw this morning." Jon could hardly hear himself speaking. "A rosewood guitar."

Chapter Fifteen

HE WOKE BEFORE the sun rose, in the gray light of a cold, early dawn.

There was no sound, no movement, from Sean's room, so he got dressed and left the apartment. Barefoot, he walked to the beach.

Even at this time of day it wasn't empty: a young couple was jogging along the waterline, the girl's ponytail bobbing with every step, their feet leaving imprints in the wet sand that were washed away by the next surge of surf, here and gone as if the sea needed to absorb their presence; a man, walking his dog, throwing a stick for him into the waves over and over, laughing at the spray of water when the pup shook himself after retrieving it.

Jon turned away from the ocean to look back at the houses. There was something special about early morning, something expectant and fresh, with the smell of coffee and fresh bread, something that allowed the world to breathe and think before the noise and pace of the day took over.

He'd wanted to call his mother, wanted to tell her about his incredible good luck and the ease with which things were happening to him, but something stopped him. Not yet, a tiny voice had whispered inside his head, wait for it. Wait. Wait until your signature is dry on that paper, until you hold it in your hands, and the check. Last night over dinner, Sal had told him that they would have to pick musicians for his band, and soon, and start rehearsing. He was popping open a bottle of champagne as he said it, with a gleeful expression on his face that made him look like a little boy.

Jon had wondered what it had been like to grow up in Las Vegas, among the bright lights in the desert. It seemed hard to imagine a normal life in such a place.

A Frisbee flew past him, and he watched the dog chasing it into the waves, barking loudly, enjoying life.

Roy and Rose had welcomed him back with delight, like an old friend who had been part of their life for a long time. Rose hadn't even tried to be her gruff self when he'd walked through the doorway but had given him that amazing, bright smile that turned her into a lovely young woman and had clapped her hands at his news. She'd torn open the door to her magic garden and yelled for her husband at the top of her lungs, telling the entire neighborhood that a new star was born, and she was there at the exact moment when it had happened.

"I knew it," she'd said to him, a little out of breath from all the shouting, her blue eyes shining. "I just knew, when you walked out of here, when I watched you walk away, there was this light around you, the aura of good luck! And how nice of you to come right back to tell us."

"Actually…" Jon had begun to say just as Roy stepped in, wiping his hands on a rag.

He couldn't say it. He'd made Sean drive him here just for this, but standing there now, facing Roy, he couldn't make himself ask for the guitar. So instead he told them about the studio and how he'd played for those producers, and how the offer of a contract had come so easily, as if they'd been waiting for him.

"They probably were," Roy had said gently. "If your manager is worth his money, they were well prepared for you, Jon. Don't think you just bowled them over with your short performance. It was just the last piece they needed to make their decision, to see you perform in person, see if you would be easy to sell. But if your music wasn't what it is, that wouldn't have meant a thing. And they knew that before you showed up, from the demos."

He'd wanted to say, maybe that was how it was, but whatever.

He'd left them with empty hands, again promising to be back soon, show them the contract once he had it; and yes, he'd have enough time for tea or lunch and a chat. Of course he would. He wanted to hold that guitar in his hands, feel the smooth grain under his fingertips and hear the sweet, mellow sound of its strings. He wanted it very badly.

THE dog whipped past, the Frisbee clamped between his teeth, drops spraying from his long, golden fur like little rainbows, to deliver it to his master.

A spike of loneliness shot through Jon, a moment of homesickness and the longing to share his news with people who knew him, who'd known him for longer than those around him now. It was almost a sense of displacement, the feeling of cold slush running down his back amid all the excitement and hope of this new day.

He shook it off. He shook it off like cobwebs and took the first step back toward the apartment, and then another; and the closer he got, the stronger the excitement about the day grew. They'd go back to the studio. There would be music, probably more music than he could stomach; and there would be musicians to meet, to put together a band. His band.

It would be his job to pick his band.

"REMEMBER," Sal said as they stood outside the record company building, "remember this moment, Jon. Yesterday you were here as an applicant. Today you walk through this door, and it is a part of you. You belong here now, and a small part of it belongs to you. One day you will have your own studio, and lots of people working for you; and you'll only come here for recording sessions, or to have lunch with your producers. But today, today is like Armstrong's first step on the moon for you. So—do it mindfully."

Jon looked down at his scruffy sneakers and the frayed hem of the jeans he was wearing. There was some sand from his morning walk still sticking to them and a clearly visible line of dried salt water. But it had been the only clean piece of clothing left. He'd have to do some laundry when they got back home later. No one seemed to mind, or even notice, though, not Sal or Sean, not even the technicians waiting for them.

Tom was there, the man who'd spoken most to them the day before. He looked like an older, thinner, more cynical version of Sal, someone who'd spent most of his life in rooms without windows and too many cigarettes, someone who'd get easily lost in a normal, everyday life.

There was another man with him today, about Jon's age: Russ, a young man with a kind face, fine brown hair, and alert eyes that watched all the proceedings as greedily as a squirrel looking for acorns.

"We've asked a few of our studio musicians to come and play with you today," Tom explained while scanning some papers that were handed to him by Russ. "Let's see how it works out."

Someone was setting up drums; someone else was tuning a bass. Jones and Sean, sitting on their stools, were chatting idly, watching the proceedings, smoking.

Jon began unpacking his own guitar, but Tom shook his head. "I want you to concentrate on the singing today. No instrument for you. Your voice is great, and it will easily be recognized on the radio, but you need to add some depth and timbre to it. I'm glad you're a baritone; there are so many tenors and what I like to call 'quackers,' but you have a real singing voice. We need to cultivate that. Maybe a few singing lessons wouldn't be a bad idea."

A mild sweat broke out on Jon's neck at those words, but he nodded gamely.

"There are more than enough mediocre singers out there," Tom went on, undeterred. "But there aren't many great ones, and even fewer with their own, unique music. So we need to cultivate you in any way we can." He squinted at Jon through the smoke of his cigarette. "Have you ever considered singing opera? You wouldn't be the best, but you could pull it off."

The prickle of sweat turned into rivulets. "No, certainly not. No. Not ever." He was stammering, and he knew it.

"Yeah, probably not a good idea anyway. We need you here. Well then. Inside you go. Your studio time, your band, let's see how it goes."

IT didn't go, and Jon knew it after the first few bars.

He took a few calming breaths and sang, his eyes closed, feeling for the music, trying to find his melodies in it; but it wasn't there.

After two songs he was ready to throw the microphone through the glass separating them from the engineering room. He had his hand clamped tightly around it, his shoulders had gone stiff with anger, and he could almost feel his voice clogging with fury.

Tom called a halt and waved to him. Wordlessly, he offered a cigarette to Jon, who took it with shaking fingers.

Only after it had been lit and he'd taken his first couple of drags did Tom ask, very quietly, "Okay, tell me."

"I don't even know." It was the truth; he didn't know.

"Those are good musicians," Tom said, "and they're trying hard."

Jon, out of words, leaned against the sound-mixing table and crossed his arms, waiting for someone else to say something intelligent.

"The thing is, how do you want your band to sound?"

They all turned toward Russ, who was sitting in the shadows in the corner, a clipboard on his knees. He blushed under the attention but went on stoutly, "You can't just dump a bunch of people in there and expect every song to sound perfect, can you? Jon needs to say how he wants his songs to sound."

Tom, his eyebrows raised, softly replied, "Very good, college boy. A very good point." And added, to Jon, "Well? You heard the intern. What shall it be? What sound? Like the Beatles? The Stones? Elton John? Or more like Neil Diamond?"

"Interesting. You only mention one American musician." Jon ground his cigarette into the mountain of butts in the overflowing ashtray.

"Oh well, here are some more: Barry Manilow? Frank Sinatra? Or maybe the Beach Boys?"

"Definitely *not* Barry Manilow." Jon shrugged. "I don't want to sound like any of those. I want to sound like myself. My own unique style."

A bright, approving smile appeared on Tom's lean face. "I like that. I like your panache, young man. You have guts. So tell me. What kind of band do you want?"

"Strings." Russ was faster than Jon. "He needs strings, and percussion. And he needs backup singers. And a third guitar, if he isn't going to play himself all the time. And he needs someone to write the score for him."

"I will do that," Sean announced. "I've claimed that job. But I'll gladly ask you to help me, if you want to, Russ."

The clipboard clattered on the floor when Russ jumped up. "Yes! I'd love to!" Again he blushed, and this time Jon grinned at him. "That is, if you don't mind."

Tom threw up his hands. "What has this world come to? Song-writers with their names barely dry on the contract calling the shots, and uppity interns putting together bands. Well, I'll just go to lunch then and let you work it out on your own. Seems I'm not really needed." His eyes were twinkling, though, and a smile tugged at his lips as he added, "Stellar moments. I love these stellar moments, and I think you'll be great together. This looks like a good mix to me. All right then, get to work. I'll come back in a couple of hours and see how you're doing."

On the point of walking out, he turned around and added, "Just call Sally. She'll get those musicians for you."

The door closed, and they were alone: Jon, Sal, Russ, Jones, and Sean; and they looked at one another, slightly dazed, until Russ cleared his throat and asked, "Strings?"

Chapter Sixteen

"YOU KNOW," SAL said, "that you're getting special treatment." He blew on his coffee. "My jaw almost hit the floor when Tom left the studio to let us do our own thing."

"You have no idea," Russ added, his face lit with enthusiasm. "I've been working with him for months now, and he's never done that before, left at such a crucial point. And I'm sure he'll come back and rip it all apart; but, man, until then it will be awesome fun."

Jon wasn't really listening. He was watching the percussionist setting up his instruments in the corner of the big recording studio. Wind chimes—there they were, and the bongos he'd always imagined for the "The River." A shiver ran down his back when the tall, dark man who had been introduced as Walter dropped his hand on them to test for the sound and it vibrated through the speakers like the promise of a thunderstorm.

Five strings and a bass, that was all they'd been able to muster in such a short time, Russ had explained, but there would be more; and if they felt they needed to move on to a bigger orchestra, they could always move the entire project to the symphonic studio. He'd cleared it with Sally, no problem there. They were, all of them, waiting with bated breath to see what would happen next.

The sound of rain.

He wanted the sound of rain on big, shiny leaves, the kind that grew in a rain forest. The kind of rain that would make the earth smell deliciously rich and fertile, that would make the ground steam.

And the bass. The heartbeat of the jungle, the call of dark, mysterious secrets, of hot skin and forbidden delights.

Ignoring the conversation flowing around him, Jon went over to Walter, who gave him a wide, relaxed grin.

"Hey," he greeted Jon. "So you're Tom's new wonder boy? He's been talking about you constantly, even before you got here. Wouldn't have surprised me if he'd rolled out a red carpet for you."

"Jungle," Jon said, ignoring the speech. "Can you make it sound like the jungle?"

Walter laughed. "Hey, look at me. I'm from Brazil. I know jungle. Which song is that?"

Jon pulled the sheets from the sheaf lying on the table. They still had the chemical smell of hastily photocopied paper, and that, more than anything else, brought home to him what was happening.

Slightly giddy, he sat on the edge of the table and looked around. There were at least twenty other people there, getting ready to play, scrutinizing his music, smoking, drinking coffee, chatting, just waiting for him to give a signal and tell them to play his songs.

He couldn't do it.

The sheets in his hands shook as he stared down at them, and he realized that someone had taken the time to type them out, that he wasn't seeing his own handwriting anymore. These were orderly, proper music sheets, the titles printed over the songs, with chord notations, text, everything, edited and ready for professional musicians. There was a box of pencils on the table and another one with erasers, paper clips, even clothespins to keep the sheets together on the stands—everything was there, everything they needed for serious studio work, including coffee and cookies.

Wordlessly, he held out the sheets to Walter, who took them with a brief nod. Glancing over the notes, he picked up his drumsticks and brought them down on the bongos with a flourish, tapping out a heartbeat rhythm, playing the intro just the way Jon had always imagined it.

His hands sweating, his ears ringing, he went to where his guitar was waiting and joined Walter, strumming the chords he had written, singing the words he had thought up on that dreary, late November afternoon while languishing at the bookstore, and how far he had come in this short time.

All talk had stopped, all attention had turned to where Jon and Walter were playing to each other, were sending each other deeper and deeper into the rhythm of "The River." Walter had discarded the sticks and was using his hands now, the beat more insistent, hotter, wilder.

Sean joined them on the electric organ, volume turned up all the way, making the glass walls of the studio tremble under the assault.

The door flew open to admit Tom, who stopped right there, watching, letting the music flood out into the hallway and through the building.

Jon turned toward the microphone with a nod at Russ, and, still playing his guitar, sang, all fear and inhibition gone, only the joy of his music left.

"AND now," Tom said when they finished, "the work begins."

He ordered more coffee, and some sandwiches, stating that no one would be leaving the studio until they were done with this one song and then he'd take them all out for dinner.

Bar by bar, chord by chord, they dissected "The River" and put together a score for it, Sean always in the lead, always saying what Jon was thinking before he could utter it himself, and all the while writing, scribbling down how they wanted to play it, trying out a passage to see if it worked the way they imagined it.

It was scary and yet exhilarating, the way these musicians worked with the melody he had created, but the most amazing part was that no one ever looked his way and laughed or asked what he had been thinking, and where did all this crap come from?

They were taking it seriously; they were accepting him as one of their club. He wasn't the dreamer anymore. He was a songwriter with a contract now, and a record label was looking after his music.

"We'll have to move to the big studio," Tom announced at some point. "I can see we'll need more than just a band. We'll need an orchestra for some of these songs. We'll work on the scores for the next few weeks, and then I'll book you into the symphonic studio for the rehearsals." He rubbed his hands together. "And we have to start the marketing pretty soon. Photo shoots. Some interviews. Announcements, teasers. And then put out a single. Let's see, it's January now." Mumbling to himself he walked away, calling for Sally.

When he returned he told them they wanted "The River" out as a single by the end of May; it would be a good summer hit, and that would leave them plenty of time for the advertising and getting it into the radio stations.

"And now, dinner. Enough for today," he called.

Jon realized that the day had slipped by without him noticing. It was almost seven.

HIS father was on the phone, and he was grumpy. Jon had forgotten about the time difference and called when they had returned from dinner, which meant it was way after midnight in New York.

"A record deal, huh," his father said. "Well, that's nice. I'm proud of you, Jon. I knew you had it in you. Now don't let that quick success go to your head, my son. Remember, every girl wants a pop star." His voice sounded raspy with sleep.

Jon wished he could touch him now, touch his father's hand for some reassurance, and to make everything feel a little more real.

"How's Jenny?" he asked instead. "Have you seen her?"

"No, we haven't." There was a stifled yawn at the other end of the phone. "No idea. But she's the past, isn't she? Was there any talk of her joining you in LA?"

"No." And now he felt stupid for bringing her up at all, as if he was trying to hold on to something that had been lost a long time ago, a piece of home amid the excitement of new beginnings.

"Are they paying you well?" His father was practical, as always.

"Yes, sir." Jon could hardly say the number out loud that he'd been promised. He'd seen it written out on the contract, and those digits had danced before his eyes like crazy little demons. It was enough to pay for Kevin's entire medical education. Enough to buy a house. Not the biggest house, or in the best part of town, but something comfortable, something to call his own, and with more than one bathroom.

For a moment there was silence. Then his father said, "Good. Now just take care you don't lose yourself in that easy fame, Jon. You're very young yet. You need to pace yourself."

"Don't worry. I won't. But…" His heart did a little jump. "But I'm going out to buy a new guitar tomorrow morning. I really need a better one."

There, and now he could say it, and even mean it. His old guitar simply wasn't good enough for the studio.

"Really?" A little more animation crept into his tone. "What kind?"

"A rosewood. A six-string concert guitar. Some nice inlay on the neck too."

"Ah." The breathing quickened a bit. "Sounds nice. Wish I could see it."

"You will, Dad. Soon." Something was stuck in Jon's throat, something that made swallowing hard and painful.

"You're very far away, Jon. I wish you were closer so we could see you from time to time. Who knows when you'll come back, if ever." Words his mother would have said, but his father—only in the middle of the night, when no one was around to see him go maudlin. "Your mom's birthday. You'll have to come home for your mom's birthday. Promise me, Jon. You have to come home then. I know she wants it very much. It would make your mom happy."

"I'll try. If I can, I will. That I'll promise. But I have no idea what will happen now." There was a tiny spider crawling up the wall, following a thin crack in the plaster like Dorothy followed the yellow brick road. "Truth is…" Jon had to chew on the words. "Truth is, Dad, I have no idea what's happening. Everyone here acts as if they'd just been waiting for me to show up. Everything is so easy, and happening so fast, I can't catch my breath or even really understand what's going on. I say I want an orchestra, and *wham*—there's an orchestra, pulled out of thin air, just for me. I say I want a bigger studio, and the next day they give us one that's big enough for the Boston Pops. It's as if… as if I've never done anything else at all, ever."

A sigh, a small cough, then: "Maybe it's meant to be that way, with your music." It sounded a little wistful and made Jon rub his eyes. "Maybe this was the way you're meant to be going. But Jon."

"Yes, Dad."

"You know what I'm going to say. You're a grown man and all that, but please be careful. An easy road is always full of seduction. Stay away from drugs, my boy. And don't let the girls get to you. Watch out for yourself. Take care." Another sigh, then he added,

"Do me a favor. If you can spare the money, buy a camera and take some pictures. Let us see where you live and how you're doing. Can you do that?"

"I'll do that. I wish you could see the sunsets here, Dad. They are amazing. It's so beautiful." Homesickness, like a big, cold wave, was trying to inundate Jon. He opened his mouth to tell his father how much he loved him, how much he missed being with his family, and how he was almost willing to throw everything away just to be in his old room again, snuggled under his quilt, waiting for his mother to call him down for breakfast.

Instead he said, "I'll do that tomorrow, I promise. As soon as I have a spare moment. They keep me pretty busy."

"Goodnight, Jon." And with that his father hung up, and he was alone again.

Chapter Seventeen

THE DAYS PASSED in a blur of music, coffee, and far too many cigarettes.

Jon could hardly tell what month it was anymore, let alone what day of the week. The music was taking up every minute, every fiber of his being, every thread of his mind.

They had taken apart "The River," dissecting it like a dead frog, gazing down at its innards, searching for its heart and veins, until Sean and Russ had retreated with a big pile of music sheets and returned hours later to dump them on the table and call for Jon, who was just then learning the intricacies of playing the bongos from Walter.

Here it was, Sean called across the studio, and they were taking it to Sally for photocopying right now.

Jon, bongos forgotten, came over to stare in bemusement at the many staff lines, at the orchestration of his song.

"You'll have to play a twelve-string if you want to play the guitar yourself," Russ said, rather diffidently, wiping his hands on his jeans in a gesture of apology. "We want it to sound full, mysterious, well, sweaty, sort of." He shrugged, with a questioning grin at Sean. "Sexy."

"Works for me." In fact, it was just what he had imagined, and seeing it written out by his new friends, Jon resolved to learn to write his own score. They had done well, but he wanted to have control, wanted to have a say in it.

"I'll take them up to Sally," he replied. "I need a break anyway." It wasn't entirely true, but he wanted the moment of waiting for the elevator to have a closer look at the music without them breathing down his neck expectantly.

SHE was in her office, headphones clamped over her ears, long, blond hair dancing down her back as she moved with the rhythm she was listening to, her fingers flying over the typewriter.

Jon stood in the doorway and listened to her humming a rather off-tune melody, oblivious to the fact that she had an observer.

"Hey," he called, but she did not react. Her fingernails were perfect, a shade of deep red, a sharp contrast to the white skin of her hands. There was no ring either.

"Sally!" He'd used his stage voice, the baritone that carried so well across the studio, and this time she did notice and turned around.

A pretty blush colored her cheeks. "I'm sorry, sorry!" Hastily, the headphones came off. "What can I do for you?"

Laughter. It was definitely laughter, bubbling in his chest, tearing to get out; and it was the easy, joyful feeling of a happy, easy instant.

Holding out the sheets to her, Jon felt some kind of sorrow he hadn't even rightly known had been there until it washed away from him. "Just a few copies. If you tell me where the machine is, I can do it myself."

"No! No way!" She jumped up, straightening her very short skirt. "Tom would kill me if I let you waste your time like that! You're to be treated like royalty, he said; you're to get everything you want, and immediately!" Again she blushed, but this time it was a dark crimson and went all the way to her throat. With a pretty trace of mischievousness she added, "But you can come along, if you want to, and keep me company, and tell me a little bit about yourself."

"Royalty, eh." He followed her down the hallway, where she opened the door to another room and turned on the light.

Jon stopped in his tracks.

"This is where you can find almost anything you need," Sally was saying. "Paper, pencils, erasers—even the odd set of guitar strings, but if they're here then they've been misplaced." She tilted her head like a little bird, like a cute canary. "Did anyone show you where to go for instruments and stuff? I'm betting they haven't. I mean, just in case you need a different guitar or something."

"You keep guitars hidden away somewhere here?" He was in paradise; Jon was pretty sure of it.

The machine was warming up, rumbling gently in its corner like a beast waking from slumber.

"Yeah, there are quite a few of them, even some Fender pieces if you want them. We keep a lot of instruments, just in case. I can show you, if you want."

"Not now, they're waiting for me, but yes, please!" His imagination was running away with him; he was certain of that. In his mind he saw her taking him into a huge vault, hidden down some stone stairs, a big brass key in her hand, swearing him to secrecy; and there it was: the stash, the magical treasure of the record company, rows of exquisite guitars, drum sets, violins and woodwinds; and in the center, as if placed there especially for him, a Steinway grand, pristine, polished, covered with a velvet spread to protect it from getting scratched.

"I'm sure you don't need anything from down there though," Sally said, handing him the requested copies. "I'm sure you have the finest guitars in the world anyway." She had dark eyes. Her hair was nearly white, an interesting shade of platinum with a hint of rose, but her eyes were as dark as those of a squirrel, and just as bright and inquisitive. She was wearing a light-blue polka-dot dress and matching ballerinas, and she was a girl.

Jon felt stupid taking the papers from her. "Thanks." No girls. Not yet. Not at this point, he didn't have time for romance. "Thank you very much, Sally."

Back out in the hallway and five steps ahead of her as if he was fleeing, he heard her call after him, "If you need anything else, you know where to find me!"

He didn't reply and took the stairs instead of waiting for the elevator.

SAL wanted to go out for dinner, but Jon declined and asked for a ride to Rose's store instead.

"A guitar maker?" Jones had overheard them. "Where? Can I come?" He was holding his black Stratocaster, ready to pack it in its case.

"Let's all go," Sal said, "and have dinner afterward. What do you think?" He waved to Russ, who was about to leave the studio. "Hey, intern. Move your butt. You're coming too."

"I'm not really an intern," Russ answered. "I just don't get paid.

Yet. Because I'm still working on my degree."

"So—you're an intern." Sal laughed at the expression on Russ's face. "Nothing wrong with that. You're good too. So move your ass to the car. Intern."

There were five of them outside Rose's store a short time later.

JON felt for the envelope in the pocket of his jacket, and for the reassuring sound of the crisp bills inside, drawn from his brand-new bank account. He'd looked at the bank statement before taking out the money, at all the digits on it, and all in the right columns too. He was wealthy. He had more cash than he had ever dreamed of, and buying a new guitar was nothing, nothing at all. He had to keep telling himself that, even now, pushing open the door to the shop. It was work. It was something he needed. It was not an indulgence.

Rose was knitting, but seeing Jon, she dropped the needles like hot potatoes and jumped up.

"Jon! You've brought friends! I'll lock up, and we'll go have tea with Roy, shall we?" As if she'd been waiting all day for him.

"You sure make friends fast," Sal murmured. "A very nice trait in someone who wants to be famous."

Jon wanted to plant his elbow in Sal's ribs but stopped short, opening the back door for them instead.

The sun was setting, and in this light the yard looked magical, very still, breathing softly, bathing in the gentle glow.

Slowly, suddenly quiet, the others walked after him along the path. Jon could hear Sean whisper a few words, say something about a secret garden, a fairy place; and that phrase snagged in his brain like bait, like a snowflake melting into his essence, like a puzzle piece finding its slot.

"So this is where you hang out when you wander off," Sal remarked. "How interesting. You are a man of mystery, Jon Stone. Leave it to you to find a place like this within days of moving here. Gosh, I'll have to frame your contract. You're quite the wizard, my friend."

Roy, slightly overwhelmed, greeted them one after the other, leaving glue residue on their hands and offered seats that weren't there.

It was Jones who wandered past him, right into the workshop, right up to the row of instruments hanging on the wall.

"This one," he called. "Oh my, this one! I want this one!" It was the rosewood. "How much are you asking for this one?"

Roy, smiling, shook his head. "I'm sorry; I can't sell you that one. You'll have to pick another."

"What? Why not?" Taking it down, Jones let his fingers slip across the strings and tuned it with fast, expert movements. "I'll pay whatever price you ask. Look at that mother-of-pearl inlay! It's exquisite, and I want to buy it!"

"Well, you can't." Roy took it from Jones and laid it on the table, where they stood around it, all of them, gazing down at the guitar.

Jon's heart pulled together in disappointment, and he had to stuff his hands into his pockets, trying not to reach out and touch it.

"You're not selling it?" He could hardly say the words. The money in the envelope seemed as heavy as clay all of a sudden.

"I didn't say I'm not selling it." Lovingly, Roy wiped the reddish surface with a chamois cloth until it shone again, every trace of Jones's touch gone. "I said I'm not selling it to *him*."

"But—" Jon brought out the money—"would you sell it to me then?"

Wordlessly, Roy vanished into the back room and returned with a black leather case, into which he laid the rosewood guitar.

"That will be forty-five hundred, please," he said.

"Oh, come on! I'm way better than he is!" Jones pointed at the guitar, and then at Jon. "I'm his bloody guitarist. I play in his band, I'm his first guitarist!" His voice shook somewhere between laughter, exasperation, and anger; but Roy ignored him and handed the case to Jon.

"You may be all that, and I'll build you any guitar you want," he replied, "but this one has been waiting for Jon for a long time. No one can make it sing and cry like Jon. A guitar is a little like a magic wand. It waits for its master, patiently, abidingly, and then one day the miracle happens: The right person walks in, and it awakens.

It gives itself the sound of jubilation; it is set free. This rosewood guitar is Jon's. It was never anyone else's, and it never will be." And added, to Jon, "It's my pleasure to sell it to you. Treat it well. Give it your best music. Come back to me when you think it needs a sister. I'll build you any guitar you want, but not one of those ugly, howling electric things. Don't ever use those, Jon. Leave those to the unprofessionals." Mischief glittering in his eyes, he turned to Jones. "You have a good eye, my friend. And Jon has great friends. Come with me. I'll show you something that might just catch your fancy."

Jon couldn't help himself. He had to open the case and take out the guitar, hold it in his hands, feel the smooth lacquer beneath his fingers. It needed a shoulder belt, and he wanted new picks, rosewood ones.

More than his first meeting with Sal, more than the trip cross-country, even more than putting his name on the contract with his new label, *this* felt like arriving, at last.

The guitar hummed softly when he touched the strings.

Chapter Eighteen

HE WAS ON the beach again, watching the pelicans, when he remembered his promise to his father that he'd buy a camera. Four of the big birds were flying in a straight line just above a cresting wave, like guards on patrol, big wings black and slow in the faint light of the rising sun. They cruised so easily over the water.

It was March, and Jon had no idea how that had happened. The days were all the same: filled with work.

"The River" had been rehearsed and recorded, ready to go on the A side of a single, and they had moved on to other songs, trying to find the right one to go on the B side. The album was being worked on at the same time and would be released soon after the single.

The photo shoot—that phrase kept returning to his mind like the shadow of a crow, like a threat that he couldn't quite grasp. He'd listened to Tom and some new people from the PR department debate where to take the photos, how to cast him; and they'd looked him up and down, their brows raised, judging, measuring.

Part of the deal, Sal had told him over dinner, it was all part of the deal; and wasn't it exciting that his photo would soon be smiling from record covers and billboards, in centerfolds and feature articles?

"You'll be a star, Jon," he'd said, and suddenly it had felt more like a threat than a promise.

"It's going so fast." It was the wrong thing to say; Jon had known it right away, seeing how Sal pulled down the corners of his mouth.

"Yeah, pretty fast" had been the response. "We're very lucky. But then again, you're very good, and hey, so am I. I'm a good manager to a good songwriter."

Fame. Funny, he'd never thought about fame. Success, yes. That he wanted very badly, but he wasn't too sure about fame.

"You'll be whipping through town in a sports car soon enough," Sal had promised. "And all the hot young things will scream when they recognize you. It's what you wanted, isn't it?" Picking up a prawn from the platter of seafood between them, he'd expertly flicked off its tail and popped it into his mouth. "That's what every musician wants: fame. That's what it's all about."

"No, for me it's the music." It had sounded lame even to him, and Jon had hidden his face behind his beer glass.

"Yeah. The music." A piece of bread had followed the prawn. "Since we're on the topic, how's it going? Any new songs? Are you writing?"

That almost made him laugh. "When do you expect me to do that? We're at the studio from morning till night, every day. There's no time to think of music, let alone lyrics. Maybe when the album is out."

The strange thing though was that the ephemeral melody he'd heard that first day when they had driven down from the hills and into the heart of LA, was still haunting him. He could still hear the tolling of that bell and the sound of the waves.

A harp. A guitar, softly strumming, and strings, an entire orchestra of strings, all of them coming together to catch the music of the ocean.

Again the yearning pulled at his heart, and he gazed out at the water and the pastel sky as if they would surrender their secrets to him if he only looked long enough. The tide was as calm as always, its rise and fall the breath of the universe itself.

"SALLY will take you shopping today," Tom said.

"Shopping?" Jon put down his coffee mug, waiting for an explanation.

Tom sighed. "Clothes, Jon. A haircut. We need to shape you now. You know, make a desirable man out of you. A dude the girls will faint for."

Sally appeared in the door, this time in a ruffled skirt and a top that was just a little too short and showed off her navel. Her hair was restrained by a red velvet bow and hung over her shoulder in a ponytail that looked like a river of light. Jon wondered if it was her natural color or if she'd gone Marilyn Monroe and dyed it, and he resolved to find out someday soon.

"Let's go," she called. "My favorite part of the job, shopping!" A little red purse was dangling from her wrist. "I've got everything we need: Cole's plastic and my car. Are you ready?"

Wordlessly, he followed her down to the garage and got into the car she indicated. It too was red, a small, foreign convertible that forced him to pull up his knees to fit into it.

"Next one," Sally said, whisking it out of its niche, "will be a Porsche, mark my words. I'll get Daddy to buy me one for my birthday."

Jon had no idea what she was talking about, so he remained silent until she flashed him a bright grin and added, "You know Cole is my dad, right?"

He hadn't known or cared. She was there when he needed anything, and she was a pretty girl.

"Why do I need new clothes?" he asked instead. "It's not as if I'm running around like a bum." In fact he rather liked the shirt he was wearing. It had been a Christmas gift from his mother.

"You look nice," Sally conceded, "but not...cool. You need to look like success. You can't look ordinary. You have to look like you're someone already, well on the road to success. I don't know how to put it. It's in the image you radiate. Success breeds success. Something like that." A pert shrug of her shoulder. "They know I have the best taste, so they always send me shopping with people like you. And I love it!"

The tires screeched a bit when she took a corner a little too fast.

"You're all the same when you get here, like young, hungry birds; you have that look of hope and confusion in your eyes. One day you're a starving, poor songwriter playing on a street corner and the next you're in a studio, and everyone adores you." Her teeth flashed. "Get used to it. It's just another job."

"It's not."

"Of course it is, Jon. It's a job. You signed contracts, you go to work every day, you have deadlines and responsibility. It's a frigging job, and you're what we're marketing. So, new, cool clothes. Let's buy you an image!"

SHE took him to stores he'd never been in before and never would have, had he remained in his old life.

Jon could almost see his mother raise her brow at the minimalist interiors and puppet-like shopgirls. For a moment he wondered if they got better pay than their counterparts at a department store just to look the way they did, or if they needed special skills, a different taste, some kind of ability that others didn't have.

"This." Sally was holding a shirt. It was very colorful, baroque, and had ruffles on the cuffs.

"Uhm," Jon said, but Sally came up to him and held it against his chest.

"You could pull this off, you know. It would look great on you, lush and exclusive. And black leather pants." Leaving the shirt in his unwilling hands, she wandered over to where the suits and trousers were displayed. "Try it on!"

Alone in the changing cubicle, Jon peered at the price tag and swallowed. He could hear Sally chatting away with the shopgirl as if it was nothing to drop this kind of money on a single piece of clothing, and his mind wandered back to Jenny and their small, hard life, to the cold nights and the meager food. They'd never gone hungry, that much was true. Her family, and his, had seen to that; but it had been tough.

And here he was now, in a shirt that cost more than they'd had to live on for an entire month, and he didn't even like it.

"Let me see," Sally called.

He felt like a fraud, like the greatest cheat in the world, when he stepped out into the store to let her have a look; but she smiled, and again there was that faint blush on her cheeks that made her look like a porcelain doll.

"Nice," she breathed, "very nice, and very sexy," and held out black leather pants to him.

Shoes, she wanted him to wear loafers, soft, expensive things that wrapped around his feet like a baby's palms.

There was a black leather jacket on a mannequin, and he asked to try it on after a moment's hesitation, fearing they would laugh at him. "Good choice," Sally cried, clapping her hands in glee. "Very good, Jon! It looks fabulous on you."

And it did.

A different man was looking back at him from the big mirrors, someone glossy and with poise, as if the new clothes hadn't just changed him outside but given him a new attitude too.

"You look like success. You have to carry your talent before you like a shield." Sally's hand was on his back, straightening the jacket, adjusting the shoulder. He liked it a lot. He liked how it ended just above the belt of the trousers, and that he could push his hands into the pockets and take a relaxed stance in it.

"Now all you need is a new car," she said. "I think you should get a Ferrari. I can see you whipping through LA in a Ferrari. Convertible, of course."

"No. Not a Ferrari." He knew exactly what he wanted. But it would have to wait. Not yet, a voice deep inside kept telling him; be cautious, wait. Wait until the first album is out, and making money. It would have to be a cheap, secondhand car until then.

"Has Tom said anything about a tour?"

Sally's words shook him from his thoughts.

"Tour?" Jon repeated stupidly, and his pulse turned a somersault. A tour. He hadn't even thought that far yet.

"Yes, Jon. There's always a tour after an album. That's how we do this. You need to take your music on the road." She shrugged. "Of course, it won't be the huge venues yet. But we have to start somewhere." A blue silk shirt had found its way into her hands, and she held it out to him. "It'll be fun! You'll get to play your songs to fans! And I'll go along and be your tour manager."

A moody face was staring back at him from the barber's mirror a while later.

His hair wasn't a lot shorter, but it fell in mannerly curls around his head. The wild mane was finally tamed.

"A manicure wouldn't hurt." Sally was sitting on the chair next to his, sipping iced tea from a big, translucent plastic cup. Jon could see slices of fruit floating around in it, all the colors whirling around one another in a rainbow dance.

Two girls got busy on his hands, soaking, snipping, clipping, and massaging, buffing his nails until they shone.

"How do you feel?" Putting down her drink, Sally moved closer and peered at him intently. "How do you feel, Jon Stone?"

"Changed. Yes, changed." He couldn't quite put his finger on it. "Better? I don't know. But—yeah, better too."

In fact, he felt comfortable, and secure, as if with the new clothes he had made an important step from Brooklyn boy to LA rocker.

"I loved that the first thing you bought with your advance was a guitar," Sally said. "It shows what's really important to you. But you also need to grow into the icon people want to see."

He didn't say that he'd always thought that part would come by itself, somehow, along the road, that he'd never thought about himself as part of the package.

A moment later, when they were back on the sidewalk, a car drove past with two girls in it. It slowed down as it went by, and the girls looked his way with attentive, curious eyes, smiling as if over a secret.

Jon smiled back, and they waved at him, laughing, before the driver stepped on the gas, and they sped away.

Chapter Nineteen

"I DON'T HAVE a special talent," Sally said, poking at the salad on her plate. "I'm just the *daughter*, and Daddy's pet. He lets me do the stuff I enjoy, like dressing up new clients, showing them around, and sometimes escorting them to a function or something. And he lets me play personal assistant if I want to. Like, I get to carry your coat or something when we travel." Her dark eyes sparkled with mirth. "I don't mind! I can have all the fun and go to as many parties as I want, and with cute guys like you too."

He'd offered her lunch, and she had accepted under the condition that she could pick the restaurant; and now they were sitting on the terrace of some fancy hotel, watching the world roll past. Jon had no idea what it was called, and he didn't really care. His only worry was if he had enough money in his pocket to pay for the outrageously overpriced, and very artfully decorated, food.

The people around them at the other tables were beautiful: tanned and sleek, well dressed, flashing jewelry, and very white teeth. The women were young, or worked very hard at remaining young; they were like an alien breed.

The most amazing thing to him though was that no one seemed to think that he was out of place. He was noticed, measured, smiled at, and then added to the space as if he belonged there. It scared him a little.

"I'm thinking" Sally went on, "I'm going to suggest that we take you to New York for the photo shoot. Somehow you don't fit on the beach and sunshine quite yet. You have something of the broody, wintery East Coast in you, and we should use that. And that song, "The River," it could be about the jungle of Manhattan, too."

"Have you ever been there?" A stab of homesickness went through his heart.

"Sure." She shrugged. "I like to fly there for some shopping or to go to a museum, especially just before Christmas. Some of my favorite stores are in Soho."

"It's a long flight." As if he knew, after driving to LA with Jones.

"Not that long. I like to take the red-eye." With an elegant movement she waved over the waiter and ordered a glass of white wine. "And you get there in the early morning, just in time for breakfast. I love breakfast in New York!" The polish on her fingernails flashed like crimson drops as she drew them through the air. "New York has this special morning smell, of coffee and fresh bread, and wet asphalt from the street cleaners; and it's so cool to watch the stores open. I just love mornings in New York." Wistfully, she sighed. "I really have to talk Cole into going to New York for your photos." Her attention returned to Jon. "Which part are you from?"

"Brooklyn. I live in Brooklyn." He looked over the street and at the palm trees lining it, their shapes like pencils against the bright-blue sky. "Used to. My family lives there."

He could see them: It would be dinnertime soon at his parents' house, and they'd all gather around the kitchen table, his siblings pouring out the stories of their day and his father, exhausted from a day at the hospital, sipping beer from a bottle while his mother put food on their plates.

Jon gazed down at his plate, at the mussels and shrimp Sally had made him order, saying it was the best in town, and at the colorful, probably very healthy and nonfattening greens on the side.

"You should come down to the beach with me in the morning." Sally stole one of the minuscule tomatoes from his salad. "I go for a run every day."

"A run?"

"Yes, I go running. You know, exercise. To keep in shape and get a tan." She wiggled her bare arm at him.

"You don't have a tan. You're as pale as a snowflake." It wasn't really a very clever comparison, but the only one he could come up with.

She rolled her eyes. "Well, I try. But I'm naturally pale. Anyway, you should come along and…" Again a shrug. "Do something for your body. Develop some muscle. You're a good-looking man, Jon, but thin. No muscle, no tone. No tan. You would look great with a tan and some muscle on your…" Her lips trembled a bit. "Body."

That made him give her a smirk. "Really. You'd appreciate that?"

"Don't get any ideas!" It came out just a little bit too loud and too fast to be convincing. "I never date clients; that's my rule. We'll work together and see each other all the time, and then if it doesn't work out it turns into a pain. I'll run on the beach with you, I'll take you shopping and pick out your clothes and turn you into a hottie, and I'll have lunch with you now and then. But that's the end of it."

The high-heeled sandal dangled from her foot when she crossed her legs and sat back in her chair. Smooth, sleek legs they were too, and quite inviting to look at.

"So no boyfriend for you?" His heart felt light. For the first time in a long while it felt light with that certain kind of gladness that only came with the bud of being in love, of feeling alive. Jon hadn't even known he'd missed it.

"I never said that. Only not one of you. Too much heartbreak, you are, you up-and-coming stars. You cling and want to be nurtured, and then when you're a celebrity, you drop me. Been there, done that, and I'm through with it."

"How old are you?" It wasn't exactly a polite question, but he wanted to know. She didn't look older than he was.

"Twenty-six," Sally replied, surprising him. "I've been working with the label for five years now, started right after college. Someday I'm going to run my own company." Her lips curled into an impish smile. "Or I'll kick Daddy out of his and take over. We'll see. I have my own ideas."

She was like a soap bubble, a light, colorful, translucent thing that was floating around his head, visible one moment and gone the next, only to touch his cheek again with a feathery stroke.

"Would you have signed me?"

Sally pursed her lips. "Yes, on the spot. You can't be passed over, Jon. You'll be a star in less than a year. I have no doubt about that whatsoever. You'll shine and rise, and if you don't stumble you'll be up there among the best forever. You'll own the stage, and the music business. It will be all about you. I'm totally certain about that." Another tomato wandered into her mouth. "You have it all:

the talent, the looks, the aura, even the naughty twinkle in your eyes. We owe Sal big-time for coming to us first. Any label would have snatched you up."

"But it can't be this easy." Jon's stomach clenched at the thought of it all. "It can't be this easy. This is ridiculous. I can't just waltz into a record company, and *wham*, that's it."

Her shoulder came up in a bored attempt at a shrug. "It happens. Not often, but it happens. But why question and wonder when it does? Don't worry. We'll take good care of you and your music." The silvery eyebrows wandered up and disappeared under her long bangs. "But you might need a little help with the lyrics from time to time. Some of them are a little edgy. We'll see."

Edgy.

"Lyrics are hard." It was so easy talking to her, as if she was a long-lost friend, someone who knew him inside and out. "They are always a struggle. Words are hard. The music just floats around me, but words…" Jon pushed his plate away, hunger forgotten. "Words are so different, and they take on a totally different meaning in a song. As if the music changes them. They look great on paper, and then when I sing them, they somehow mean something else. I feel like the words and the music should be one thing, should create one bigger thing, together."

"Yes." She smiled, and it was the sweetest smile he'd seen on a girl in a long time. "Yes, that's how it should be. You're good, Jon Stone. You're really very good. Don't make me fall in love with you. I'd hate that."

"I'll try that running thing with you," Jon said, and she laughed.

HE wanted a place of his own. He wanted to be able to get up and look around and know he was in his own place, even if it was a tiny apartment, or a shack; and it must to be on the beach. From now on, Jon swore to himself, he'd always live on the beach. He needed a view of the surf and the ocean as much as breathing. Every morning when he opened the balcony door and stepped outside, he felt his soul expand, felt it reach out for the great stretch of water, his heart beating in the rhythm of the waves.

His daily routine changed with the promise to Sally. He met her early, just after sunrise, to jog on the beach and go for a swim. The water was surprisingly cold despite its pastel color; but he made himself swim through the surf and out into the calmer stretches, where he turned around and looked at the city, at the misty hills and the huge, shimmering orb of the sun floating over them.

California, and life, was as easy and light as cotton candy. There was no worry, no effort, no pain—just the music, people who cared for him, and eternal sunshine.

And yet, whenever he stopped moving and listened to the tolling of that great bell inside his head, he found a lonely place, empty, and hollow where something should be that wasn't there. He had no idea what it was; he had everything: a new guitar, new clothes, new friends, now his own car. He moved through life in LA like a fish through a colorful, coral reef, exploring all its nooks and hollows, finding spots where he paused a bit, basking in the sun, dreaming under the stars and all the time; it was about the music.

He heard "The River" played by an orchestra, a real orchestra, backing up his growing band; and he'd been part of the process when Tom and Russ picked backup singers for him: three of them with voices that dwarfed his own, wonderful singers who knew their business.

That was when he agreed to singing lessons, and what an eye-opener that had been.

On the day they were to go to New York for the photo shoot, Jon stood before the mirror in Sean's bathroom and gazed at his reflection.

He had a tan all right, and he had muscles. Sally hadn't stopped at running. She had given him weights to lift and showed him how to do proper push-ups too. He looked like a Californian: fit, healthy, relaxed, and at ease with himself.

Jon liked it a lot.

Chapter Twenty

IT DIDN'T FEEL like coming home at all.

The New York sky was drenched with rain, pouring gray on a gray city landscape. Crossing the Pulaski Skyway on their way to Manhattan from Newark airport he looked out at the city looming in the murk of dawn, and it seemed like a strange, new place, a realm yet to be discovered.

Rainy streets and fairy tales…new words ran through his head as the van sped toward the Holland Tunnel toll station, and he whispered them against the clouded windows of the car: "Of nights that never end."

"What?" Sally turned to look at him, her eyes wide with curiosity. She looked perky in the short red leather coat and high boots, her hair piled into a knot.

"Nothing. Just words."

But they went on, those words. A cold, gray dawn, a forgotten smile…

He wanted paper, and a pencil, before they drifted away again.

"Sally."

Again she turned, this time waiting, listening.

"Do you have a piece of paper?" He felt more than foolish. "And something to write with?"

But as always, she was magical. A notebook appeared in her hand, easily pulled from her big purse, and with it a pen. "Tell me."

"It's just snippets," Jon said, trying to evade her; but she smiled, so he repeated the lyrics to her, and she wrote them down.

"That's what I'm here for, Jon." The notebook disappeared. "If you need anything, tell me. That's why I'm here. Anything at all." Pen still in hand, she paused. "Have you told your family you'll be in town? We should make time for you to see them."

"No." He shrugged when she blinked at him. "I want to surprise them. You know, just pop in and… be there." It had seemed like a good idea, but now, seeing Sally's face, he wasn't so sure. He'd brought the rosewood guitar to show his father. Waiting to board at LAX, the guitar case propped against the side of his chair, he'd watched people walk by and glance at him, watched the question flit across their faces at seeing him surrounded by Sal, Tom, Sean, Jones and Sally, as if they were his entourage.

Sally had walked a few steps away and taken photos of him while he talked to Sal, drank coffee, smoked a cigarette, and one of him putting his hand protectively on the guitar case when someone came too close. He wondered where and when those snapshots would be used, but he didn't ask. He'd learned to let it go, to let her decide which images were good enough to publish and which would wander into his private stash.

"On the road," she'd called it, and gone on photographing him on the plane until he turned away and put on his sunglasses, hiding from the inquisitive eye of the camera.

Sean, Jones, and Tom hadn't come along. They'd been there to see them off, just for fun.

"Well, you should totally see your family."

They were on Canal, on the way to the hotel. It seemed weird, staying at a hotel when his family lived here, but it was also exciting: He was now a visitor in his own hometown.

"Yes, of course I will see them! I was thinking tonight, if you don't have any other plans for me." He would go over and show up for dinner. How that would fluster his mother! The thought alone was enough to make him grin and feel like a schoolboy again.

"You can use the van. No need to grab a cab." Sally, still shaking her head, talked to their driver, who nodded.

She wanted, Sally explained, to go to places where he'd hung out before he came to LA. She wanted him photographed in his old surroundings, as the searching, lonely young man, the one still dreaming of a music career.

Streets, subway stations, a park, a diner. Those kind of places; places that told his story.

So Jon told her about his job at the bookstore, about the hot dog stand on Union Square where he'd often had lunch, and that was where they went after checking in at the hotel and grabbing a fast breakfast at a coffee shop.

While someone was putting makeup on his face and fussing with his hair Jon watched people walk by, giving him short, curious glances before moving on in the typical New York way, too busy with their own lives, too hurried to care.

"I used to come this way every day," he told Sally, "and pick up a bagel or something for breakfast. Then I'd walk the two blocks to the bookstore, and I'd be there all day, trying to do as little as possible while writing songs. Most of the time it worked. But some days there were customers from morning to night. Lots of tourists too." He pointed down Broadway. "Right there. You can see it from here."

"So that's where we go next," she answered, and peered down the street. "Good, a corner too. Maybe we can get the store manager to let us take some pictures inside? Now, that would be great."

The thought of facing Mr. Brown made Jon fidget, and the makeup artist hissed softly at him.

He was wearing the black leather jacket and one of the silk turtlenecks he'd discovered for himself a couple of weeks ago, light, smooth things that were comfortable to wear and didn't need ironing. Sally frowned at his penchant for black clothes, saying he looked much better in colors; but it made him feel safe, and less conspicuous.

Together they walked down to the store, Jon pointing out spots to her, telling her little anecdotes about his former life. Just like then, he was carrying a guitar case with him, only now it was a nice one and the guitar inside his precious rosewood and not the old, cheap, battered thing he'd played since childhood.

She was laughing at his story of the day when he'd written "The River" and the woman who had dripped rain all over the hardwood floor, and Mr. Brown had sneaked up on him.

"And she said I should rhyme *heartbeat* with *feet*. I was tempted to use it too." Jon loved how she looked, how she was like a pretty flower in the melancholy of a New York day in her bright colors and that silvery hair. It was her natural color, that much he knew by now. He'd asked her one night, after sharing a bottle of tequila and a huge bowl of deviled shrimp on the deck of a seaside grill.

Naughty, she had called him, and nosy, and replied that yes, it was her natural color. Her cheeks had blushed that lovely rose that made him want to reach out for her hand and hold her fingers between his. He imagined them to be soft and cool, just the kind of fingers he wanted to hold; but he didn't, and the moment passed.

"Let's have lunch later," he offered when they stopped outside the bookstore. "I'll take you to my favorite deli and buy you a pastrami sandwich."

"It would have to be Carnegie's for that," Sally said, "and that's too far away for a lunch foray today, Jon. We'd have to drag all the others with us, and where would be the fun in that. But yes, I'll go to lunch with you. I know a nice little Italian place not too far from here. I need to make time for shopping too. A girl can't go to New York and not buy a new purse, can she?"

He didn't comment on that. To Jon it seemed as if she carried a different one every day of the month.

"Jon?"

Sally gazed past him, eyebrows in silver arches.

"Jon, is that really you?" Jenny was standing there like a sepia print of herself. "I didn't know you were coming home." There was a trace of guilt in her voice, and some accusation. "You never said you were coming home."

"Jen. Hi." He had no idea what to say to her. She looked tired, faded, as colorless as the murky spring day. Sally, next to her, shone with all the sun of California, with a healthy glow of happiness.

"We're only here for a photo shoot."

She nodded as if she'd known all along, as if he was telling her an old secret. "You look well." A small gesture at his jacket. "Nice clothes. Things seem to be going well for you."

"Yeah. Quite well." Anger was building in his chest at her tone, and he didn't even know why. "I'm doing great. We're only here for a couple of days. My first single will be out shortly, and I have a lot of work waiting for me in LA." He wanted it to sound arrogant, and he wanted it to hurt.

She was carrying a lunch bag, and now she pressed it to her chest like a shield and nodded. "Good. Nice. I'm glad your dream is coming true. You worked hard enough for it." Her glance drifted toward the store entrance. "I have to get back inside. A couple of people called in sick; there's a lot of work."

Sally was watching them intently, as if she was trying to glean some information about him out of this awkward, halting exchange.

"What have you been up to?" His heart shivered a bit, and he found he really wanted to know.

Jenny gave him a small shrug. "Not much. Work. I'd meant to go back to school, but somehow..." Her eyes followed a stretch limo that floated past, its tinted glass reflecting the shop windows. "Somehow it wasn't the right moment, or whatever. And I'm happy here anyway."

"Right. I'm glad you're happy, Jenny. Really." He wanted to bang his head against the doorframe, push it into the gutter, hide in his guitar case; but most of all, he wanted Sally's scrutiny gone from this appalling scene.

"You're the old girlfriend!" Sally's voice sounded as clear as a spring in a forest glade. "You're *that* Jenny! He told me all about you. Hello, it's nice to meet you." She held out her hand, arm outstretched, and smiled her best California smile. "A pity you couldn't come out to LA when Jon made the move. I'm sure you'd love it there. Did he tell you he's learning to surf? And a fine figure he is on that board! We're turning him into a regular beach boy!"

Jenny stared down at the hand with the red nail polish and the fine, white skin, at the charm bracelet gracing the slim wrist, and the expensive purse, and grabbed her brown paper bag even tighter. "Pleased, yes. Are you... do you work with Jon?"

"Oh." Sally tilted her head. "Sort of. Yes, you could say that. We work together. I look after him. I buy his clothes and take him to business lunches, and we run and surf together. Sometimes we even have breakfast together."

"You're his manager?" Jenny's voice sounded dull, listless.

"His manager? No, I'm not his manager. Sal is his manager. We're a little more involved than that." Jon didn't move when Sally hooked her arm through his. "He needs someone to take care of him, doesn't he? He's so wonderfully talented, we can't let him fend for himself. Someone like Jon can have any girl at all, and they're all running after him in California." A brilliant smile blossomed on her face. "I'm his girlfriend now."

Chapter Twenty-one

"YOU'RE NOT MY girlfriend."

Sally brought out her lipstick and a small mirror. "No, but I could be. Theoretically. I mean, there's nothing stopping us, except me saying no. So, theoretically, I'm your girlfriend."

His head was spinning.

She smiled up at him. "I'm right, am I not? I'd be your girlfriend if I let you."

"I don't know."

That made her stop and frown. "What, you don't know? You don't want me as your girlfriend?"

The door to the bookstore opened, and Mr. Brown appeared. He was wearing the same jacket Jon had last seen him in, and he had the same stern expression on his face. "You're blocking the entrance with your circus," he said. "Do you have a permit for this?"

"We have everything we need," Sally replied, "and thank you for your patience."

This was not going the way Jon had envisioned it at all. In his dreams, coming back to New York had always been triumphant, a glorious moment of joy, when everyone would at last recognize his talent and praise him for taking that daring step; but it wasn't like that at all.

He felt like an outcast. He felt like something forgotten, something that had gotten out of sync, and now, re-entering this world jarred with its regular flow. The seams had closed behind him, and he was no longer welcome.

"Come on." Sally was tugging his sleeve to catch his attention. "Don't stand there dreaming. It's not that nice a corner, Jon. I have a feeling your old cronies don't give a damn about your success."

He followed her back to the van and sat, staring out at the rain-washed streets as they moved uptown, back to the hotel where they were staying. There was no talk of that Italian place and lunch anymore, but he was sure he didn't want to stay in the neighborhood anyway and run into anyone else from the store.

"I'm a stranger," he said to Sally when they stopped outside the hotel. "I'm a stranger in my own city. It's the weirdest feeling."

"You're not a stranger, Jon; that's nonsense." Standing on the sidewalk, she was waiting for him to climb out, and again she reminded him of a lovely, bright flower. "You've moved into a different sphere is all. You return on business, you stay at a nice hotel, you have a purpose. You return with a name, and an altered status. That's all there is to it. In a few weeks they'll see your face on a record sleeve, and soon on billboards and in tabloids. It's not you. It's them. They feel left behind, betrayed, shut out. You did what they dream of doing, but they lack the guts. Your Jenny, that poor, gray mouse. She's even now crying into her lunch bag, kicking her butt and probably whining about not going with you when she had the chance."

The car door slammed shut behind him, and she took his arm again. "Now let's talk some more about that girlfriend thing. That was your old flame? That tired little mouse? Really, Jon?"

"She's not a mouse." Defending Jenny, and to Sally, too. Those last bitter days were still so vivid in his memory, all the ugly, desperate things she had said to him, almost wishing for him to fail just so he would have to come crawling back to her, defeated. "She wanted a different life for us. She's a good person, and all she wanted was a regular, normal life with a husband who'd care for her, who'd come home at night and take her to the movies. Only..."

"Only you're not that man, Jon." Sally finished the sentence for him, a trace of impatience in her voice. "Good heavens, Jon, how could she even think that? How did she think she'd be able to contain you? No one will be able to." Her smile wobbled a bit. "No one at all."

THEY had a quick lunch at a deli, standing together under the awning and watching the rain and the people hurrying by while eating a sandwich stuffed with pastrami and mustard; and again it felt as if he was standing on the other side of a divide, watching his old life through a stranger's eyes.

Sally was talking about doing some shopping later in the day, or maybe going to a show in the evening and taking some nighttime shots in subway stations, when they were emptier and they could spread out, but he shook his head. He wanted to go home and see his parents, and as soon as possible. He needed to find out if at least there he was still himself, still the same man.

"Can I come?"

The question woke him from his thoughts.

"Can I come with you and meet your parents?" Sally repeated. "I'd like to see where you grew up."

He was on the point of saying that no, she couldn't; it was too intimate, and they weren't lovers after all, but then he changed his mind.

"Yeah, why not. Come along and meet my family." As if it mattered. As if it would change anything now. "I wanted to take her, you know."

Sally hid her face behind her coffee cup.

"I wanted to take her. I kept asking her to come along, even after she'd more or less told me to go to hell. I went back and asked again. I never meant to betray her, or leave her behind." That, at least was his memory of things. "I promised everything would be all right, but she didn't believe me."

"She didn't trust you." The half-eaten sandwich wandered into a nearby trash can, followed by the paper cup. "It's not about you betraying her, Jon. It's about her not trusting you to follow up on your promises. Totally different story. And that's the reason she's so pissed now. She knows it's her own fault. She could have been the rock star's wife. Now she's nothing more than a bookstore clerk, and that's all she will ever be. She threw it away."

"I don't know." He couldn't see Jenny in his new surroundings. He couldn't see her running with him on the beach in the morning or going shopping on Rodeo Drive. He couldn't see her meeting Tom and Cole, or sitting with him in the studio while they recorded his songs, hour after hour, day after day; and he positively hated the image of her waiting at home for him to show up, tired and hyped from a long day of music, to listen to her complain of boredom and emptiness.

"Can we talk about that girlfriend thing now?" Sally brought him out of his murky bubble with her question.

"Why do you keep going on about that, I want to know?" Jon zipped up his jacket and turned up the collar against the wet wind. "You're such a tease. You said you didn't want to be a client's girlfriend, and now you're talking about it all the time. Did Jenny do that? I'll have to go back and buy her a cupcake if she changed your mind."

"I didn't say I changed my mind. You're putting words into my mouth."

"Why speculate, then? It's not as if you're begging to be kissed." He wanted a piece of the cheesecake they had in the deli, and a cup of coffee in a quiet corner where it was warm and not raining.

"It's fun." She followed him back inside. "It's just fun to think how it would go."

"Well, it's a temptation and nothing else. So stop it." There was a table way in the back, right next to the restroom doors, and Jon went there to squeeze himself into the chair in the corner. His back to the wall, he felt safe and unobserved while he watched everything going on around them. They'd ruined the cheesecake for him: There was hot fudge on it and strawberries on the side. Morosely he wondered why he couldn't have a slice of plain cheesecake without some fancy dressing, just like his life. All he wanted was to write music, play it, and not be bothered by matters of the heart.

"You're too young to be this cynical. You should be in love with someone." Sally poked at the cupcake on her plate. It was a pink thing with a little chocolate heart tucked into the icing, much too pretty to eat.

"I will be. Don't worry. Don't worry about my soul, Sally. I'm fine. I don't need anyone right now. I'm much too busy to be romancing any girl." His thoughts flew back to his last conversation with Tom and Sal before he had left for New York, and how his heart had beaten hard and fast when Tom, rather off-handedly, speculated about the best time for a concert tour. Everything else could wait.

"Jenny is a good girl." The fudge was actually quite good, and it complemented the soft moistness of the cake in a pleasant way. "She always worried about me. She wanted me to lead a stable life, a quiet, ordered life. A house, a car, two kids, and a regular income. She wants to settle down and raise a family. Can't blame her for that. It's what most girls want. I'm sure she'll be a great wife and mom someday."

Sally was busy licking icing off the chocolate heart, but now she laid it aside and clasped her hands in her lap.

"But you wouldn't be happy that way," she said. "It's not your life, Jon. You would have wilted and died a little more inside every day. You would have watched your dreams slip away while trying to work in an office and support your family. You'd have crept through life and watched your music fade, and then one day, just before your fiftieth birthday, you'd have woken up and realized that everything you ever cared about was gone forever; and that day, your life would have ended."

Every word she was saying was true, and he knew it, could feel it by the way it resonated in his heart. The image was so dismal it almost made him choke.

"She said a woman would always be second to my music, and she couldn't take that." There, and it sounded every bit as dramatic as it had when Jenny said it.

"Well, of course. That's how it's supposed to be. How can you be a success if you don't pour all your passion and love into your music? You aren't a real estate agent or insurance salesman, Jon. You're the creator of something beautiful, and always will be." Without asking, she picked up his coffee and took a sip. "It's the same, old, stupid thing; and I haven't managed to figure it out yet. People—I mean ordinary, normal people—always think art and creativity are things that one should have on the side, like that fudge on your cheesecake. They take it for granted, and for some reason I just can't figure out, they expect it to be free. But it isn't. Bottom line, you create something, and someone else wants it, you get paid. It's the same for cars, furniture, clothes, food, and art. No difference. You want it—you buy it." She gave him a long, thoughtful look. "I don't know why people are willing to pay a lawyer or doctor a good salary but balk when it comes to artists. That's the part I've never understood."

A whiff of bathroom caught them when the door opened and a young woman stepped out. Sally grimaced.

"Let's get the hell out of here," she said, "and back to work. Then we'll go see your family."

Chapter Twenty-two

HIS SISTER OPENED the door.

She stood and stared at him as if she didn't recognize him, and then peered around Jon and Sally at the black van with the tinted glass pulling away from the sidewalk.

"What are you doing here?" Val asked in her usual brisk manner.

"I wanted to see my family, Val. Even you." Things weren't going the way he'd expected. He'd thought that he'd return in triumph, but this wasn't it at all. "May we come in?"

The rain had stopped, and the clouds had drifted away to leave the sky bare; and now, just before sunset, it looked washed-out, like a violet that had been exposed to sunlight for too long. There was this special smell in the air, that scent of rain on earth, and he always forgot the name for it. Birds were singing in the sycamore trees lining the small street, and it was quiet. Down the road, just two blocks away, if he stepped back just a little, Jon could see the glittering skyline of Manhattan on the other side of the river.

He loved this time of the day in his hometown: the colors, the lights, the sounds, the constant song of the big city on its island, the horns of ships, the thrum of traffic from the bridge. It was so different from balmy LA, and for a second he stood on that sidewalk, torn between the two images, and utterly lost.

His mother appeared in the door. "Jon!" And at last, seeing the sudden joy in her face, it felt as if he'd come home.

He'd bought her flowers and a big box of her favorite chocolates, something he'd never been able to do before because they'd been well beyond his means; and he held them out now, as proud as a schoolboy.

"You should have called," Helen said, looking at Sally behind him. "There's nothing special for dinner, just sausages and mashed potatoes! I'd have made a roast for you!"

Her small, slim body felt warm and good in his hug. Jon hadn't even realized how much he'd missed home.

"We're only here for a couple of days," he replied, his face in his mother's hair, "but I wanted to see you at all costs."

HELEN rushed around, talking the whole time, nervous in Sally's presence, not looking at her yet measuring her when she thought Sally wasn't looking, until Jon explained that she was coordinating the photo shoot, and no, she wasn't his girlfriend but worked for his record label. His father was watching with an amused glint in his eyes, the newspaper in his hands, reading the sports section as he had done every night; and Jon, sitting next to him at the big kitchen table, felt as comfortable as a kid. There was the same kind of bread sitting on the cutting board in front of him, and the same knife waiting to dive into it; and he could just see his mother going out earlier in the day to go and buy it at the French bakery on Atlantic. For so many years that had been her routine: She'd seen them off to school, already in her coat and with her shopping bag in hand to head off in the other direction. Seeing her standing there on the sidewalk, waving after them, was like a promise that he would always be secure, warm, loved. They'd sit together around this kitchen table for dinner and talk about the day until his father nodded off and his mother chased them away for an hour of TV before bed.

She was giving Val orders, telling her in a fluttery voice to run and fetch some salad and dessert from the Italian restaurant across the street, but Sally interrupted her, asking her to leave it—they'd had a huge lunch and hadn't come to eat but so Jon could see them.

"He's doing so well; you should be proud of him." And Sally went on to talk about how he was working so hard on his music. How proud they were of him, she said, her eyes turning to Jon and smiling at him warmly; he was so talented and so wonderful to work with.

Helen, listening, sank down into a chair and gazed from one to the other, speechless and blushing.

"He's such an outstanding talent, your Jon," Sally ended her accolade in a soft, kind voice, laying her hand on Jon's. "Such an incredible musician."

It had been just three months since he moved to LA, and everything had changed.

"We are proud of him." His father put down the newspaper. "We always were, even before he decided to give up everything else for the music. We're proud of all our children."

"But Jon is special. Jon will be a huge star. Just wait and see. You'll get into your car and turn on the radio, and there will be your son's voice, and someone raving about his songs. You'll see his face everywhere, and you'll read about him in the newspapers and magazines." Her fingers curled around Jon's, and he gripped them.

"I'm not sure I want that for him," Helen mumbled. "What a burden that would be. Can you even lead your own life anymore with all that? Can you go where you please and do as you want?"

"Oh." Sally took the knife and cut off the end of the bread. "He'll be going anywhere he wants, whenever he wants. He'll own the world. He'll have a penthouse on Park Avenue and a mansion in Malibu."

His parents were watching, bemused. It felt as if he and Sally were speeding past on a broad, straight highway, and his parents were standing on the shoulder, seen and lost again in the blink of an eye, their faces blank, their eyes full of questions.

Val came to stand in the doorway, her glasses pushed down on her nose, a book in her hand, to listen.

"Surely you're exaggerating." Helen brought the steaming pot of potatoes to the table. "No one does all that in this brief a time. It will take him years, if ever. Give the boy a break."

"No. We just provide the means: a studio and musicians, sound engineers, marketing. But at the core of it all, the beating heart of this miracle, that's Jon himself, and his music. None of this would be happening without that."

"You're in love with my brother, California girl." Of course it would be Val, bursting the emotional bubble with her brusque tone.

Sally popped the piece of bread into her mouth, the wistfulness of just a second earlier gone. "He's astounding, beautiful, a dashing figure; and when he's in the studio and opens his mouth to sing, I want to die, every time. I want to lie down on that ugly carpet and close my eyes and drift off on his voice, and die. There's nothing more beautiful than hearing Jon sing."

THE van came to pick them up.

As easy as it had been for Jon to leave New York with Jones, this time it was hard. His entire family was standing on the doorstep, watching as he climbed in after Sally, his mother with her hand over her mouth, his father waving, and Val with her arms crossed, refusing to show any feelings.

Kevin had the eternally exhausted frown of his profession on his brow as he called after Jon, asking if he could come out to LA when he had a few days off, if Jon would take him surfing. Heck, he could use the sunshine and warmth to ease his tired bones.

"Whenever you want," Jon replied, then the door shut between him and the people he loved, and he was on the way back across the bridge to Manhattan.

Like living, breathing entities they seemed, those towers, like creatures from another world that had come together on this narrow island and now stood, huddled and yet majestic, looking out over the strange place they had found.

Sal was in the bar with a few people from the photographer's crew, nursing a beer and a cigarette.

Jon held Sally back when she began to walk toward them.

"Wait," he said, and she stopped. "I want to know this now. You keep telling the world that you're my girlfriend and in love with me. Why don't you tell me too?"

"Because it's not that kind of love, Jon. I'm not in love with you as a man. I'm in love with the musician, the composer, the singer, maybe even the centerfold model. But I'd rather have my tongue ripped out than admit I'm in love with the man. You'd have to drag me naked down the entire length of Broadway before I'd admit that."

"Broadway is a mighty long road, my dear."

"I know it is. I've walked it from end to end, and it took me two days." She flicked her wrist at the traffic outside the hotel lobby. "I bought three pairs of shoes, four dresses, and five purses in those two days. So don't tell *me* about Broadway." Her silver hair shone in the light of the chandelier above their heads. It shone like tinsel, and it seemed just as smooth and glossy.

"You could, you know." Jon wanted to touch that hair very much. "You could just say it, and we'd be lovers. I know I'm in love with you, Sally."

A ripple of laughter and an onyx flash of her dark eyes. "You know no such thing, Jon Stone. You believe that because I'm nice to you, and because you think I'm available. Yes to the first, no to the second."

"You could let yourself fall in love with me though." His heart was beating fast; his palms were sweaty with the excitement. "You could just admit that you want me too, and we'd go upstairs and into my room, and..."

"You're getting ahead of yourself, wonder boy. I'm going to join Sal and the guys for a drink now, and you can come along or stand here and steam. But I'm definitely not going to bed with you."

With that she marched off, ponytail bobbing, and called out to Sal to please order her a mimosa, and if they didn't have that, then a Long Island iced tea would do.

Chapter Twenty-three

THE FIRST TIME Jon heard "The River" on the radio he was driving to Venice Beach to see Roy.

He'd been listening with one ear to the dj blather on about the weather, the surfing conditions, and a new bar that promised to be the new hot spot for celebrities, and then, without any warning, there were the opening chords of his song, and he nearly swerved off the pavement. Braking wildly, he managed to bring the car to a stop and pull off the road, and there he sat while the music flowed around him and the sun beat down on his head and neck. His voice, he was listening to his own voice coming at him from the loudspeakers. He whispered the words to himself, while around him the noonday traffic roared as if nothing at all had happened.

"A new voice with a new sound," the announcer said, "and I can tell you, I'm already in love with this young man's style. I'll be one of the first to stand in line when his album is released next month."

It was unreal.

Jon sat, staring at the cars and trucks, each of them shaking his convertible as it passed. He put his hands on the steering wheel of the old car, trying to feel something, anything, that belonged in the real world, something that would be a kind of anchor. Slowly, very slowly, the real world returned, allowing him to start the car and drive on, still shaky but collected again.

"They had nothing but good things to say," he said to Roy after his first sip of tea. His back felt sweaty again at the thought of it. "All this praise, and I feel like..." He had to search for the right word. "Like a fraud or a magician who has charmed the crowd, and I'm the only one who knows the truth. It's all one big show, and one day they'll wake up and find out, and I'll have to pay."

Roy was holding a guitar in his lap, a new instrument made of a strange, marbled wood that Jon had never seen before, its grain like tightly rippled curls of auburn hair. It was a twelve-string, a beautiful, unique piece of art, and he coveted it.

"It's a strange thing, creativity," Roy replied, moving his fingers along the curve of the guitar, polishing, stroking, searching for imperfections. "Those who have it can't measure its value. It's a part of them, and creating is in their souls. Those who don't have it think it's play, something outside the real world. You and your music, for you it's no effort to come up with lovely melodies, so you don't see its worth. You never will. You can only see the impact it has on others, and there's no way for you to tell how much it really does for them. You will see people flock to your concerts, or stand in line to buy your albums, but the doubt will never go away." He picked up a chamois and wiped the back of the guitar. "There is no security. There is no point you'll reach where you can relax and say you've done it all." Again he ran his palm along the shape of the guitar. The slow caress reminded Jon of a woman's body, of female curves under his touch, and he had to clear his throat.

"The really good ones," Roy said, "never realize how good they are. They only see ways to improve, always trying new things to get even better. They see their flaws and feel insecure about their art." He grinned. "I think you're doing just fine. Here."

Jon took the instrument from him. It was heavier than the rosewood, a serious, mature thing that wouldn't easily tolerate nonsense; and it had the full, sated sound of a well-fed, complacent beast. A male beast.

Roy held out a pick, but he shook his head and played, using his fingers to feel the thrum on his skin. The vibration rippled through his body like the echo of laughter, like the echo of his pulse.

"I want it." Jon heard the rough edge of greed in his voice and coughed.

Roy nodded. "Of course you do. I've been working on this one for years. Somehow I never managed to finish it; there always seemed to be something missing, some ingredient that was essential but wouldn't reveal itself. Then you showed up, and I knew how it wanted to sound. It's not a plaything, Jon. This guitar means business. She'll rip you apart if you mistreat her."

As if.

"I'll come by tomorrow and bring you the money. Keep her safe for me until then." He could hardly bear to let go of the guitar. He'd play "The River" on this one, play it during concerts and not feel locked out of the music by just singing.

"I don't want to be one of those performers who play with the microphone and croon to the audience." There, he'd said it, and again Roy nodded.

"You're not the best guitarist in the world" was his response, "but you're good enough to add your own sound to your band, and that's as it should be. Don't let them back you up. Be part of them."

The warmth of a California spring afternoon lay over the yard and flooded through the open doorway of the workshop. Dust motes were dancing in the sunbeams that fell through the grimy windows; a bumblebee danced deliriously around the hollyhocks. From far away they could hear the sounds of the street, and even the rhythm of the surf.

"I wish I could live here," Jon said. "It's such a quiet place, hidden inside the turmoil of this huge city. It makes me tranquil just sitting here with you. I always come away calm."

Roy poured more tea. "That's good, then. Everyone needs a place where they can relax and let go. You need a place of your own, Jon. You need a retreat where you can let go and just be yourself. And it has to be safe too. You'll be noticed now. People will know your face soon enough."

He hadn't thought about this part of being famous yet. It was too new, too awkward, and too embarrassing.

"I want something on the water. Doesn't have to be big or fancy, but I want to be able to step out and be on the beach."

That made Roy nod and smile. "Of course you do, but I'm afraid you'll have to make a lot more money before you'll be able to afford one of those mansions in Malibu." He tilted his head and looked at Jon through narrowed eyes. "I can see you living there someday in a huge, old house with high walls around it. A stone driveway, and cameras on the gate like gargoyles. Yes, I can see that."

Uncomfortable now, Jon moved his shoulders as if to shake off that image. It was a grand vision, but there was a sadness some-where in it that he didn't want to acknowledge.

"Anyway"—Roy took the guitar from him to put it into its case—"you can take her with you. Pay me tomorrow. I trust you.

"On second thought," Roy added, "leave her here. I'll put your monogram on the back of the neck for you. How's the rosewood?"

"Fine," Jon replied, "just fine." He would be the envy of many with that instrument.

Solemnly, Roy closed the case. "You are a child of the gods, Jon Stone. Everyone who looks at you properly can see it. You bear their mark on your forehead. It shines like a gem. Don't throw it away."

Fear prickled Jon's neck. "I'm not…I'm nothing like that." He couldn't sit any longer; fear was crawling on his skin like a million tiny mites. "I mean, really. Look at me. I'm a New York boy who likes to write songs, and I'm getting the royal treatment from all of you. Do you know how that feels? It's pressure! I haven't written a new song since I came here. Not even the melody I came into your shop to write down, not even that is a finished piece. It's as if everything else is more important now. There's never a moment's rest."

Unperturbed, Roy pushed aside his teacup. "Stop whining, Jon. You have what many dream of, and yes, it's harsh right now. But you'll settle into it." With a crooked grin he added, "You'll find a balance soon enough, and you'll be in control; I have no doubt about it. Don't let it overwhelm you. Keep a piece of yourself back, to yourself. Don't give everything away. You'll be fine. You got your heart's desire. Now be a man and shape your life."

Cold shame washed away the sting of fear. "Yes. Yes. You're right." Jon pushed his fingers through his hair.

"With great success comes responsibility, Jon. You're responsible for your life now. Don't waste it on fear and second-guessing. Walk, don't crawl."

That nearly made him laugh. "Yes, sir. I won't crawl."

THEY were all there: Sally, Tom, Cole, Sal, even Jones and Sean, as if they'd been waiting for him to show up at the studio.

Had he heard, Tom asked, his face full of glee, what had been said about him on the radio? This was just the beginning. Now he would take off, and hey, it was high time to start planning a tour.

"Easy," Cole chimed in. "Let's take it easy. Let's wait a bit. Let's go for the bigger venues. If we wait until next summer we'll be able to make the hop across the pond; until then, there's TV, and well-placed appearances. Also, both albums will be out by then."

Blood rushed through Jon's ears fast and hard, canceling out their voices. He could see the glow on Sally's face, her pride in him, and Sal's wide grin, the joy of success in his musicians' eyes.

Responsible. He was responsible for them all, for their well-being, and their careers.

His shoulders felt wider, stronger, as he stood up straight and said, "I think this calls for a small celebration. Come on, guys; I'll buy you a late lunch. This party is on me."

He held out his hand to Sally, who took it and leaned into him. She felt as soft and warm as a kitten, and putting his arm around her waist seemed natural.

They followed him to the Mexican restaurant down the street and piled in, calling for margaritas, guacamole, nachos, and a big bowl of pico de gallo.

"Champagne," Jon said, "I think we should have champagne. Today my first record was played on the radio. This day will never come again."

And Sal, who still hadn't said a word, nodded and clasped his shoulder in the tight grip of friendship.

Chapter Twenty-four

"HERE."

Cole had come down to the studio himself for this, and now he held out the album to Jon, who took it as if it was made of the thinnest crystal.

His photo was on it; it was one they'd taken outside the bookstore, one that showed him staring moodily down the street, the guitar case leaning against his leg and the collar of his jacket turned up. In the background, a line of cabs standing at a red light was visible; and there, slightly blurry, and only recognized by him, Jenny, entering the store.

"Do you like it?" Cole asked. "Are you pleased?"

"Yeah." Of course he was pleased. Of course he liked it: he was holding his dream in his hands, at long last. Carefully Jon pulled out the record to see the label, and the list of songs on it, on both sides. They had been generous with the cover, printing more photos on the back, a collage of him in New York, visiting places from his childhood; and inside the jacket was a booklet with his lyrics.

"It came out great. I'm really happy with it. There's a box of them waiting for you in Sally's office. I'm sure you want to send some home, and to friends. Give Sally the addresses and she'll ship them for you."

"Thank you." Jon made his way slowly to Sally's office, trying to figure out to whom to send the album. His parents, yes, he would send them more than one so they could give them to Val and Kevin and maybe some friends, but beyond that he had no idea.

Jenny.

In the elevator, he turned over the album in his hands, looking at the photos again, but there was nothing new to be gleaned from them. He knew every corner of those streets, every shop, every streetlight. A wave of homesickness washed over him, a longing for those gritty New York streets and familiar faces, for his mother's roast and his sister's acerbic voice.

July, and he had no idea how that had happened. He'd been in LA for six months, and it still felt strange, fresh, not like home at all. Transitory, that was how it felt, and in a weird, scary way, lonely.

SALLY handed him a fresh mug of coffee.

"I'm going to a party in a couple of weeks," she said. "Want to come? I think you should show your face in public more often."

"A party?"

"Yeah, a big one. It's a movie premiere thing, I think. Cole gets these invitations all the time, and I'm asking you to escort me. It's in a fancy hotel; it will be fun! And the food will be glorious." She eyed him critically. "Of course, you need to dress up for this. Do you own a tux, Jon Stone?"

Jon shook his head. He'd never owned a tuxedo in his life. So far, his life hadn't called for anything like that.

"Oh well. More shopping then." She was already angling for her purse. "Let's go. You can buy me lunch. You do that very well."

"Sally, no."

Surprised, she stopped in her tracks.

"Not right now. I'm not up to shopping with you right now. I'll take you out for lunch though, if you want." He waved at the door. "Let's find a nice place somewhere on the shore and have lunch. Maybe some place up or down the coast? I still haven't seen much of California outside of LA."

"Well, it's a big state." Sally thought for a moment and then said, "All right. Come with me. I know just the place you need now. We can go tux shopping on the way back."

She steered him out of the office and into the parking garage, where she handed him the keys to her car and hopped into the passenger seat.

"A date" were her words. "Well—sort of. Let's go."

They bought a picnic lunch at her favorite restaurant, and even a bottle of red wine, then Sally made him drive in a direction he hadn't gone before. It wasn't a very long drive, and he knew right away where they were.

"The Greek Theatre." Jon stopped the car at the gate to the stage entrance compound. "We're at the Greek Theatre."

"Yes." Sally waved at the guard who was coming over to let them in. "Have you been here yet?"

He hadn't. It had been a decision, a willful and obstinate decision, that he wouldn't come to this place as a spectator, not until he'd been on the stage himself and played to an audience. This was the one place in the world where he wanted to perform, and he wouldn't come here as a supplicant.

"I figured you hadn't come here yet." Grabbing the bag with their lunch, Sally got out of the car and walked toward the back door. "I can just see you smoldering at concert posters, even of artists you'd actually like to see, and not go. You know I can get you into almost every show here, right? You don't even have to buy a ticket. But you wouldn't come because you want to own the place and not just watch."

She was holding the door for him. He could see past her into the dimness of a hallway, could even see shadows of people moving around, and he stopped.

"You know me too well. I want to perform here. I want to be on that stage more than anything." The sun was hot on his back. "This was my dream, Sally, and it still is. Not Madison Square Garden, not the Royal Albert Hall in London, but this."

"I know, I know. The sky is your limit. Now, let's go have that lunch."

Jon looked down at his feet as he crossed the threshold. It was one step, just a single step, and he was inside the venue, and the heavy metal door fell shut behind him. He stood, waiting, listening to the sounds echoing through the guts of the building. It almost felt as if they were in a spaceship belonging to an alien race: They were somewhere in the labyrinth of tunnels, going about their business. Sally was calling for him to come on, don't just stand there and gawk. He wanted to see the stage, didn't he?

Goose bumps broke out on his arms. He could hear snatches of music, the twang of an electric guitar and the rugged breath of a snare, a woman's laugh.

"It's one of our bands," Sally said when he caught up with her.

"They have a show tonight. And when you said you weren't in the mood for Rodeo Drive, I thought I'd bring you here and give you a taste of what's waiting for you, wonder boy. I know this is your dream. And you'll get it, don't worry."

They stepped out into blinding light.

Jon, shading his eyes with his hand, looked up at the ascending rows of seats, at the bowl of glimmering sunshine and the trees lining the surrounding hills, at the sky like an upside-down brass bowl, throwing heat at them. The air smelled of dry earth and pine needles, of cedar and the dust of the stage, and he was sure he was in heaven.

He imagined the place at night: the seats filled with people and the stars shining above, a cool wind coming down the hillside and the trees standing like sentinels against the dark sky while the music flowed from the stage out into space. He saw himself making that music, standing on the edge of the stage so he could see the audience and their reaction to his songs, see how he made them happy for a couple of hours. A feeling of joy flooded him, more than the shot he'd felt when Cole had handed him the album, more than when he'd signed the contracts. This was basic, immediate, and all he'd ever wanted.

"I know you." The strange voice shook him out of his thoughts. The drummer of the band had pushed up his sunglasses and was gazing at him. "You're that new kid everyone is talking about, Jon Stone. Hey, nice to meet you!"

"Hey."

The other people on the stage were turning toward him, listening curiously.

"That's a nice song you put out. My name is Mortimer." The drummer held out his hand. He was wearing a battered t-shirt that showed well-muscled, tattooed arms.

"Yeah, thanks. The album will be released next week. I'm really glad about the way it turned out." He'd left it in Sally's office. "I was lucky with my band too."

"You got Jones, eh. He's fabulous." Mortimer nodded. "You got yourself a first-class lead guitarist there. And your keyboarder, Sean. Good man."

He was talking shop. He was on the stage of the Greek Theatre, talking about his album and his band with a fellow musician, and it felt as if he'd been doing it forever. His eyes caught Sally's. She'd left the stage and was slowly moving up the aisle to the last row of seats where there was some shade from the trees. The sun glinted on her hair and shone through the thin skirt she was wearing, showing the shape of her legs. She had taken off her sandals and was walking barefoot, the paper bag with their lunch in her hand.

"I have to go." Jon pointed in her direction. "Sally has our lunch."

Mortimer laughed. "Going out for lunch with Sally. You *are* a very lucky man, Jon. She never does that. She's very good at playing aloof. At one time, we had bet on seeing if any of us could entice her out, but she never succumbed to our charms. Must be because you're from New York."

"She thinks I need to be taken in hand. I'm sort of her pet right now." Jon pushed his hands into his jeans pockets.

The other laughed. "Don't let her take too much of you in hand. You want to be in control of your life and not the label's puppet."

There was a serious warning underlying the easily spoken words, something that resonated within Jon and made him nod thoughtfully.

"Thanks," he replied, "I'm not letting them walk all over me. But I'm sure they know what they're doing." Once again there was that pull, the yearning to sing to thousands, for a huge audience to love his music; and ashamed, he looked away. "I'm grateful for everything Sally does. She wants to help, and I'm grateful."

"Yeah, I'm sure." Mortimer pointed one of his drumsticks in Sally's direction. "She's got ambition, that one. She's waiting for the right guy to show up, the one who'll cement her career. She wants to own her own company. I'm sure she'd steal you away from her father's label if you agreed to work for her."

"Nah. I'm happy the way things are." Jon moved to the edge of the stage.

He could see it. He could see the bowl filled with people and him up here, singing, and it wasn't scary at all.

His heart burned with yearning for that day.

Chapter Twenty-five

SHE HANDED HIM a sandwich and a bottle of iced tea.

"Unsweetened," Sally said, "and there's a lot of healthy stuff on the sandwich too. No more eating like a New York street boy."

"I love pastrami." The spread on the bread looked suspiciously vegetarian, and very colorful. Jon sniffed it cautiously, but there was just the scent of basil and fresh tomatoes. "And I'm healthy enough."

"You are now." Sally had a salad with a lot of fruit in it, and shrimp. "But in a couple of years your new life will start to take a toll on you, Jon. You should start looking after yourself now, when it's still easy and you're young. Exercise. Lots of sleep. Good, healthy food." She threw him a sidelong glance. "And not too many parties. You'd be surprised how careful and quiet many rock stars' private lives are. There's way less sex and drugs than you'd think."

There was avocado on his sandwich. Jon bit into the soft, green flesh and wondered why anyone bothered to eat it at all. It was pretty flavorless, and the texture was slightly disgusting.

"Tell me more about that ex-girlfriend of yours, Jenny."

He nearly choked.

"Did you love her? I mean, did it hurt to leave her behind?" Sally's dark eyes shone as bright and lively as a squirrel's.

Jon recalled how Jenny had stood there in their old apartment, a crumpled tissue in her hand, her frayed bathrobe pulled around her like armor, and how he'd walked out on her, his heart bursting with anger and sorrow.

"I loved her. And I wanted her to come with me." He put down the half-eaten sandwich, tired of the mushy taste of avocado and veggies. "She was good for me. Jenny was always the practical one; she kept me grounded when my dreams ran away with me. We had a good time despite being dirt poor. I'd love to have her here now and give her a different life, a life in the sun, with enough money to have some fun."

149

Down on the stage they had begun to play. The music filled the theater like water in a pool. Jon imagined the audience drowning in it, floating in it like little fishes would in a swaying forest of seaweed. His fingers tapped out the rhythm. He knew the song. He'd heard it on the radio just this morning, while having breakfast.

"But music is not her thing, and Jenny and LA… I don't know."

Sally was busy peeling the label off her water bottle. "It's hard to imagine," she said, "a girl not being charmed by you. Especially one who says she loves you. I'm having a hard time with that."

That made him smile. "Really? I'm not very good with girls. I'm hoping being famous and a rock star will change that. I'm hoping there will be lots of girls."

She gazed at him. "There will be, don't worry. The question is, will they really love you, or the rock star?"

"Is there a difference? I'll always be me, no matter how successful I am. There'll always be Jon Stone underneath the glamour."

Sally smiled and shook her head at him. "That's entirely up to you. Some give themselves over to their fame and forget who they are. Some don't. I'm thinking you belong to that group. It's sad when people lose themselves."

The moment when they'd met Jenny outside the bookstore came back to him. How bleak and tired she had looked, standing there in the rain with her little lunch bag. Then he'd wanted to lash out at her, show her he had indeed done it, had realized his dreams. "You're making me feel sad, and very lonely. I thought I'd never be lonely again once I had a record deal."

Very carefully, Sally rolled the peeled-off label into a tiny funnel. She held it to her eye and pretended to look through it at the stage.

"You'll rarely be alone, but I don't know about lonely. Everyone is lonely now and then." With a sigh, she tossed the paper into the bag. "That's about as much philosophy as I can take on a sunny day."

RUSS and Sal were waiting at the studio.

Jon wondered if they ever left it or if they had put beds somewhere in an unused room where they now slept.

They had, they informed him, been setting up a number of concerts for him for the fall, both here and in New York, and in a couple of other cities; nothing really big as yet, but they were certain he'd draw a couple thousand at each place. The company was promoting the album enthusiastically.

"Which means," Russ said, "from now until we leave, you'll have to rehearse the songs you want to perform. And we need more than just those on the released album. We're going to include some from the new record, to promote that while you're onstage. Let's start putting together the playlist."

They sat in the studio that was now theirs—Jon, Sal, Russ, and Sean—the list of songs between them, and debated which one to use for the opening and how to keep the impetus going without ignoring the slower pieces.

Jon leaned back in his chair. A sense of displacement threatened to inundate him, listening to these three men debate his songs, what order they would place them in, and their impact on the audience. His songs. He recalled how Jenny had always rolled her eyes at him when he'd written a new one and wanted to play it for her. She had barely found the patience, saying over and over that it was all very well and nice, and yes, it was a pretty song, but really, he would never make any money with it.

Even now, after more than six months, the memory still made him angry.

He looked around: They were in the record company's studio. Granted, it wasn't the biggest company in the market, but it had a name all the same, and they had managed to launch his single successfully.

His album was on the table in front of him, and he picked it up. It had that special, unique smell of freshly printed paper.

It was strange. He knew his voice was on that record; he remembered every minute of the recording sessions, how he had felt, how the concentration and hard work had overtaken the sense of wonder at some point, and here was the result; yet all he felt was a kind of displacement. It was as if, the moment Cole had handed him the album, it had slipped away from him, a finished, done thing that no longer had anything to do with him, a trophy for something completed and now in the past. He turned it over, slipped it out of the jacket, looking at the black disc with the label; but he couldn't glean anything new, any excitement from it.

It was done. And it was out in the world at this very moment.

He had given a number of interviews by now, always carefully coached by Sal and Sally about how much to give away and what to keep back. Sally collected the articles and photos. She'd even pinned a centerfold to her office wall, one that he hated more than all other pictures; but she loved it, stating that it showed what the girls wanted to see: a moody, slightly lost boy with unruly hair and a guitar, in the sunset, on the beach.

"It's perfection," she'd said, glee in her voice. "They'll slobber over that one."

Disgusted, he'd left her office and sworn not to return until she took it down, but she had only laughed at him.

"'THE River' as an encore," Russ said, waking him from his thoughts.

"Not as opener?" Jon put down the album. "I'd have used it as the opener."

"Nope. That's your best-known song, and people are expecting to hear it. They are waiting to hear you perform it. You need to build up to it, make them wait. But you're right: we need a fast number as an opener. I was thinking 'The Road I'm On,' do a slow start, the band only; and then you walk on and rock the stage. 'Wilted Love' would be a good second, and then a fluid transition into 'Statue of Liberty.' After that a few slower numbers, then we pick up the tempo again."

"What are you gonna wear?" Pursing his lips, Sal gazed at Jon. "You can't go onstage in jeans and a shirt."

"Why ever not? What am I supposed to wear? A suit? A tux?" The question irritated Jon more than he wanted to admit.

"No, but something a little flashy. Something that will catch the eye." Nodding to himself, Sal went on, "I think I have the perfect thing for you in mind. And Jon, not jeans. You'll have to wear something that shows off your butt a little better."

"You've got to be kidding me." Embarrassed, sure that he was blushing, Jon pushed the record away.

"Absolutely not," Russ added, his hair standing up in excitement. "Sal is right. The girls want to see your...your... Well, you have to show them something." His face turned dark red. "I know it sounds sort of sordid, but that's how it works. A good concert is more than just getting up there and singing. It has to be a good show too. You want them swooning, don't you."

"Uhm." He'd never thought about it like that, and he wasn't sure he wanted to now.

"Don't worry about it," Sal said. He patted Jon's shoulder. "After the first few times you'll get used to it, and I'm sure, knowing you, you'll also get a feel for what works on the stage. You'll do just fine."

"So." Russ crossed his arms. "Here you are. A budding superstar. It's kind of fun to watch the process. Things just seem to come naturally to you, without any effort. Is it always like that?"

Jon grinned. "I have no idea. It's the first time for me too. And I have a feeling I won't go through this again. I don't intend to either. There's only one direction from here, and that's up."

"Damn." Unfolding his limbs, Russ touched the album lying on the table between them like a trophy, like an offering. "How I wish I could travel that road with you. But I'm just an intern, and a foreigner at that. Eventually I have to go back to England."

"Unless, of course..." Jon's heart beat hard and fast at what he was going to say. "Unless I hire you as my producer. I like the way you see and do things. You have a sharp mind, and you seem to *get* what I want. Would you like to work for me?"

It was almost ridiculous how Russ's hair always seemed electrified when he got excited, and it made Jon smile when he replied.

"Do I want to? You have to ask? It would be a dream come true! Yes, of course I want to!"

Jon rose from his chair and stretched. He picked up the album. It felt like picking up his life, like taking control, like gathering up loose threads and knitting them into reins.

"Right. It's done, then. Now I'll go tell Cole that I want you hired, and working for me. See you later, Russ."

From the door, he turned around and added, "Oh, and tell Sean and Sal we're going down to the beach for dinner, will you? I have a hankering for a big bowl of shrimp."

Chapter Twenty-six

IT WAS SO different it almost paralyzed him.

This was no dingy, communal dressing room with a dirty toilet, and no bar owner grunting at him to hurry up. Now it was all about making him feel comfortable and at ease.

Sally was there, and Russ and Sal; and he had a room to himself, a nice room with a couch and proper lighting around the mirror. A makeup artist was waiting for him while Sally got him coffee and a sandwich. Russ asked him how he wanted his guitars arranged—the old one he'd brought from New York, the rosewood, and his new love, the koa twelve-string—and did he want Jones to tune them for him? They had even thought to bring along a dozen picks and place them on Sean's keyboard in a little bowl so he could reach them easily.

There was a rack with his stage clothes, shirts and black slacks, for him to pick from. Jon wasn't convinced that he wanted to wear any of it though. Neither the bright colors of the shirts nor the tight fit of the trousers appealed to him. He was standing there, staring at them in dismay, when Russ walked in.

"Are you excited?" he asked, and Jon shook his head.

"Nah. Not really. Not excited. Scared, yes. But not excited." Red. He slipped the red shirt on. "To be honest, I'm scared to death."

Russ gestured for him to hold out his arms so he could fasten the cufflinks. "Don't be scared, Jon. Nothing can go wrong. You've rehearsed long and hard, and the audience is in a really good mood. All you have to do is go out there and give them your best. You'll be fantastic." Together they walked to the stairs leading up to the stage. "Sal and I will be right there, at the side of the stage. Don't worry; we'll look after everything. All you have to do is go up there and be gorgeous." Russ grinned at Jon's sidelong glance. "No, really. Go out there and shine, and sing, and win their hearts. That's all. Sing your soul out, Jon Stone."

And with a slight slap on the back he sent Jon off.

Those stairs seemed endless, and seemed to be leading into a black hole, into an unknown world.

During the soundcheck in the afternoon he'd felt the exhilaration of a big stage and his own voice filling the empty auditorium; but now, with the murmur of a thousand people filling the space, his pulse was racing and sweat was gathering on his back.

Get them with your first chord, Sal had emphasized, get them right away or they'll drift away from you. Make them love you with the first word you utter.

The first word, and that was *sunrise.* "Sunrise," he whispered to himself.

Sean was playing the intro. They had practiced it endlessly; he knew exactly when he was supposed to enter so the stage lights would catch him.

He was alone, standing in the darkness. For a moment it felt as if everyone had deserted him, had left him in this dark, dusty place to rot, to be the laughingstock of the mass of people out there. The tiny, cold claws of panic crawled up his spine, ripping into his skin.

To shake it off, Jon hummed along with the music, waiting for it to surge, waiting for his cue, and with that all fear vanished. Squaring his shoulders, he stepped out into the blinding light and sang.

THERE were girls.

They clung to the edge of the stage as if it was the side of a lifeboat and he had come to rescue them, their faces shining with rapture and desire, stretching out their hands to him every time he came a little closer, calling his name.

He'd won the audience, all right. In fact, they had even surprised him, singing along with many of his songs, especially the girls at the front, cheering crazily as soon as they recognized the next number.

They didn't want to let him go either. Three encores, those had been well planned, but the applause didn't die down. By then he'd left the stage, exhausted, drenched in sweat, his voice hoarse from two hours of singing and talking. Sally was there to wrap him in a bathrobe, and Russ handed him a bottle of water.

"You'll have to go out again," Sal said. "They won't stop calling for you." His eyes were gleaming. "Can you do one more?"

"Yeah." The cold water felt good in his throat, soothing. "I'll do something quiet. That should send them off."

"Do 'Not Like You' again." There was a sweet smile on Sally's face. "That's my favorite, I think. And it always breaks my heart when I listen to it."

"No, that's too sad. What about 'Forever.' There's promise in that one, and they'll take that away instead of a song about loss." Russ took the bottle when Jon held it out. "Promise them your love, forever. You haven't done it yet tonight. Give them an extra."

And that was what he did. He sent the band off and pulled his stool up to the microphone, settled the rosewood on his knee, and said to the audience: "Now it's just you and me. I wrote this song for a girlfriend, a long time ago. Back then, I thought we'd get married someday and live happily ever after. But it wasn't meant to be. So now I'm here, singing it to you, in gratitude for showing up tonight."

He began to play, picking the chords gently, singing the words softly, thinking of Jenny and how she had looked when he'd last seen her outside the bookstore, and how his heart had felt so heavy despite his anger and pride. Sadness crept into his voice, and wistfulness, regret for what he had lost. It became very still in the big auditorium as they listened, and the applause, when he ended, was as gentle and thoughtful as the song had been.

Guitar in hand, Jon bowed to his audience and left the stage.

They were waiting for him, Sal, Russ, Sally, and Tom, staring at him silently.

"What?" Jon handed Russ the guitar. "What did I do?"

It took Tom a moment, then he said gently, "Nothing, everything. You're such a natural, Jon. I don't know what to say, except, I'm looking forward to the other concerts. You really know how to play them."

"I'm being honest, that's all." He wanted out of the sweaty shirt more than anything. "I told them the truth. They understand those feelings. That's all."

"Yeah, that's all. Right." Shaking his head, Tom followed him into the dressing room. "It's not so much what you tell them, Jon. It's the way you do it. You're amazing."

For some reason he couldn't figure out, the constant praise was beginning to irritate him.

"Oh, get out of here," Jon replied, waving at the open door, "and stop that. I'm beginning to feel like I'm an alien or something. Stop telling me how wonderful I am. It's the loneliest thing in the world, being praised all the time, and I hate feeling lonely. Now let me take a shower and get into my normal clothes!"

He only realized who he'd said those words to when Tom laughed.

"I'm sorry, Tom," Jon began to say, but Tom shook his head and raised his hand to stop him.

"No, it's totally okay. You're right, and I understand what you're saying. Get changed, Jon. You must be starving. We'll go have dinner someplace nice, and quiet. Nothing fancy. Just food."

"Burgers would be great. And fries. Comfort food. I feel like comfort food and a beer." He dropped the shirt on the dressing table. "And I want my friends around me. Not my manager and producer."

"And you shall have them." With another nod Tom left, closing the door behind him.

THERE were girls at the backstage door. Security was holding them back, but as soon as they saw him they screamed his name, begging for autographs.

"Do you want to?" Sal asked. "I have a pen, and Sally has a stack of promo photos."

Jon dithered. He was tired and hungry, and he wanted a rest. The bus was waiting for them, the members of the band inside already.

"Okay. But just for five minutes." He took the pen from Sal and began walking toward the fans.

"I don't think you'll have to worry about having a date ever again." Sal, beside him, smirked. "You can take your pick, my friend."

That thought was even scarier than facing them now, with only a rope and a couple of sturdy men between him and them.

"Looks more like they want to rip me apart, if you ask me."

That made Sal laugh. "Love sometimes takes weird roads, Jon. Very weird roads indeed. And sometimes adoring someone and hurting him isn't as far apart as you'd like." He fell silent, pondering. "We'll have to start worrying about security for you sooner than I thought. A pity. I'd hoped, for your sake, that you'd have a grace period. But I also knew you'd be an instant success. Really a pity. You can't stay in that apartment with Sean much longer. You need new, private digs. I'll look around."

One of the girls reminded him a lot of Jenny. Her hair was the same color, her nose the same cute shape. Only she was smiling at him, adoration in her lovely blue eyes and a flush of excitement on her cheeks.

"Hello, darling," he said to her, putting his name on the concert ticket she was holding out to him. "Did you enjoy the show?"

The girls around her giggled and cooed.

"What's your name?" Jon pushed. "I'm sure it's something pretty."

"Liz," she breathed, blushing even harder.

"Well, Liz." He handed back the ticket. "Thank you for coming. Get home safely, okay?"

"You're impossible." Sal groaned when they were back on their way to the bus. "Flirting with your fans, Jon; shame on you!" But he was laughing. "That chick won't be able to sleep tonight!"

"Yeah. I hope so. You want me to sell, don't you?" The bus door hissed closed behind them, and Jon dropped into a seat. It was the first time in almost four hours that he was able to sit down. He felt exhausted, drained, tired like never before; and somewhere deep down inside there was a tiny drop of melancholia, a diffuse kind of sadness mixed with a feeling of loneliness that he couldn't quite explain.

He looked around. They were all here: Sean, Jones, Sal, Russ and Sally, Tom, Rodney and Walter, people he called friends. And yet he was sad, despite being pleased and happy.

Jon closed his eyes.

Something was missing. Something he needed to survive, to be content, and it was missing. He could feel it like a hollow place in his heart, a spot where his voice echoed and his songs got lost.

Again he looked at those around him. They smiled back when their eyes met, and there was love in their smiles, admiration, care.

"A drink would be nice," he said, and they nodded, all of them, happy to know there was something they could do to make him happy too.

"And tomorrow, no work. I need a day to rest."

Again they nodded, and Tom replied, "Or two. We fly to New York in four days. Take a break, Jon. You need rest; you're right."

It wasn't them at all.

The realization took him by surprise, and he turned away to look out into the night and the passing lights of the highway.

It wasn't his friends; it was him.

It wasn't the love of others he was lacking. The hole in his heart, the thing he was missing, it was his own love, the kind of love he needed to give to someone else.

Listening to the voices of the people around him, Jon felt the veil of loneliness settling on his face.

Chapter Twenty-seven

THE LEAVES WERE falling; the sky was gray.

Jon gazed out the bus window. New York looked dreary in the feeble light, tired, gritty. They had landed at JFK this time, and were so close to his parents' house that he was tempted to ask the driver to drop him off at home so he could spend the night in his own bed instead of going to the hotel in Manhattan with the others. But then, turning around, seeing the others looking at the skyline, seeing the excitement on their faces, he knew he couldn't do it. He was part of this group now, and it wouldn't be right to leave them.

On the plane, Sally had asked him if he'd thought to call his family, and he'd nodded gamely. He had called, and they'd all be there for the concert. Tom had given him a handful of tickets a few weeks before they'd left, saying they were for friends and family back in New York, and did he want them mailed to his parents?

It was the small things that caught Jon by surprise over and over again, the things he didn't think about himself but seemed natural to others. He'd called his mother, telling her he would be giving a concert in New York and that he'd try to get tickets for her and the family, only he didn't know how just yet. The thought that he was entitled to a number of free tickets had never crossed his mind.

"Backstage," Tom had gone on, "who do you want passes for? Your family? Any friends? We'll get them made. Give me a list. But mind you, not too many. They'll mess with our routine."

Just his parents, Jon had replied; he didn't want his sister's scrutiny right before a show. It was embarrassing enough to think of his entire family seeing him perform, but there was no way he'd let Val see him up close, in his stage clothes, with makeup on his face. He'd never hear the end of it.

"*Eyeliner?*" he could hear her say in her sharpest tone. "What has the world come to, my brother with painted eyes? Aren't you pretty enough without makeup?" But her eyes would be shining, and a

161

smile would be tugging at the corners of her mouth, and he'd know it was her way of showing her pride in him.

At least he hoped so. He hoped they would be proud of him for what he had achieved, and acknowledge that indeed he now had a career and was no longer the college dropout and loser.

FROM his hotel room he could look toward Brooklyn and the line of trees along the Promenade. He was almost sure he could see the break in that line where his parent's street intersected it, and he caught a glimpse of the big white house standing on the corner, secure behind its ivy-covered fence and the old sycamore trees.

He loved that house with its big garden. Owning it had always been his dream, and now he was one step closer.

He looked around the room; it was large, with a wide, comfortable bed and a jetted tub in the bathroom. On the table there was a bowl of fruit and a box of chocolates, with a welcome note from the management. A maid had come by earlier to turn down his bed and ask if he wanted anything, and he'd known he was supposed to tip her, only he had no idea how much. So he'd pressed a ten-dollar bill into her hand and thanked her, and she had whisked off, a blush on her face.

Jon wondered why girls had this tendency to blush when he smiled at them.

Jenny had never blushed when he smiled. Often enough, her reply had been to turn her head away and do something else, as if she didn't want him to see a loving response. As if she'd always known they'd come to an end, and because of that she'd held back her heart.

His fingers twitched. Something made him want to call her, ask her to come to the concert and see how far he had come in such a short time, but then he pushed his hands into his jeans pockets to keep them from picking up the phone. It was childish; he didn't have anything to prove to Jenny. Nothing at all. He didn't owe her, and he didn't care.

Telling himself that, Jon grabbed his jacket and wallet, the key to his room, and left the hotel.

New York City, and he was alone in it.

Standing in the hotel entrance, he looked up and down the street. Rush-hour traffic was heavy. A huddle of cabs was stuck right in front of him; they looked like a cluster of yellow beetles gathered on a blossom to catch the last rays of light before the sun dropped below the horizon. The air was full of New York, a smell he always associated with this city. It was a mix of exhaust fumes, brackish water, and the refuse and garbage rotting in the alleys between the tall buildings.

On an impulse, Jon returned to his room to get his rosewood guitar.

The case in hand, he hailed a cab and gave the driver the address.

HIS timing was perfect. The bar was full of people who worked in the city, people who wanted a drink or beer before going home.

Jon didn't take the back entrance this time. He walked inside and up to the counter where Bob was busy filling beer glasses.

"Hey," he said, but Bob, without looking up, called, "I'll be right with you!"

The stage was empty, but a microphone was set up, and the lights were on. Dust motes were dancing in tired beams like tiny fairies, as if the magic of music and the yearning of every artist who'd ever performed here had been caught in them.

A wave of nostalgia swept over Jon at the sight of the old piano against the wall and the yellowed posters of past shows stuck to the paneling over it.

"All right, what can I get you?"

Bob's voice woke him from his reverie, and he turned around. A slow, unbelieving smile crept over the bar owner's round face.

"Look at you! I hardly recognized you, my friend! It's been almost a year since you were here last, and now, just look at you! The scrawny, hungry look is gone! You look great, Jon! Tan and fit, and no longer in that frayed old coat of yours but a leather jacket that screams Fifth Avenue. Never thought you'd find your way back to this old den."

Jon hoisted the guitar case onto the counter. "Actually, I'm here because I wanted to repay you for your kindness. Is there a slot open tonight? If there is, I'd like to fill it."

Bob's hand came down on the fine leather of the case in a careful caress. "You want to play, here? You? Do you know you're in the top ten of the charts with your album? You don't come here and play for free, Jon Stone. Not you, not anymore."

His heart felt light. A happiness was flooding it that he hadn't felt in a long time, and for a second Jon wondered why that was, with all the wonderful things that had been happening to him.

"Yeah, I want to play here, and for free. All night long, if you want. Call it a warm-up for tomorrow night, if you want." That reminded him of something else, and he dug into the pocket of his jacket. "Here." He laid down two tickets for the concert on the following evening. "For you. And I mean for you, Bob. Don't give them away. I want to see you down there in the first row."

Bob stared at the tickets with Jon's portrait on them. "You've come a long way in such a short time, Jon. The Winter Garden, really? You're going to fill the Winter Garden?"

Jon shrugged to hide his pride. "Yeah, three nights in a row, all of them sold out. I have good management."

"Good management, nothing." Picking up the tickets to put them into the drawer, Bob said, "Of course the slots are all taken, but I couldn't care less. I'll offer those young whippersnappers a beer and let them watch you; maybe they'll learn something. The stage is all yours, if you want it. Hey, I have a star in my bar tonight. Incredible. Tell me what you need!"

Nothing, Jon replied, he needed nothing. Maybe a glass of water, but that was all. He just wanted to be on that small, dusty stage once more, just to relive old feelings.

Bob threw him a shrewd glare. "Old feelings, right. I'm thinking you want to nail your new reality by taking note of the difference for you, now and then. But I couldn't care less, Jon. Your reasons are your own. Go on, the stage is yours."

JON didn't even take his jacket to the dressing room; he just dropped it on the piano bench.

The stool on the stage was the same rickety old thing he'd sat on the night he'd met Sal and Sean. Even the microphone was the same battered one he recalled so well. He wondered how many young singers had left their spit in its fine metal mesh. At the studio in LA, he had his own microphone now, a beautiful, matte-gray thing that felt solid and hefty in his hand and produced a clear, unspoiled sound.

Tuning his guitar, he looked out over the room. No one was taking any notice of him. People were discussing their day, sipping beers and cocktails, their backs turned to the stage. The tables were all taken. A good audience. A full house. And no one knew who he was.

He wanted it that way.

Without introducing himself he began to play, softly at first, a gentle, probing intro, enjoying the pure sound of the guitar; and it brought back the comforting scent of wood and warm dust of that day in Roy's workshop.

"*Take me down to the river,*" Jon sang, but this time it was a slow invitation, not the hot jungle night. "*Let me listen to its song.*"

The noise of voices died away as people noticed and shifted to look at him.

"*Can't you hear the river's heartbeat, it's the place where I belong.*"

Something changed. It was like a ripple of wind going through a forest, like a flash of sunlight through thick clouds.

"…Stone," he heard someone say. "It's him!" It was a woman's voice, louder than necessary, loud enough to carry.

Jon smiled and moved closer to the microphone. "Good evening," he called. "Don't tell anyone. I'm here for some fun, and to give you a small, secret concert. Let's enjoy some music, people."

The pick came down on the strings, strumming out the opening chord to "The River" one more time.

Chapter Twenty-eight

SALLY WAS WAITING for him in the lobby, an untouched cup of coffee on the low table in front of her. Her hair was in an untidy braid, and her clothes looked thrown on in haste.

"Where have you been?" She rose when he came toward her, fists on her hips. "We've been worried to death! You can't just walk off like that, Jon, and not tell anyone! Don't you know how dangerous that is? What if someone kidnaps you? Or is out to harm you?"

"Give me a break. Seriously? You're worried about something like that?" Jon dropped onto the couch and took a sip of her coffee. "Who in the world would want to kidnap me?"

Sally stood before him, her face clouded in fury. For once she was without her red lipstick, which made her look even more formidable, in a natural, almost nude way. There was nothing of the sleek, always glamorous Hollywood girl. She was just an angry young woman with worry in her dark eyes.

"Come on, Sally." Jon tried to calm her. "It's no big deal. This is my hometown. I know every alley and dark corner, and I survived quite well here before I moved to LA. I know how to look after myself." He patted the couch. "Come on, sit down and stop fuming at me, and I'll tell you where I was."

"I don't give a damn where you were! I do care about you running out on your own without letting us know." She ignored his invitation to sit. Her eyes were darting from the hotel entrance to the elevator and back, as if she was checking to make sure no one overheard them. "Come on, let's go. I know Sal and Tom are discussing getting a bodyguard for you right away so at least you'll have someone with you when you decide to go on an adventure."

"Oh, hang on." Anger rose in him like a slow tide. "You're doing nothing of the kind. I decide where I go, and with whom. You're not going to have someone follow me around."

Her eyes narrowed to slits of fury, Sally leaned toward him. "Not follow you, Jon. Escort you. Drive you. In a car that belongs to us and not just any old cab. Watch out for you. Don't act like you don't know what I'm talking about."

Grabbing his guitar, Jon got up and moved toward the elevators, forcing her to trail after him.

"Actually," he drawled, "I didn't call a cab to come back here. I took the subway."

Sally threw up her hands. "Are you out of your mind, Jon? I never thought you were this naive." A long, deep sigh escaped her, and with it the rigidity of her fury. "You aren't who you were when you left here anymore. You're not Jon Stone, struggling songwriter anymore. You're Jon Stone at the top of the charts now!"

Jon opened his mouth to reply, but she shook her head.

"No, Jon. I know exactly what's going on with you. You know and accept that you're all that in LA. You live accordingly too. But you just can't accept that it might be the same here. It's your home turf, you know people, you're used to getting around on your own. But things have changed, Jon! Your face is on billboards and posters, your album is prominently displayed in stores, they talk about you on the radio. You are not just anyone anymore."

Mortified, Jon looked away from her and watched the jumping lights of the floor numbers on the buttons.

"So where were you, and why did you take the rosewood?" Her voice was mellower now, more patient.

"Nowhere special," Jon muttered. She made him feel like a miscreant, like he deserved to be locked up for his adventure. "I went down to Bob's and made some music."

"You what?"

The elevator hissed to a stop and opened. Jon stepped out. "I went to Bob's, a bar where I used to play before. Well, you know. And I did what I used to do back then, for a few bucks; I played and sang. It was fun! People didn't know who I was." He shrugged. "Well, at first they didn't. Then someone recognized me, and the party really took off. It was great fun. They were lovely, the audience, and Bob. I gave quite a few autographs. Someone bought me a drink. A couple of women wanted to know if I was free tonight.

Bob insisted on paying me my usual fee. Here it is!" From his jeans pocket, Jon drew out the grubby twenty-dollar bills Bob had given him. "He wouldn't hear of me not taking them. Said that thanks to me the place had been busier than it had in months."

"You gave autographs." She didn't even look at the money. "You gave autographs after you'd been recognized, alone, in a New York bar. And *then* you took the subway back to the hotel." Casting a furtive glance around, she pushed him toward Sal's room. "We'll have to call reception and tell them to field any calls or requests for you. Silly man. Stupid, silly man."

Jon had no idea what she was talking about.

The door opened to reveal Sal's face. "Where were you?" he asked, and Jon gave up.

HE couldn't do this, Sal and Tom repeated, nearly finishing each other's sentences in their attempt to make him see sense; he couldn't just walk off alone without at least informing them. He shouldn't—and this sounded like a less violent repetition of Sally's harangue—go out without an escort; too many bad things could happen. Didn't he realize how many crazies there were out there, fans waiting to run into their star, waiting for a chance to meet him alone? And no, not every fan wanted just an autograph and a smile. Was it really necessary for him to learn the hard way, or would he, please God, believe them?

A glass of bourbon in hand, Jon stood near the window and looked out at the night traffic on the street below.

His hometown, and he'd never felt afraid for a moment moving through New York, regardless of where. He'd walked across Manhattan when the weather was nice, sometimes all the way across the Brooklyn Bridge instead of taking the subway, enjoying the pulse of the city, the sounds, and yes, even the smells. It was like a huge symphony, baroque and opulent, unrestrained like a naked woman dancing on a lonely beach. He loved it, he realized, and it was totally different from the love he felt for LA.

There he was free, a different person, but here he was at home.

He could see the bridge in the distance, it's Gothic arches shimmering like gates into another world. A line of light was winding its way up the ramp to them like a glowing snake, the cars leaving town on their trek home.

Jon wanted to be in one of them, wanted to be in the anonymous herd of humanity instead of listening to his friends' admonishments.

"We have a basement," Tom was saying, pulling him out of his thoughts, "at the studio. We have a room down there full of fan mail. We keep the ugly ones, we catalog and store them, just in case something happens, so we'll have proof that there was a threat beforehand. Your name isn't on one of those shelves yet, Jon. But it won't be long now. So yes, you do have to take this seriously. Everything seems fun and easy now; but there will come a time when you'll see that your new life bears its own dangers, and they are not to be underestimated."

"Oh, come on." Jon sighed, turning toward them, and stopped at the expression on their faces. Sal and Tom were looking at him with kindness, and a trace of regret; and they were serious in a way he'd never seen before, not even during his contract negotiations. Even then there had always been time for a smile, the love for their job and excitement sparkling in their eyes, but there was none of that now.

"At least take me," Sal ended, taking a deep breath. He reached for the bourbon and poured himself a stiff drink. "Now. I need dinner. It's a bit late, but heck, I need dinner. Who's coming with me? Jon? Sally? Tom? Russ?"

He was hungry indeed. Jon realized they'd skipped lunch, and that his impromptu concert had chased away any thought of food.

SEAN and Jones agreed to come along, and they piled into the van, discussing where to go.

Sally, wedged in the back seat between the door and Sean, said she wanted to go to Carnegie's for pastrami; but Tom shook his head.

If she wanted pastrami, he replied, it would be Katz's or nothing. It was a matter of belief, he added, and he, personally, believed Katz's had the best pastrami.

Katz's. Jon remembered how he'd taken Jenny there one Sunday afternoon after their shift at the bookstore. She'd ordered chicken soup and half a Reuben sandwich while he had enjoyed the warm, succulent pastrami and the pickles. She'd taken a sip of his German beer and declared it to be awful, bitter and thin, but he'd loved the tartness, so different from any American beer he'd ever tasted.

On their way out they'd bought a jar of pickles to take home, and Jenny had joked about how he'd have to come here every week once they were married and expecting their first child. He'd promised to get her anything she craved, no matter what time of day it was; and they'd laughed together, hand in hand, waiting for the subway.

They'd never returned, and he'd never brought her another jar of pickles.

"SO were there girls?" Sal's voice brought Jon out of the dark pit of his memories.

"Girls?" he asked, puzzled.

"Yeah, at Bob's. Were the girls flocking to the edge of the stage, like in LA?" Sal was laughing at him, laughing at how dense he was.

"Oh. Yes. There were girls." Mortified, Jon turned his face away. "Yeah, girls."

"And?" Sal prompted, but Jon only shrugged. His thoughts were still with Jenny and that night when the world had looked good to him, and he had believed in a future with her.

"I'm careful with girls," Jon said. "You know. Don't want to get stuck with the wrong one."

They had arrived. Sally was the first to jump out. She stood on the sidewalk in her red coat, her hair like a river of silver over her shoulder, a small red patent leather purse in her hands. A couple of young men walking past stared at her legs.

"Don't tell me you believe in that one true love crap." Critically she watched as Jon closed his jacket against the rain-soaked wind. "Really, Jon? You're waiting for that one girl of your dreams?"

"I thought I'd found her," he replied. "I wanted to believe it very much. Only she wasn't the one. She didn't love me at all, I think. I wonder why she stuck with me for so long." Old sadness clawed at his heart. "I wonder why she didn't leave me a lot sooner. She should have seen I wasn't going to lead the life she wanted. She should have pulled out. But she stuck with me until I left. And then blamed me for leaving her. It wasn't fair."

"You're such a silly bastard." Sal, coming up, slapped his shoulder. "Has no one told you that that's exactly what women do? They'll always wait until they get a chance to blame you for whatever happened. That's the way the world works, my friend. And your girl, she was no different. The way things went she can always say that you walked out on her. Come on. I'll buy you a beer."

Jon hesitated, and Sally, noticing, waited.

"Yes," he said softly so only she could hear, "I do believe in that one true love. I know it's somewhere out there, and I'm convinced I'll know when the moment is right. Only I haven't met her yet. But trust me, Sally. I'll know her when I see her."

She gave him a small, sad smile and entered the restaurant while he held the door for her.

"WHAT were you talking about out there?" Sal handed the menu back to the young waiter.

Jon wondered if he was a college student, or maybe an artist like himself, trying to keep his head above water while waiting for someone to pay him for his art. He looked scrawny enough for it in his black polyester trousers.

"Jon says he believes in true love." Biting into one of the pickles the boy had left on the table for them, Sally said, her mouth full, "And he said he'd know it when he saw it."

"Romantic." Sal snatched a pickle before she pulled the small bowl in her direction. "How do you think you'll know? I mean, how do you think this will happen?" He waved at the entrance door. "You believe if the right woman walked in now you'd know her? You'd feel it somehow, and then get up and walk over to her and say, 'Hey, I know you're my one true love. Let's get married!' Something like that?"

Defensively, Jon drew up his shoulders. "I don't know. I just know that I'll know when I meet her. It will be different. Special."

Just then the door flew open and a girl walked in, a slim, delicate girl with long, black locks that tumbled down her back all the way to her hips. She was wrapped in a blue coat that ended just above her knees and displayed slim, well-shaped legs. Her face was turned away from them; she was laughing at something the man behind her had said, her head held at an elegant angle that showed the graceful curve of her throat.

Jon's ears were ringing. The air around him seemed to thicken, making breathing a painful thing for a moment.

"Yeah," he said, speaking through the haze. "Yeah, I really believe that. I believe something will tell me when the moment is right. I'll look up and see the one, and I'll know."

The girl in the blue coat had moved to the counter and was studying the menu on the wall above it, pointing, asking her escort something, and then laughed. It was a soft sound, and it moved across his heart with the frisson of foreboding, almost fear, as if someone had left a door open and a breeze of cool air was touching him.

"I will know," Jon repeated, watching the girl pick up a tray and walk to the rear of the restaurant, where she sat down with her back to them.

"I believe there's no way I can't know. My heart will probably stop, and my breath will feel like ice in my chest. I'll reach out to her, and she'll know too. It will be that easy, and that miraculous. It will be a moment outside of time; the universe will stop for us. Yes."

He broke off. They were all staring at him, frozen, their eyes locked on him.

"What?" Jon reached for his bottle of beer. "What did I say?"

The waiter was bringing their food. Strange, it was strangely painful to see him put down a bowl of chicken soup with matzo swimming in it in front of Sally, and half a sandwich. It wasn't a Reuben but pastrami, and yet.

"You're such a romantic," Tom said slowly. "This is a side of you I've never seen, Jon. You're so matter-of-fact about your music, so straightforward when it comes to business; yet here you are spilling your heart out about a kind of love no one ever finds, except in mushy romance novels. I'm surprised."

"Really?" The beer was icy, much too cold for a chilly day like this. "I don't think you can be a songwriter without a trace of romance in your heart." Jon grinned at Tom. "How else would I be able to write love songs? I need a romantic side." He paused to take a bite of his pastrami sandwich. It was warm, juicy, with just the right amount of mustard and a nice rim of fat on the meat. How he'd missed this. There was no pastrami like this in LA.

"Although I have to say, lyrics are hard. I'd hoped it would get easier with time, but I'm still battling with the rhymes." There, he'd said it, and to Tom.

"I think your lyrics are great," Russ threw in, blushing as always when he dared to speak up in the company of his boss. "They have just the right edge of ruggedness to make them appealing to guys and not just the girls. Wrestle with them, if you must, but they are really good." Looking from Tom to Jon, and then to Sal, he added, "But your music is better yet. That's true."

He wanted to see the face of the girl, but she didn't turn their way. Her entire attention was focused on the man she was with. Their hands kept meeting across the table, entwined for a moment, and then they'd separate again, like a slow dance, a ritual of movements.

A line of words formed in Jon's head, sad, soft words of good-bye, and lost love. He forced himself to look away from the couple and concentrate on his food and his friends.

Sally was gazing at him thoughtfully, her elbow on the table, the spoon in her hand. "So. For you it's true love or nothing?" Her eyes were sparkling with a challenge, but Jon ignored it.

"I didn't say that." He was tempted to lick the meaty juice off his fingers but grabbed a napkin instead. "I didn't say that I'm not having fun meeting girls. I'm just saying that so far, I haven't met the one who will capture my heart."

Sally's gaze slid away from him. It was as if the sun had vanished behind clouds, as if the joy had gone out of her.

"But you haven't written any songs about that yet," Tom said, oblivious to Sally's reaction. "Why is that, I wonder. You write about lost love, about broken promises and chance encounters on a desert highway. You sing about dark and lonely Sunday afternoons in New York, but where is that bright spark of hope? The utter belief that someday you'll find the one who will own your heart? I think you should write about that, Jon."

"I've tried." His beer bottle was empty, and he wanted another one. Instead of calling the waiter he got up and went to the counter to get one himself. The girl in the blue coat was talking to her escort, her hands moving through the air in animation, her laughter rippling through the noisy room like a little brook of forest water.

Hope, and love, and yearning. The empty space in his heart ached when he grappled for words to fill it.

"I will wait for you," Jon whispered, watching the man behind the counter as he got a fresh bottle from the fridge behind him. "If it takes all my life, I will wait for you."

There was no song there. In a strange, eerie way it felt as if all the songs in his head danced around this one, as if there was a silent place in his soul that he couldn't reach, let alone turn into music. It wasn't a dark or scary place. But it was empty, a big white bubble in the center of his heart.

Chapter Twenty-nine

A KNOCK WOKE him.

It was still dark outside, the traffic not yet in rush-hour mode, and for a second he was disoriented, not knowing where he was. Jon stumbled to the door without turning on the lights.

Sally was standing in the hallway, dressed in flannel pajamas with kittens printed on them, glaring at him. She didn't wait for an invitation but walked past him into his room and sat on his bed.

Jon realized he was in his shorts. The hotel bathrobe was still in its plastic wrapping; he had never found any use for bathrobes yet. Hastily, mortified, he pulled on his jeans and a shirt. His mind wasn't awake yet. "Do you want me to ring for coffee?"

"No, forget the stupid coffee." Her fist came down on the blanket. "I'm tired of being professional and civilized. Can we talk about it now, before I lose my nerve?"

"Talk about what?" His stomach was curling up. "And why in the middle of the night?"

There was enough light from outside, from the skyscrapers surrounding them, to see her. Her long mane shone like liquid moonlight, and her skin glowed like a pearl. Carefully, Jon perched on the edge of the bed, far enough away so he wouldn't be able to touch her.

"Talk about us." Sally's voice shook a bit. The usual bravado and brisk firmness was completely missing from it. "What you said at dinner. I'm quite upset about it."

"What did I say?" He remembered the girl in the blue coat, and feeling very stuffed after the huge sandwich he'd eaten. "We talked about the job. About what Tom wants me to write." Slowly, his brain was waking up. "And I said that I believe in true love."

"Yes, you did. You talked about an imaginary someone and how you'd fall in love instantly when you met her, and how that love would last forever. As if we're in a stupid fairy tale and you are Prince Charming. Who am I in your fairy tale, Jon?"

Jon ran his hand through his hair, and when that wasn't enough, rubbed his face. He hadn't shaved the day before; the stubbles on his chin made a rasping sound under his palm. "I'm not Prince Charming. And I haven't the slightest idea what you want from me at this time of night. Do us all a favor and go back to your room, Sally. I'm tired." He sighed. "You've told me a million times that you never get involved with clients, as you so kindly put it. So what would be the point of falling in love with you? I'm done with unhappy love affairs. I can wait until the right girl comes along."

"But you make out with your fans. I'm surprised there isn't one here tonight." She gazed around in the dark, still room.

"Yes. I do. Sometimes." With a shrug, Jon began to button his shirt. "And why ever not. It's not as if there's someone in my life I want to be faithful to. It's not as if I'm in love."

"Where does that leave me?" It came out in such a small, soft voice that Jon stopped fussing with his shirt and looked up.

"Sally." How to tell her without inflicting pain, how to explain without driving her away? "Sally, when we met, I was ready to fall in love with you. You were like the answer to a dream: uncomplicated, sunny, pretty, and you understood me. I wanted to fall in love with you very badly. You are a part of my new life, and most of all, you are the one part that makes that new life real for me."

He recalled how they'd gone to that movie premiere party together, he in the new tux she had picked out for him, freshly barbered and manicured, and Sally on his arm, in a narrow dress covered with silver sequins. She'd looked like a mermaid, like a selkie just risen from the ocean, her hair a pale, glinting stream down her back, its color mingling with the glitter from the dress. She had danced with him, her body a sweet warmth in his embrace, and he'd wished with all his heart that she'd been his girlfriend, his to claim. But as always, she'd been friendly, funny, kind, and taken care that he presented himself in his best light, a budding star, a future icon, her responsibility.

"I wanted to fall in love with you the same way I'm in love with LA, with the beach and the sunshine. But you never offered me a chink in that armor. In fact, I imagined us together, climbing the mountain of success together. I could see it."

Jon rose from the bed to get the phone and call room service for coffee and, if they could manage it despite the early hour, breakfast.

That had been another hard thing to learn. No going down for breakfast for him if he wanted to eat in peace. Someone would recognize him and come over to ask for an autograph. At first he'd been awkward, asking the person how they knew him; now, with the posters all over New York City, he didn't have to anymore. All his shows were sold out. Tom, Sal, and Cole were discussing a European tour for the following summer. He was ready to conquer the world.

"But you never made a move!" It sounded like an accusation. "You never told me any of this!"

Jon opened his mouth to reply and then closed it, nearly biting his tongue.

He had to chew on the answer for a moment. Then he said, carefully, "Of course not. I didn't want to risk our relationship, Sally. We are good together, it's fun, and we get a lot of things accomplished. Why would I go and ruin that?" What a lie that was. "You're Cole's daughter. I'd rather freeze in hell than antagonize your old man." Not that much of a lie, but still. "I love what I'm doing. I wouldn't jeopardize that for a fling with you."

Sally tilted her head at him, making her long hair ripple like sunlight on wet leaves. "You're such a coward."

Slowly, Jon sat down next to her so he could take her hand. "You're special, Sally, and different. In the beginning, when we first met, I wanted to...well, I wanted to get involved with you very much. You were always there, tantalizing like a piece of music that's dancing in my mind. You're very lovely, a lovely girl, and I wanted you badly. I wanted you in my bed. But the longer we worked together, the longer I knew you, the more I realized that it wouldn't be a good thing. Your friendship is something I treasure, and I don't want it ruined." That statement pulled at his lips, forcing him to smile. "Hey, will you listen to me? I sound like someone much older, and much cheesier."

"You sound like an idiot, Jon, if you want to know." Sally drew her hand out of his. It felt like a sleek little animal slipping from his grasp. "Like an idiot making cheap excuses. Seriously. And you're not even being honest. I think I deserve honesty from you."

The tiny, bitter worm of anger was making its way from his heart to his mouth.

"Honesty, really?" Again he got up to walk away, but this time not to order coffee or food. Pacing the carpet between the door and the bed, Jon pushed his hands into his pockets. They felt safer there.

"You can have honest from me. I'm so sick and tired of women wanting things from me that I can't give. First Jenny, who wanted to turn me into a banker or insurance broker; and now you, after repeating for months that you don't want an affair with me, whatever that means, expecting me to tell you that yes, you're the one love of my life and to forget all others. Well, you're both not getting what you want. At least not from me. I'm done with people telling me how to be, what to do, and who to love. I'm done. I'm done with being who you all want me to be!"

"Oh goodness, the drama." Sally left the bed, pulling at the sleeves of her pajama top in a gesture of shame. "An affair was never on my mind, Jon. But I wouldn't have minded something better, something lasting. I thought if I kept you away in the beginning, if we didn't slide into some hurried thing, we'd have a chance at something lasting. I get it; I miscalculated. I'm never going to be that one true love you keep going on about. So. Go back to bed and get some more sleep. Today will be tough enough, with the TV interview in the morning and the show tonight. I'll leave you to it."

"Sit down." Jon pointed at the bed, at the spot that still seemed to radiate her body warmth. "You're going to have breakfast with me now. I ordered it, and it's expensive enough in this stupid place, so you're going to eat it. And we're going to make up and be friends again, or else. I'm much too grumpy and tired to go on arguing."

She stood there next to the door like a little girl, a bit forlorn, exhausted, and yet still very pretty.

"Sally."

"All right, all right." She didn't return to the bed but sat on the

180

couch instead, her legs primly crossed, her arms wrapped around her chest.

"I don't even know what brought this on." He pulled over a chair. "What happened to bring this on?"

A small shrug, an obstinate tilt of her chin. "You. You brought it on, with your constant ramble about love, and miracles, and stuff. Do you seriously believe all that crap, Jon? Really?"

His heart pulled together, squeezing out all the blood. "Yes, I do. I want to believe that someone will appear in my life someday. That she will stop my breath, make me forget my name, make me even forget my music, everything, for that instant. For her, I'll be willing to lay it all down: my life, my music, my heart. And I know that because I'm made that way. I'll allow that love to overwhelm me, to let it rule my life. I'm willing to give all of myself to it." The pain was easing; he could draw a careful breath. "It will be like the sound of a large bell—clear, loud, and beautiful—and…"

The bell, he remembered how he'd heard it on the beach in Santa Monica, that first night in LA, and how he'd thought he'd heard a faraway whisper, the echo of a voice, and no one had been there. His heart had ached then too for something he hadn't known he was missing.

"And I'll know it," Jon went on softly. "I'll know it, because it will be the perfect sound, a flawless, melodious heartbeat, one you can only hear when two hearts that should be beating as one finally meet."

There was a knock on the door.

"Oh." Jon jumped up. "Breakfast. I hope the bacon is nice and crisp. I ordered a double portion. Eggs, bacon, and hash browns. The ultimate early-morning breakfast!"

Busy signing the check, he didn't see the silent tears dropping from Sally's eyes onto the kittens on her pajamas.

Chapter Thirty

STANDING IN THE gray, early light, a cup of coffee from the deli next door between his hands warming them, Jon decided never to do this again. No morning interviews if there was a show the same day. No morning appearances at all, if there was a show that night.

The weight of a hundred decisions dampened his mood, decisions he alone had to make and then get others to accept.

Traffic was picking up. The sidewalks were filling with people on their way to work. It was funny how no one seemed to stir in New York before six in the morning; in fact, it seemed like an unspoken agreement, arrived at to give everyone a chance to enjoy the evenings. New York didn't care for early risers.

Sean, Jones, and the core of the band were already inside, setting up their instruments, tuning the guitars, and getting ready for their three minutes on the morning TV show. Russ and Sal were there to help, but not Sally. He hadn't seen her at all after she stormed out of his room. They'd eaten breakfast together, but it had been a silent, joyless affair while the sun rose and shone into the room. He'd risen to open the curtains, and that had made her flinch as if he was about to hit her. That one movement had hurt more than the angry words that had been spoken.

"You're out on your own again." Sal had come out of the building looking for him. "You're inviting trouble."

"I'm fine." Jon tossed the empty paper cup into a trash can on the brink of overflowing. "Don't worry about me, Sal. I'm fine. I'll always go out on my own, no matter how famous I get."

He could see Sal take a breath to respond, and how the air left him again.

"Fine," Sal said, "have it your way. If you won't listen to our advice you'll just have to learn the hard way. I'd hoped I could spare you that. Your ride has been so smooth until now, but it seems like you're headed for a reality check sooner rather than later. Go ahead and get yourself into trouble. I'll be there to help get you out of it when the time comes though. I've invested too much in you to see you end up in the gutter."

"Why..." He didn't even know how to respond. Anger was choking him, anger and a weird kind of disappointment. "Why is everyone out to create drama today? What have I done to you and Sally? All I'm saying is that I'm perfectly capable of looking after myself—especially in my own hometown—and I'll decide on my own who to love, and when. Give it a rest already!"

A smirk appeared on Sal's face. "Oh, so that's it. I was wondering what was making you so morose today. A lovers' tiff with Sally, is that it?"

"It wasn't a lovers' tiff because we aren't lovers, and it's none of your business either."

Sean was coming through the doorway, a cigarette in his hand. He stopped to light it, blinking in the sunlight.

"It's none of my business, that's true. But it is my business to see to it that you deliver a good performance. This interview is important, Jon. It's national. This is the number one–rated morning show that you'll be on. Don't mess this up because you've decided to have an attitude. This is *not* the time." Sal's voice had a steely edge to it that Jon had rarely heard, and never directed at him.

"Don't worry." He held out his hand to Sean, who put a cigarette in it. "I won't mess up, and neither will the others. You'll be happy, I promise. But, Sal." Steely voice, he could do that too. And even a bit more. "I'm only saying this once. Don't get involved in my love life. Ever."

Surprised, Sal pulled up his eyebrows.

"I draw the line where my private life is concerned. It's messy enough as it is; I really don't need your input." The cigarette tasted bitter and stale. He dropped it into the gutter, where it mingled with other debris.

"All right, all right, calm down, for heaven's sake!" Sal raised his hands in a show of defeat. "I wasn't even asking as your manager, I was asking as your friend. Jon? I thought we were friends."

"Yeah, we are. But you delivered it along with dire threats about my security and your panic about messing up this morning's appearance on TV." Jon shook his shoulders, trying to get rid of the black mood and sadness along with the stiffness in his neck. "That was not fun with Sally." He looked around, but there was only Sean, who was listening with his head turned away, his eyes on the traffic. "She showed up in my room in the middle of the night. I don't know what she wanted, to be honest. And I have no idea why I'm telling you either."

"Because we're your friends, and because you want to hear some-one else's opinion," Sean said softly. "That's what friends are for, Jon. You're getting it all confused because we work together too. But we're still your friends, and we care about you, as a person."

"Yeah." He knew. Of course he knew, but somehow his mind had forgotten for a moment what his heart knew so well. "She was upset because of what I said over dinner. She wanted to know if I really believed in love at first sight and there being one true love."

"On, interesting!" Sean took a step closer. "I was actually going to ask you the same thing today. You were so sincere about it, as if you were ready to open your veins and lie down to die for it right there. Really, Jon? I mean, that's so utterly romantic."

"Dunno." Something was turning over in his chest; it felt as if a sleeping animal was burrowing deeper into its nest. "I think I want to believe it. I want something in this world to be true down to its bare bones and still true when everything else crumbles. If that isn't the case, then nothing else makes sense. What good are love songs if they are about a thing that doesn't exist? It would be the saddest thing ever."

They stared at him, Sean and Sal, mesmerized, ignoring the thickening stream of pedestrians around them, ignoring Russ, who'd come outside to tell them that it was time, that they needed to be in the studio.

"I don't get," Sal said, a smile in his tone, "why you keep going on about not being able to write good lyrics. You speak them all the time. Can't you make the connection or what?" Jon waved him away and followed Russ inside, humming the song he was going to sing in a few minutes.

JON had to knock twice before Sally opened her door.

She was still in the same pajamas she'd been wearing during her surprise visit to his room. Defensively she pulled the top closer around her body and crossed her arms.

"What?" she asked, taking a step back from the door but not far enough for Jon to enter.

"You didn't show up for the interview. I was worried about you." He leaned against the wall. "It went well, if you care. And now we're back, and it's nearly time for lunch, and I want to take you out. So are you coming?"

"I'm not dressed." She waved at the bed somewhere behind her in the dim room. "I was in bed, and I know the interview went well. I saw you on TV. Nice performance too."

A small, awkward silence fell while they avoided looking at each other, waiting for the other to speak first.

Jon was the first to give in. "Okay," he said, "all right. You're mad at me. I'm sorry. I should have known, and I didn't. I should have seen that you wanted more, and I didn't. I listened to what you were saying to me all the time when instead I should have believed what I was seeing."

"Seeing?" Sally, wiping her face with the back of her hand, stepped to one side to let him inside, but Jon remained where he was.

"Yeah. I should have ignored your talk and just gone for it, tried my luck with you, and I didn't, because I believed what you said. Men aren't good at this, Sally. You can't tell them one thing and expect them to do the other, especially not in a situation like ours."

"Oh, whatever." Her body slumping, she turned away from him, leaving the door open. "Do as you please. I'm going back to bed."

"No, you're not. Get dressed. We're going out for lunch, and a stroll up Fifth Avenue. The weather is much too nice to spend the day moping in your room. I'm giving you ten minutes. Get going."

A trace of life returned to her posture. "Strong words, Jon Stone! Are you finally getting a backbone?" It sounded a little sharper than necessary, but her face had softened. "Okay then, you win. Give me ten minutes, and I'll be with you."

"I'll wait in the lobby, so you can't sneak past me."

Jon heard the door close as he reached the elevators.

HE sat on one of the couches in the lobby and asked for a cup of coffee when a waiter came by. It was a cozy niche; he could see the entrance and the desk but wasn't visible himself. The sun was falling on the red carpet in long, mellow beams, the typical golden light of a nice fall day on the East Coast. On their way back from the studio, he'd noticed some maple trees in their full glory, flaunting red and yellow leaves, proclaiming their beauty. It had made him homesick for New York, for seasons, but the yearning for the beach and the flaming sunsets won.

He wanted a house on the beach, but not one of those modern, clustered glass shells that clung to each other along the shore; he wanted something solid, with land around it, something private, and built to last.

THERE was movement in the entrance, a figure disturbing the light beams, and he looked up.

A woman was standing there, dressed in jeans and a short, white coat, sunglasses dangling from her fingers. Her long hair was in a braid falling over her shoulder, the lovely auburn gleaming in the sun. She was waiting for something, for someone, her head turned away from him so Jon couldn't see her face properly.

Once again, like the night before when the girl in the blue coat had walked into the restaurant, a strange feeling ran through him.

He couldn't say what it was really, that echo, that weird feeling of remembering something that hadn't even happened yet.

He wanted to get up and go over to that woman, ask her who she was and why she was making him feel so strange, but before he could, Sally stepped in front of him and blocked his vision. She looked as if nothing had happened. Dapper as always, she was in a coat with polka dots. A ruffled blouse showed in the neckline.

"Here I am," she said. "Now for lunch. Where are we going?"

Chapter Thirty-one

THE LAST TIME they'd been in New York there hadn't been time for walks and shopping sprees. But now the sun was shining brightly, bathing the buildings and streets in the mild, golden light of a late Indian summer day. Jon regretted not having more time in his hometown.

Fifth Avenue had never been one of his usual haunts. He'd never had the money to shop there, and looking at windows full of things he knew he would covet and couldn't afford was a kind of self-torture that he didn't need. A few times, when he'd been in a particularly black mood, he'd come here and hung out, watching the tourists, the rich and the beautiful, stroll in and out of the stores full of pretty things.

Now, walking down the street with Sally, everything was different. For her it was the next best thing to Rodeo Drive, and, while eating an ice cream cone, she threw desultory glances at the winter fashions displayed in the shop windows.

"Nothing new," she said, waving at the storefronts. "Nothing we don't have in LA too. And then some. New York is getting stale."

They stopped outside Tiffany's. A flock of Japanese tourists was blocking the sidewalk, taking photographs, chatting excitedly, pointing. Some were carrying the telltale little blue bags, showing them off to one another, even posing with them in front of the entrance.

"They can forever thank Audrey Hepburn for that," Sally commented sourly. "This place is so tacky now. Just another tourist trap, like so many others in New York."

"I don't know. It's still a classic." Jon stopped to gaze into the window.

"Listen to you. A New Yorker, defending one of the New York hallmarks. Seriously, Jon. You can get much nicer stuff elsewhere, and cheaper too." She waved at the diamond earrings and necklaces in the display. "Always with the Art Deco designs. Who'd wear

189

that other than tourists, and they buy it because of the name, not because they actually like it."

"I like it." It did sound a bit defensive, he had to admit. "I like Tiffany's. They have a certain kind of style, elegant. I like it."

Once, only once, had he been here. He recalled that day very well; it had been one like this, and just over a year ago.

He'd decided to buy Jenny a ring. He'd woken up with the sunlight in his eyes, and there she'd been, her reddish hair like strands of rose gold on his pillow, her shoulder so fragile and sweet under his touch. She had not woken but stirred like a kitten, murmuring something he couldn't understand. That was when he had decided to ask her.

So he'd gone out without telling her where he was off to, and he'd even ignored her calling after him to bring back some bread and not to forget it, please. The world had seemed fresh and glorious to him as he walked to the subway, his pocket full of money secretly saved from his earnings. He'd gone to the bank to have all those grubby, small bills exchanged for neat, crisp twenties so that he wouldn't look too pathetic at the store.

Dressed in his best shirt, shoes polished, and wearing the coat his mother had given him instead of his beloved but well-worn leather jacket, he'd walked into Tiffany's. They'd been kind and patient with him, and they hadn't made him ask for a ring that he could afford but had discreetly shown him the entire range. No one had smirked or rolled their eyes when he picked the cheapest one, a slim band with a diamond that was as tiny as a spark of light on a raindrop. It had been handed to him wrapped up in the signature light-blue box and white ribbon, and in one of their little paper bags. His bills had been accepted graciously too. He hadn't once felt inferior to the men in their well-tailored suits and expensive watches.

His wife would wear Tiffany's and nothing less. This was the statement that he wanted to make to the world.

"I bought an engagement ring for Jenny here," he said, "but I never gave it to her."

Sally, about to take another bite of her ice cream, stopped to look up at him, her eyes round and curious.

Jon shrugged. "Yeah, I know. It was a couple of weeks before I met Sal and Sean. I was waiting for the right moment, and it never came. And then, suddenly, everything was over." He moved toward the entrance of the store. "So stupid. I still have that ring. Would you believe it? I never gave it to her, and I never parted with it. It took me so long to save up all that money. And it was for nothing. I even brought it with me on this trip. It's a reminder to wait for the right girl, for real love that's received and returned in kind."

"I'm sorry, about last night," Jon said softly.

Sally nodded. "Yeah, me too. You were right; it's my fault. I treated you as if you were an innocent teenager. I teased you, flirted, and told you to stay away at the same time. I honestly misjudged you, Jon, and for that I'm sorrier than you can imagine."

"Yeah." He wasn't sure what to say. "Maybe we should try and forget that whole episode, pretend it never happened. Me, I'm not in the mood to rehash everything we said last night. Wouldn't change anything anyway."

She gave him a thoughtful glance. "You're a strange man, Jon. You're as hard as nails when it comes to your work, yet with girls you're as mushy as melting ice cream. It's weird, and had I known earlier what a softie you really are, I'd have tackled this differently. You hide your heart well."

"You get that way when you have to defend your dreams and ambitions to everyone around you." The sun had vanished behind a bank of clouds. Fifth Avenue looked as gray and joyless as any other part of the city for a moment. "You lock up your dreams and desires deep inside so they can't be ripped from you. You hold on to them like you'd hold on to your last breath, because they're all you have." Jon zipped up his jacket against a sudden gust of sharp wind. "It's the only way to keep those dreams alive. It's either that or you give up on them. And then nothing is left behind. You're an empty shell. I swore to myself that I'd never give up my dream of being a successful songwriter. I was prepared to work hard, work until I bled. I'd have given up anything and anyone for it. Turns out I did."

They began to walk down the sidewalk, back toward the hotel. After a while Sally pushed her arm through his, and Jon let her. She stopped walking when they reached Fifty-third and pointed at a billboard above the subway entrance. "Look!"

There it was, the proof. His face, his name in bold, proud letters, the dates of his concerts, and, plastered over them, a sign that said SOLD OUT.

"You know," Jon said slowly, "I want one of those. My first big appearance in New York City. I want one of those posters."

Sally laughed. "Really, Jon. If that's all you want, that's easily done. I'll call the office when we get back to the hotel."

SAL and Tom were waiting. It was nearly time to go to the venue for the soundcheck and rehearsal.

The sound and light people had gone ahead. Russ looked flustered as always, but his voice sounded cool enough with its relaxed, British accent. "We go now," he said. "Dinner will be catered. There's a good hospitality room where we can gather after the soundcheck." He gave Jon a brief glance. "You'll have to get used to this, Jon. When we're on the road, we don't leave the venue once we get there, not until after the show. It would be too much of a risk for various reasons. We'll see to it that you'll always have a comfortable dressing room so you can relax before the concert. Now. Is there anything that you want done, procured, or arranged before we leave?"

"My guitars." That was the only thing he could think of.

"They've been taken care of. They're going to the venue with the other instruments, right now." Russ ticked off an item on his clipboard.

"No."

Surprised, they all looked at Jon.

"My guitars go with me. I won't risk losing them." The thought alone was enough to give him goose bumps. "All the other instruments are going with their owners. Mine will be the only unattended ones."

"Good point," Russ answered before Sal had even taken a breath.

"I'm glad you brought it up. In fact, they aren't unattended. Jones is taking them, and he'll also tune them for you. We also sent along your little bowl and a bag full of picks. Jones recommended that. He said you like to drop the things. Can't have you scrabbling all over the stage searching for your guitar pick."

"Right." Mortified, Jon grinned at them. "Sorry."

"Don't worry about it. It's all been taken care of. Your stage clothes are there too. We put out a choice of shirts for you. You can pick out whatever you like; it can be laundered by tomorrow night, so even if you want to wear it again for some reason it'll be okay." Digging into a briefcase on the couch behind him, Russ pulled out some backstage passes. "For your parents. Anyone else you want to admit?"

Jon thought about it for a moment. "Nah. I don't know anyone else who'd want to come backstage to see me."

A round of laughter was all the response he got.

Chapter Thirty-two

"I'VE NEVER UNDERSTOOD the appeal of autographs," Jon mused, watching the cluster of fans around the backstage entrance of the theater. "What do they want with it? I mean, it's just a name scribbled on a piece of paper."

"You obviously aren't a star yet." Sally handed him a pen and a pack of postcards with his image on them.

Jon hated that photo; it had been taken on the beach, just after sunrise, only him and some pelicans.

"The fisherman image," Sal had called it derisively, "as if you're ready to go out to catch some fish for dinner."

He had been wearing an artfully ragged shirt and frayed linen pants, and, staring into the distance, he looked like a beach bum. At least his arms were tan and muscular, thanks to Sally's relentless workout plan.

The pelicans and he had all been thinking of breakfast just then, to hell with the sunrise on that surprisingly chilly morning.

"Go on, make them happy!" Sal urged.

Jon shook off the memory and took two steps toward the group. Security was holding them back, but a susurration of excitement went through them like a breeze through reeds along a lakeshore. Most of them were young women, girls, their faces radiant with expectation, their hands fluttering, holding out photos or concert tickets for him to sign.

"An autograph," Sally went on while they strolled toward the fans, "is proof of your humanity; didn't you know? It means you actually touched something that they own. You and they, you held the same object in your hands. They can take that home and hold on to it, and know you're not just a figment of their imagination. It's a trophy."

"Oh, will you shut up." It was a disgusting thought, and it made him feel unreal, somehow like a fraud.

"Smile, Jon. Be Prince Charming." Her fist pressed into his back.

"Woo them. Make them swoon. Sell yourself."

A very nasty word indeed was forming on his lips, but she smiled at him so sweetly that he just threw her a venomous glare and bared his teeth.

"Yes, that too," Sally added. "Once we're back home we'll have to get an appointment with a dentist for you. Your teeth need bleaching."

"Good grief. The things you think about at a moment like this. Here, hold these for me." He handed her back the stack of cards. "And make a note to bring a clipboard or something for me to write on in the future. I'm not going to use your back, much less a fan's."

"Jon."

The voice made him swivel around.

There she was, and she looked much the same as always. The collar of her coat was turned up, the ends of her hair curling around it. Her hands were sunk in the pockets; she looked cold and very, very young.

"Jenny. Hi."

A few flashbulbs went off, catching the moment until Jon realized that he was staring, and so was everyone else, waiting for what was going to happen. It even seemed as if they were holding their breath, waiting for some kind of scandal. It was Sally, though, who caught herself first.

"Jenny!" she called, and reached out to grab her sleeve. "What are you doing out here? Come on in, darling! Why didn't you call ahead and tell us you'd be here?"

The line of guards opened for her, and Sally pulled her forward.

"I'm going inside with Jen," she said to Jon. "We'll have a cup of coffee while you chat with your fans." With that she waved to Sal and Russ, who rapidly came over and joined Jon.

Dazed, still not sure what had just happened, Jon scrawled his name on everything that was pushed his way, including some bare arms and a forehead.

After what seemed like an eternity, Sal patted his shoulder. "We have to go, Jon." He pointed at his watch. "They're waiting for you."

Connecting with the fans had never been hard until now. He'd even been able to chat easily with the people at the TV studios before an interview or short appearance. He didn't feel nervous. He felt like himself, and that's what he presented. That was the way he wanted it. He didn't want to create an artificial, public persona. He wanted people to love him for himself.

"Your feelings are written all over your face, Jon," Sal remarked once the heavy backstage door had shut behind them. "I'm glad that Sally kept her cool and knew what to do. What was that all about? Who's that girl? An old flame?"

The hallway in which they were standing was rather dingy. It looked old, as if many generations of singers and dancers had walked through it, as if their whispers could still be heard through the walls and under the rafters.

"Yeah, an old flame." It was surprising how much that short sentence hurt. "I'll say hello to her and then we'll start the soundcheck, all right?"

Russ was watching him doubtfully.

"I have to," Jon went on. "I really have to. If I don't get this out of the way now I won't be able to concentrate on the music. Just give me a few minutes."

They entered the hospitality room. The caterers were still busy setting up the coffee urns and soda cans, and there was no food visible as yet.

Sean, Jones, and Walter were sitting together over some music, discussing the set list, going over their solo parts. From somewhere deep in the building Jon could hear the telltale sounds of the stage still being set up.

Since his first live concert in LA, things had changed: It wasn't an unplugged, simple roadshow anymore. They brought along their own light and sound systems now. It still wasn't what he wanted, but they were getting there. He wanted light effects to enhance the mood of the songs and beams playing over the audience so he could get a glimpse of who he was singing to, and he wanted them in different colors too.

Patiently Tom had replied to his list of requests; he'd get everything he wanted in good time, but first they had to figure out how his concerts would go. This tour would be minimalistic, a trial; but, he added laughing, they'd never send him overseas like that. No worries.

SALLY and Jenny were sitting in a corner, hugging paper cups of coffee. Both were looking his way, Sally with her lips in a thin, white line, her dark eyes sparkling, and Jenny with a strange mix of sorrow, exhaustion, and curiosity.

"Is everything in my dressing room?" Jon asked; when Sal nodded, he added, "Call me when they're ready, okay?"

Sal vanished into the dim hallway.

Ten easy steps. Ten steps across the room, and he'd be facing her. The old anger churned in his stomach, its tentacles reaching up toward the tip of his heart with their needle-sharp points. He could feel them raking it gently, in a teasing caress, like a kitten testing a new toy just before it buried its teeth in it.

"Well then," Jon said, "Jenny. Shall we talk? Please come this way. Sally, my dressing room, please. Where is it?" Words as cold as shards of ice, freezing on his tongue, clinking against his teeth like pebbles before they dropped from his lips.

Sally led them to a door with a star on it, and for a second Jon stood, mesmerized by the symbol. It was made of metal and painted gold, an old thing, like the entire building; the metal almost melted into the door surrounded by so many layers of paint. Inside, it looked just as he had always imagined a dressing room should look, just like in the movies: a table with a huge mirror over it; bulbs running along both of its sides, creating an unflattering, white glare. There was a couch and, a new addition to the old splendor, the rack with his clothes. Someone had placed a bouquet of flowers on the table, some bottles of water, and a stack of towels. Another door led into a small bathroom with a shower stall, and again there were towels, a fresh bar of soap, a small bottle of shampoo.

The heating was making a strange, clattering sound, rather like the rumbling of a sleeping beast.

Jenny was still standing in the middle of the room, waiting, silent, uncertain.

"Please." He pointed at the couch. "Sit."

She did as she was told. Her eyes kept darting around, taking in where she was, taking in a reality that was new and strange to her.

"You did it," Jenny said softly. "You're really a star."

"Yes. I guess. What do you want, Jenny? Why did you stand out there with the fans?" He plunged his right hand into his pocket. There it was. The small blue box with the name stamped on it: TIFFANY & CO.

"You look well." Her voice sounded shaky, scared, as if she had to walk over the words carefully, picking them out of a bed of shards. "You look even better than you did when you were here in the spring. Taller somehow, grown-up, and glossy."

The senseless prattling was irritating him. A brief glance at his watch—time was running out. Jon cursed Sally for bringing her inside. "Jenny, say what you have to say. I have to get out there soon for the soundcheck. What did you want?" Rude. He sounded rude, and it made him feel ashamed. "What can I do for you?"

A small hiccup escaped her. "Nothing at all, Jon. I just wanted to see you." The hint of a smile crossed her face. "Besides, I guess I was curious to see what has become of you."

"But what do you want?" From the stage came the sound of a bass being tuned. It was a deep, satisfying sound; and Jon, recognizing the chord that was being played, felt his shoulders relax. He waited for the drums and the keyboard to join in, the music rising in him, the lyrics forming on his lips. The good, vibrant excitement he always felt before he was going to sing wrapped around him, warming his blood, softening his heart.

"What do you want, Jenny?"

"I never thought you'd be able to pull this off." She shrugged in a small gesture of defeat. "I came to apologize. When we met outside the bookstore, when I saw you standing there in the light of the cameras and all those people around you, focused on you, I could hardly believe my eyes. I could hardly believe you'd come back like that, or that I'd ever see you again. Our parting was so angry."

"Tell me about it." Those tentacles around his heart were squeezing harder.

"Yes, but at least you got to go away, start a new life. All I had was the empty apartment and memories of you and me." Jenny unbuttoned her coat and peeled it off. "I was the one left behind."

"Like hell you were! You tossed me out, Jenny. You refused to even give this a chance. I clearly remember begging you to come with me to LA. I remember begging quite a lot, actually. And I remember you letting my begging roll off you as if it meant nothing. You broke my heart, Jenny. You made me go away."

"And I'm sorry about that. I really am. I just couldn't grasp the idea that someone like you could fly off to Hollywood and be a big star a year later. That's dream stuff, Jon, not hard reality. I thought you'd go down, and I didn't want to go down with you." Her hands clasped together in her lap, she was looking up at him, her eyes swimming with unshed tears. "I was afraid. I didn't have the courage to go with you."

"I know," Jon said softly, "I know. I wasn't angry at you. Not ever." A lie so bad that it almost blistered on his tongue.

There was a knock on the door, Sal calling that it was time.

"I have to go." Jon pushed the little box deeper into his jeans pocket. "Come on, come along. You'll get to see what my job is really like."

Chapter Thirty-three

"SIT HER DOWN somewhere and keep an eye on her," Jon told Sal when he and Jenny emerged. "If she wants something, get it."

He didn't care that it sounded rude and impersonal.

There was so much more to say. Jon wanted to fling all his fury at her, wanted her to feel the pain and desolation he'd felt when she'd asked him to go. That day was so clear in his memory. He'd walked out of their apartment, her last words still echoing in his mind, the expression on her face etched onto the back of his eyelids. Like a ghost, he'd stood there in the street, wondering if he was doing the right thing. And then a miracle had happened: With every step he took away from their door, the certainty grew that he was doing the right thing.

And now she was here, in his new life, watching him pick up his guitar and settle it against his body.

Sal sat her in the third row and gave her another cup of coffee. She sat there like a lonely little girl, all alone, lost in the big auditorium.

Jon could see the technicians in their box at the back of the room, Tom among them, trying out the spotlights, pointing them his way, as if they'd read his mind. He wanted for a moment to be the star on the stage, while Jenny watched.

"We'll start with 'Wilted Love,'" he said into the microphone, and right away, Sean began playing the intro. Jon loved him for it, loved how attuned Sean was to him and his music. Most of the others weren't bad either—they knew his songs—but Sean seemed to sense how he felt every moment they were onstage. He turned slightly so he could see the two girls doing backup and smiled. They had fallen into the slow dance step of the song already, the one they had rehearsed with Sean for fun during a break in a recording session. There had been a lot of giggling and flirting involved, and it had ended as always, with all of them going out for dinner together.

"It's basically slow fox," Sean had explained to Jon. "I'm surprised you don't know it. Let the girls move a bit, nothing fancy, just a few steps on the spot, but it'll look less static." And he'd been right.

Sally appeared from backstage and put down a bottle of water next to his guitars. Jon thanked her with a nod before he stepped up to the microphone and drew the deep breath he needed to sing.

> *"... and when you look again, I will be gone*
> *The door will close, you'll be alone.*
> *Your wilted love's too much to take*
> *your silences, your smile's a fake*
> *you drowned my love in bitter words*
> *and cut my heartstrings with your swords*
> *of fear and doubt and misery*
> *It wasn't you, it wasn't me, can't blame the rain, can't*
> *blame the day*
> *Maybe it was just that time, I knew I had to walk away."*

He flung the words out into the dark, empty space of the theater, threw them at Jenny with all the bitterness and sorrow that had been eating at his heart without him even realizing it.

> *"You watched me go, you let me leave, you let me stand*
> *there in the cold*
> *You said your tears were only yours.*
> *Well, baby, ain't that sentence old."*

He wanted to kick something. The lyrics bothered him; as often as he had gone over them, sung them, they lacked the depth of what he wanted to say. Every single word was true, but the rhymes seemed gritty, awkward, not as smooth and elegant as he wanted them too, and not as poetic either.

Halfway through the song he broke off. The band fell silent, waiting for his verdict.

"We're leaving this one out," Jon said, his voice gravelly from singing, deep from disappointment. "Let's start on the set list." He nodded at Sean, who began the intro. Right away, the lighting techs picked it up and drenched the stage in the colors of a sunrise, and with that, at last, Jon relaxed. He fell into the comfort and ease of the well-rehearsed routine, of starting out on all the songs and going through them until the sound engineer and Tom were pleased, and the lights had all been adjusted.

It took them less than an hour before Russ called a break. He came up to the stage and planted his elbows on the edge. "Sounds really great back there now," he announced. "This place isn't bad! Come on down, guys. We're done for now. Jon, a word."

Jon followed him to the other end of the stage and hunkered down, well out of range of the microphones and people.

"I know I'm the junior member of this team and all," Russ said, his voice lowered and soft, "but can I say this? You're too angry on the stage today. I have an idea why that may be, but, Jon. You can't let your audience see it. You're a very furious man right now. Is there any way we can resolve this?" When there was no reply, he went on. "I know you can be very professional, and I hope you will be tonight. But I'd rather see you in an easier mood right now. Is there anything I can do?"

"No." Jon sat down on the edge of the stage and let his legs dangle. "Thanks, Russ, but no. I'll have to sort this out on my own. Thank you for offering."

Russ gazed at him thoughtfully, then said, "It's not just about you, Jon. It's like this: The people around you, the band, they will all pick up on your mood before a concert. They need to be attuned to you during a show, and if you leave the stage after a rehearsal in a dark mood, then so will they, and they'll carry it into the show." He took a deep breath and squared his shoulders. "So, no. You don't have to sort out anything on your own right now. That's why you have Sal, and me, and Sally. We're going to keep anything and anyone away from you that you don't want to deal with. We are the bulwark between you and the rest of the world and, if need be, all the time. So please, tell me what you want done."

"Hell, Russ."

With a small smile, Russ slapped his knee. "We're like a family when we're on tour. Like a clan. And we protect our leader. In your case, it's a great pleasure too. We all love you, Jon."

"I'm not your leader! Seriously, Russ!" It felt like a compliment, but one that came with a lot of responsibility.

"Yes, you are. This entire tour thing wouldn't be happening if not for you. So tell us your wishes. We're at your command, O clan chief." Russ nodded in Jenny's direction. "You want her out? We'll throw her out."

"I'll deal with this, Russ." Jon had to think for a moment. "But here's something you can do for me. I want the band, everyone who'll go onstage with me, gathered in a separate room ten minutes before the show. And I want to meet with them alone. No one else is allowed inside, just the band."

"As you wish."

Jon wasn't entirely sure, but he thought he'd seen a gleam of surprise and respect in Russ's eyes just before he turned away. With a sigh, he dropped off the stage, calling, "All right, Jenny. My dressing room. Let's get this over with."

HE didn't even wait for her to follow, but once they were in his room and alone, he slammed the door.

The box with the ring had pressed against his leg the entire time he'd been onstage. Now he took it out and held it in his open hand.

"I bought this for you," Jon said, "a couple of weeks before we broke up. I'd saved up my money for it for a long time. Even then, even though you'd been telling me for quite a while that you didn't believe in me, I still wanted to marry you, because I loved you, Jenny. I loved you even though you wanted me to be someone else. Here."

He tossed the box at her. Surprised, she didn't reach out for it, and it dropped to the floor at her feet.

"You can have it." Jon watched as she picked it up and opened it. "I'm giving it to you. I have no use for it. Throw it away for all I care, or have the engraving removed and pretend you found it somewhere on the beach."

"It's so pretty." Her voice sounded wobbly, hurt. "It's beautiful, Jon."

She took the ring from the box and slipped it on her finger, where it sparkled sweetly.

"I'd love to wear it for you, Jon." Her hand, the ring on it, reached out to him. "Can't you forgive me? Can't you see that I was scared out of my wits by your plans? I never stopped loving you."

Big, fat toads. The words on his tongue, the words he was trying not to say, felt like big, slimy toads stuck to the roof of his mouth, their bitter juice dripping down his throat.

"I know I loved you," Jon said. "I wanted a life with you. But, Jenny. How can you expect me to take you back?" It was so ludicrous, he felt like throwing open the door to let the others witness it. "Now you want me back? Now you come to me, crawling, pleading? Now that you know I've made it, after seeing my face on posters and in magazines, after you know I'm making a lot of money? Or was it the girls gathered out there, screaming and sighing at the sight of me? You seriously think we have a chance now?"

He took a step in her direction, and she retreated, her head bowed.

Russ's words rang in Jon's head, and he took a calming breath. They would all be there. All he had to do was shout out a name and this scene would be over, and never repeated.

"I think," he said, a lot gentler now, "you should leave. Find that life you were always talking about. Find that bank manager or car dealer, Jenny, and settle down. You have no place in the kind of life I'm leading now."

That made her look up. "Oh, so it's the pretty blond, is it?" There was venom in her tone, and anger.

Jon shook his head. "No. You just don't get it, do you? It was always about the music, all the time. I thought you'd understand if you saw a rehearsal and realized how unglamorous that is." He waved at the room, at the mirror and the sharp lights surrounding it. "This is my life, Jenny. Tight schedules, a lot of work, and a very hard two hours on the stage in the evening. It's not about me or you or anyone else. It's always been about the music, and the joy it brings to others."

He pulled open the door, and there they were: Sal, Russ, Sally, looking his way, waiting for him, ready to do his bidding.

"Sally isn't my girlfriend. I don't have a girlfriend or lover right now, if you must know." Jon had no idea why he was telling her, or why he wanted the others to hear it. "I just know that someday I'll find her. She won't judge me the way you do. She will see right through the glamour and everything else. She'll see only me, Jon Stone. And I'll love her for that, forever."

Without another word, Jenny walked out. The only thing that remained of her was a whiff of lemony perfume.

Chapter Thirty-four

THEY REMINDED HIM a bit of the Seven Dwarfs waiting for Snow White to show up, the way they were perched on the chairs and the couch, all of them gazing at him, curious about what he wanted. It had been an impulse, a spur-of-the-moment thing born out of Russ's little speech, and here he was now, dressed for the show, his face powdered and his hair brushed and held in place with hair spray and gel.

"I want to thank you," Jon said.

A sigh of relief went through them and, relaxed, they leaned back.

"Russ said something interesting today. Something that made me stop and realize something. I'm really grateful for having met you all. I think we have the chance to do something big, if we stick together and work hard."

Pompous. He sounded like an old, pompous entertainer, not like a young and fresh songwriter.

"What I'm trying to say, is…" He began again and stopped, seeing the smile on Sean's face. "Hell, what I'm trying to say is, I love making music with you guys."

"I like your shirt, man," Walter interrupted him. "That's a cool shade of blue, and the embroidery, nice. Where do you get them?"

"Yeah," Jones added, "and why do you need an entire bowl of picks? Do you still have the one I gave you?"

"And I think a last smoke, before we go onstage, would be good." Sean rose, picking up a pack of cigarettes. "Outside? Who's coming? Jon?"

It had begun to rain. A cold wind whipped the drops into the alley where they stood and smoked in silence, their minds in the music already. Jon could see it: Sean's fingers were dancing against his leg, playing out the first bars of their opening song; Walter's tall frame was moving in a silent rhythm. Jones was standing with his back to them, his face turned toward the street, where the heavy evening traffic had come to a stop.

207

"Broadway," he mumbled, "we're on freaking Broadway. We're playing in New York City, and it's not some dingy bar but Broadway. Dig that."

"I just want to say," Jon began again, but the backstage door opened; it was Russ.

"Two minutes," he said. "Jon, your hair."

Once again the makeup artist fussed around him, producing even more powder dust, even more hair spray smell. The band filed by, each of them touching him, either slapping his shoulder or briefly clasping his arm before they walked onto the stage.

Jon could hear the applause. It sounded like surf, like the murmur of the sea when the tide rose, like the wind in an old forest.

The first chords of the intro broke into that sound, pushing it back, dimming it out.

"Now." Russ was holding the rosewood, waiting for Jon to take it. "Good luck. Break a leg."

Old words, a ritual, making Jon nod in acceptance. Four steps to the door, another two to the stairs that led up to the stage, and there he was, in the blinding light, amid the sea of music and cheers; and all he had to do was raise the hand holding the pick.

The song took off.

He could see his family in the front row, standing, clapping, cheering with the crowd; and at one point Jon was sure his sister was singing along with him, like most of the other girls. It made him smile; he knew he was going to tease her about it later, and she would never admit to it. She'd always pretended that she didn't care for his music, had scoffed at his dream; but here she was, dancing and singing like a teenager, even waving when he threw her a kiss.

His heart expanded at seeing all the happy faces, at seeing how well his songs were received, how he made the audience happy.

The band behind him was having fun too, toying with the music, adding little flourishes to it, throwing the chords at one another like rubber balls. At the side of the stage, hidden from the audience by the curtains, stood Sally, her hands folded under her chin, a sweet, satisfied smile on her face.

He had come home to New York. And he was rocking it.

HE woke up to loud knocking on his door.

Confused, still half-asleep, Jon stumbled across the room, trying to slip on his jeans on the way. Muttering, he opened the door to find Sal standing there, a stack of newspapers in his hands. "Well, golden boy," he crowed. "Wake up, order coffee, read what the critics have to say, and bask in the glory of the praise!"

Jon blinked at him. This, he hadn't even thought about. In LA it seemed normal to see news about the music or movie business in the papers, but somehow he hadn't expected it here.

Sal walked past him into the room and dropped onto the couch. "'Our very own Jon Stone,' they're calling you. And here," He held up one of the papers. "'The New York boy who rocks the world.' I really love that one!"

Rubbing his eyes, Jon listened to Sal's enthusiastic words. He hadn't slept well, his night filled with even worse dreams. A strange, bitter taste clung to his tongue and made it feel furry, dry.

"What time is it?" The sun shone brightly, making him squint when he drew back the curtains. New York looked the same as always: busy, crowded. He'd promised his mother he'd spend some time at home, have lunch with her, tell her about his life.

"Just after eleven." Sal picked up the phone and ordered coffee for both of them. "I know you need your sleep after a show, and a slow start, but this was just too good not to share with you. You've worked hard for this, Jon. You deserve the praise. And maybe you want to take the papers to show your family. They'll be proud of you."

"Yeah." The dream was coming back to him. Jon remembered why he was feeling so groggy.

There had been a show in his dream too, a big one; and in it he had rehashed the time right after last night's concert when he'd come off the stage, exhilarated, exhausted, sore from singing. Sally had been there, holding a bathrobe to wrap around him, and Russ, with a bottle of cold water.

He'd been ready to wave them away, but then he'd felt the comforting warmth of the bathrobe on his shoulders and the soothing coolness of the water in his throat, and had nodded in gratitude.

He'd wanted a hot shower to ease his tired muscles, wanted the hot water to run down his back for hours. And so the dressing-room door had closed behind him, leaving him alone, and that had been the moment when the truth had hit him: He was alone.

In that instant, when the door shut, when the noise and bustle of the hallway was locked out and he stood there in the silence, he'd felt alone as never before. The burden of responsibility had settled on his shoulders, the realization that all that was happening was really because of him, because of his songs; and it was threatening to suffocate him.

Jon had been on the point of turning around, of fleeing to the band's dressing room and pretending he was one of them, but he knew he wasn't.

He was their employer, their leader. They were exchangeable; he was not.

It was a strange and lonely insight, and it seemed like a steep price to pay for success.

In his dream, that moment of solitude had been played out. He'd stepped out of the dressing room to find everyone else gone. The theater was dark, deserted, a cold and mute place. He'd wandered through the corridors, calling the names of his friends, but no one had answered. At last he'd gone to the stage; and there they'd been, waiting for him, their bodies frozen, their stares blank and without a soul until he picked up his guitar and strummed a chord. They'd looked just like puppets, and he was the only one who could wake them.

"…what I'm saying? Jon?"

"Yes. Yes." He shook off the traces of dread as best as he could. "Sorry. What did you say?"

Sal was watching him, a crease of worry between his eyes. "Are you okay?"

"I'm fine. A bad night, that's all. Must have been all that excitement, and too much booze after the show."

There had indeed been a lot of drinks. Elated as they'd been, there had been no way they were going to sleep. They'd commandeered the rented van, and Sean had driven them down to Bob's, where they'd hogged the stage and gone on with their music until even Bob was too tired for them and turned out the lights.

"I said," Sal repeated patiently, "I want you to let the van take you if you're going to Brooklyn to see your family. Your subway days are over. Just tell me when you want it."

And there it was again, that threatening sound of solitude, of being isolated from life.

"Yes, right. I'd like to leave right after we've had that coffee." At least for a few hours, at least until the next show began that night, he wanted to feel like himself.

HELEN had made him roast beef. His favorite homemade dish, and she was still flustered and hot from standing in the kitchen all morning.

Jon wondered when she'd gotten out of bed and started on it, and who had gone and bought the French bread from the bakery.

She had set the table in the dining room for the two of them, even bringing out the good china.

"Mom." Jon didn't know how to tell her. "Mom, really, we could have eaten in the kitchen."

"Nonsense." She came to stand beside him. "We have something to celebrate. You're a star now, and I won't let you eat in the kitchen. Here, sit down. I'll bring you some coffee."

It was more than he could take. Again he was locked out, isolated, even by his own mother.

"Mom, no. Let's sit in the kitchen. Please."

The shadow of disappointment crossed Helen's face, but then she shrugged. "If that's what you want, all right. I wanted to do something special for you."

"Yeah, I know, Mom." Jon put his arms around her. "Thanks for that; it's a lovely table." Together they returned to the warm, steamy kitchen. "But here's the thing. I don't want you to do nice things for me. I want to come home and just be myself, your son, and not a

211

celebrity visitor. Can we please do that? I need one place where I can just be myself, and if it isn't here, then where?"

Helen, her head bowed so he couldn't see her face, nodded.

"I'm sorry to disappoint you, Mom." He reached for her hand, but she pulled it away and knitted it around a kitchen towel. "Please don't be disappointed. But I don't want to change. I need you, I need my family, to make me feel real, to know I'm still Jon and not that guy on the stage who can't even take the subway anymore to visit his own mother. I need you, Mom."

"No, Jon." Her back turned to him, Helen started cutting the bread and placed it on the big kitchen table in the same old basket she'd used for as long as he could remember. "I'm the one who is sorry." She wiped her eyes with the back of her hand. "I'm the one who must apologize. I thought you wouldn't want to come home anymore now that you're a star, and I'm glad I'm wrong." A wobbly smile appeared on her face. "Of course we can eat in the kitchen. And before we do, please be so kind as to take out the trash. If you don't mind."

One of his most-hated chores as a kid. How he'd hated being called down from his room just to take out the trash; and here he was, a grown man, a Hollywood celebrity, and he was rushing to do her bidding.

Just when he was about to step out the back door, he heard her say, in a quiet, serious voice, "I'm proud of you, Jon."

The day didn't seem quite so lonely anymore.

Chapter Thirty-five

EARLY ONE MORNING in December Sal showed up at Sean's apartment, a box of doughnuts in one hand, a briefcase in the other.

"Make coffee," he ordered, "and do it quickly. We have something to do today."

Jon, still in his pajama bottoms, blinked at him. Fuzzy from being dragged out of bed so suddenly, he stumbled into the kitchen and did as he was told.

Sal opened the briefcase and brought out some photos and papers while the coffeemaker burbled in the background.

"I've found you a house," he said, and rubbed his hands in glee. "I've found the perfect house, and we're going over to have a look. If you like it and everything goes well, it will soon be yours." He laid out the photos on the kitchen table. "Didn't you say you wanted a house on the beach? One with enough space around it to be private? Like a huge, unkempt park? Is that what you want?"

"Yeah. Sort of." It was chilly in the apartment. They'd left the balcony door open to let in some air, but now it was uncomfortable, and Jon went to fetch a sweater. "Where is this gem of a house?" he asked when he returned. "And how am I supposed to pay for it?"

Sal rolled his eyes at Jon. "Have you looked at your bank account recently? You have more than enough to make a decent down payment, and buy that frigging Porsche you keep talking about. And the rest, well, the rest...I'm sure I know someone who'll gladly give you a loan for that." He grinned at Jon over the rim of his coffee mug. "You'll have to face reality, my friend. You're a star now."

THE air had that fresh, moist aroma that Jon always associated with early spring back in New York, the few weeks between slushy, murky winter and humid, blistering summer. He stopped at the curb a moment before getting into Sal's car to breathe it in.

He'd be flying home the day before Christmas to spend the holidays with his family. Sally had arranged everything: She'd take him to the airport herself and show him to the first-class seat she'd booked for him. In New York, a van would be waiting for him and would take him directly to his parents' house.

"Don't run around in the city too much," she'd said, handing him the ticket. "I'm worried about you. Your face is too well-known for lonely forays now."

Driving along the shore with Sal, the sea scent in his nose, Jon wondered about her constant admonishments. People were kind, friendly, enthusiastic, but never threatening. He liked the attention he got from the girls, he couldn't deny it. Sally called it inviting trouble, but he had a hard time believing her. A couple of times now he'd even brought a girl to the studio to listen and watch while they worked, flirting with her during the breaks, getting her coffee and cookies, until Sally had left, disgust and sorrow painted clearly on her face while she mouthed "Trouble" at him, shaking her head.

Once, he'd followed her out into the hallway, cornering her before she could vanish into the elevator.

"What kind of trouble?" he'd asked, gripping her shoulder, keeping her from moving away. "You toss those threats at me, but they're just that, words. So what are we talking about here?"

But she hadn't replied and pulled out of his hold like a monkey. When the elevator doors opened, she'd waved at him to come along. She'd taken him to the basement of the building instead of to her office.

Wordlessly, Sally had turned on the light and unlocking a door, led him into a space like a vault. There had been a musty smell, and the silence of a tomb. Shelves lined the walls, and more shelves separated the floor into squares. They were filled with boxes and folders, some of them yellowed and old, some new and pristine.

Sally had taken his hand and led him to a shelf on the left and pointed. There was a name tag, and his name, written out in a neat handwriting, was on it.

"As you can see," she'd said, "we made a lot of room for you. We expect a lot of mail. Heck, there's a lot, even now."

Love letters written on pink paper, adorned with hand-painted flowers, doodles, little hearts, some with photos attached, some of them less than decent, but all of them declaring undying devotion and heart-burning passion. He thought he recognized one or two of the faces, a lovely girl with blond hair, smiling at him somewhere, but he couldn't remember where.

"These are kind of nice," Sally had gone on, "and not too offensive. But the bad ones will come, Jon. No one gets spared, not even you. There's a fine line separating devotion from erotomaniac behavior. We're doing our best to look out for you. But it's not a good idea to bring dates to the studio unless you're pretty serious about the girl."

"I thought you were jealous." His words had sounded muted and hollow in the unfriendly, cold surroundings. "I thought you didn't want them there because you felt slighted."

Her dark eyes had flashed in fury. "You're learning rather quickly how to be a conceited bastard, Jon Stone. I'm not jealous. It's my job to take care of you. I hope you realize that!"

She'd stalked out of the room, leaving him alone with his fans' declarations of love.

"HERE."

Sal stopped the car in front of a tall, wrought-iron gate. High walls marched away on both sides, leaving a view of treetops and a red roof.

"I like how it's so hidden," Sal said when the gate swung open to admit them. "Privacy. You can't have enough of it, and soon too."

The gravel driveway wasn't long but took a slight turn toward the beach before the house itself was visible. Like a great white ship the building loomed over bushes of jasmine and bougainvillea. Palm trees and cedars surrounded it, giving shade to the many balconies and what looked like a roof garden. What should have been a well-kept yard, maybe even a small park, was a wilderness of green, with a narrow path leading to where Jon surmised the beach would be.

"You're crazy." Jon got out of the car when they stopped in the open space in front of the main entrance to the house. "What am I going to do with this? It's huge, Sal! This isn't a house; it's a frigging mansion! How many rooms does it have? You're insane."

"Seventeen rooms," Sal replied joyfully. "Yes, it is huge, really huge. But Jon, it's on the market for far less than it's actually worth because of the neglected grounds. I think you should buy it. If you get the yard cleaned up, this will be a paradise! You could ask your mother to come out and help you settle in; I'm sure she'd love that." He produced a set of keys from his pocket and unlocked the door. "This house used to belong to some movie star or other; I forget which one. They didn't take a lot of interest in it though, and preferred living in Paris." The door swung open. "Which is something I'll never understand. How could anyone give up a property like this for an apartment in a city where you don't even understand the language? Ah well."

Cool, dim silence greeted them. Jon, standing in the lofty hallway, had the feeling that the house was holding its breath, watching them, waiting for his verdict. He moved to the living room on his left, another huge, empty space leading onto a deep, tiled porch.

"I think this used to be the library," Sal called, and opened a door into another room. "It would be perfect for a private studio. You can easily fit a piano in here, and everything you want. You and the band could even rehearse here."

It was so quiet, and the traffic so far away, that he could hear the surf even though he couldn't see it.

The kitchen was dated, but roomy and sunny, and the ground-floor bathroom clean and comfortable.

Upstairs, and he stood for a moment, unsure where to go first. The hallway seemed endless, offering too many choices.

There was a door to his left, and it seemed to whisper, beckoning him, so he opened it. The bright sunlight made him blink.

Through a gap in the trees he could see the ocean, the sun glinting on the water, and a sailboat as it skimmed over the waves. Entranced, he crossed the room and opened the glass French doors. They led to a roof garden, a space between the two wings of the house, an outside room all by itself, hidden from view but allowing spectacular views of the Pacific and, on the other side, of the hills to the east.

"I want it," Jon said, but there was no one there to hear him.

Slowly, his heart beating hard, he returned inside and carefully shut the glass doors. The sun shone on the dark hardwood floor of the room, making it glint like his koa guitar, like the black hair of a beautiful woman.

"I want it," he said again, and this time it felt as if the walls breathed a sigh of relief.

He didn't even care about the other rooms or the many possibilities Sal saw. The house had reached out to him and touched his heart, and he knew he wanted to live here.

"Let's go down to the beach," he suggested, walking ahead.

They followed the path, jasmine blossoms snagging in their hair, touching them with curious fingers, releasing their enticing perfume. A sudden gust of wind made the trees rustle and sing, made the cedars talk to the palm trees; and looking up at them, Jon had the impression that they were talking about him, watching him like curious sentinels, deciding if they would let him in or not.

A fence with a locked gate separated the property from the beach. Jon, peering through the mesh, could see surfers riding the waves and the shadows of dolphins among them, playing with their human friends.

He could imagine coming down here at dawn for a run along the waterline before retreating into his own little paradise for breakfast and quiet hours of composing.

"I want it," he repeated. "Thank you for finding this, Sal. You were right. It must be mine."

"Just think of the parties you can throw here." Sal rubbed his hands in glee. "So much space, and it will all belong to you!"

Strangely, the thought of parties didn't appeal to Jon at all. Frowning, he looked up at the facade of the house, at the balconies and windows, at the porch, at the serenity the mansion seemed to exude.

"Yeah, parties." The trees seemed to bend toward him, listening closely. "We'll see about parties." He pointed at the roof garden and the room hidden behind it. "That will be my bedroom. I'll go to sleep with the sound of the ocean in my ears."

"What a waste!" Sal frowned against the sun. "That roof garden would make a perfect spot for parties."

"Not happening." His heart sang at the certainty he felt. "That will be mine alone. No one else will go up there unless I invite them."

A sprig of jasmine touched his check in a feathery caress.

"It will be mine, and my wife's. Our private little paradise." The words came from his lips like sparkling jewels, like a truth he knew deep in his heart.

"Your wife," Sal muttered. "I'll believe that when I see it."

But Jon wasn't listening. He could have sworn that just for an instant, just for the length of a heartbeat, he'd seen lace curtains gently moving in the breeze up there, up in the bedroom window; and behind them, hidden in shadow, a figure had turned, a female figure with long, black hair.

Chapter Thirty-six

HE HAD A bed, and a couch. There were a couple of stools pushed up against the kitchen counter, but that was it.

He didn't mind. All he needed was the studio with a Steinway grand in it, stands for his guitars along the wall, and a shelf with staff paper and a box of pencils. Through the open porch door he could see across a terrace and a smallish square of unkempt lawn to where the blooming bushes and palm trees were waiting to take back the gardened terrain. Like silent predators they had gathered at the edge of the clearing, staring at it, hardly breathing, waiting for their moment.

"You can't have it," Jon had told them during one of his evening strolls. "Do with the rest of the property as you wish, but leave me this small spot so I get some sunlight too."

They had obeyed, but unwillingly, and in return had opened another small path, one he hadn't noticed before. It led him to a natural arbor amid swaying jasmine. A stone bench stood there, partly covered by moss, hidden from the world, a fairy place. He'd sat down and watched as the colors of the leaves changed, how far above him the stars came out against the darkening sky, and listened to the soft sounds of the garden: a bird singing a gentle song, a cicada tuning its wings, the whisper of the trees talking to one another. The blossoms around him opened their petals to release their perfume. It wound around him like fairies' veils, like an enticing cobweb, and he drew in a deep breath. His heart slowed until it seemed to beat in rhythm with the surf, until he felt as one with the planet turning beneath his feet.

The beach beckoned; the real estate agent had given him a thick ring of keys and pointed out the one that was for the gate in the fence.

"There's only one," he'd said, "so be careful where you keep it until you have some copies made."

There was a hook on a wall in the kitchen, right next to the fridge, and that was where he had put it.

It was like opening a forbidden door to a hidden kingdom when he put the key in the lock now and turned it.

The beach was empty, sunset over. Black sky met the black sea in the unfathomable distance; the waves thundered against a shore that was almost as dark. There was no moon out; the night sky hid itself behind the net of stars.

Jon listened, waiting for the familiar sound of the big bell, but it wouldn't come. There was nothing but the beat of the surf, the wind on the sand, and his breathing.

Silent, the world was silent.

Wrapping his heart in that silence, Jon returned to his wilderness, locked the gate behind him, and walked along the winding path back to his big, empty house.

He took a shower and lay on his bed, wrapped in the blankets, watching the tops of the trees dancing in the breeze, their whisper trying to sing him to sleep. Around him, the house settled into the night, its joints creaking a bit as the warmth of the day crept out of them.

Someone was calling his name; he was quite certain of it. The voice reached into his dreams with wispy fingers, touched his lips tenderly, brushed over his temples, and came to rest on his outstretched arm like the precious weight of a beloved woman.

For the length of two heartbeats, loneliness gripped his dreaming mind, then the music of the trees, the beach, and the stars put him back to sleep.

"NOW you need to decorate and furnish it," Sally said. She was sitting on the table in the corner of the studio, legs dangling, eating yogurt and fruit from a Styrofoam cup while the orchestra was warming up.

Jon wasn't listening. He was watching Sean and Jones debating over the pages of the song he'd finished only that morning. Sean had a pencil in his hand, nodding at what Jones was saying, while scribbling comments, trying out segments on his keyboard.

"Will you try and do that on your own, or do you need any help?"

"Huh?" He turned his head to look at her.

"I said," Sally repeated, rolling her eyes at him, "do you need help with your house? With the decorating?"

"No!" It came out a little faster and a lot more vehemently than he'd wanted it to, but panic had won over. "Thanks, I'm fine. No help. I'll do it on my own."

"Are you sure?" She sounded doubtful, but Jon nodded.

"Yeah. Totally. Thanks for offering, but I want it to feel like my home and not look like an interior designer's dream." He sighed, seeing her face fall. "I'm sorry, Sally. But I want to do this on my own. My mother offered to come out, and I told her no too. It's my house. I want it to look the way I want. End of story."

"You're getting so willful." Pouting, she tossed the empty cup into the trash can. "You were a lot more fun when you first got here."

"I need to grow up sometime, don't I? You won't be around forever to tell me what to do and when to do it." Sean was moving his way, and Jon stepped away from her.

"What do you mean, I won't be around forever? Do you know something I don't?" She tried to make it sound light and fun, but Jon could hear the tremble in her voice.

"Sally." Ignoring Sean, Jon placed his hands on her shoulders. "Sally, you have better things to do than babysit me. You have a career to consider. And me, honestly? I don't want to be babysat anymore. I know it's all concern for my welfare, and to give the right impression in public and all that, but underneath all the marketing crap I'm still a person."

His eyes wandered to the gold album on the wall behind her. His first and, he was certain, not his last. He remembered how he'd been handed the framed gilded record in a little ceremony, and how hollow it had felt.

Weird, it was weird. He had everything he'd ever wanted—his second album was in the works, he was the prized centerpiece of every Hollywood party these days—and yet it felt weird. Success didn't bring the satisfaction he'd imagined. The music was the only place where he felt the joy and fulfillment he craved.

"And I want to stay the person I am. I'm drawing the line here.

My home is my own and not another showpiece for a magazine," he ended his little speech.

"You call our marketing strategies crap? Really, Jon?" A steely edge had crept into her tone. "Because, you know, we invest a lot of time and money in making you look good." Her finger flew out to point to the golden disc on the wall. "Do you think you got that all on your own? Your songs could be as wonderful as the music of angels, but if there was nobody to market it, they would be worthless."

He needed three deep breaths before he could answer in a civilized voice. "I know that, Sally, and I appreciate it." Another two breaths until he felt the knot of anger in his stomach unwind. "No one is more grateful, but my house and my private life will not be used for any kind of marketing, ever. That's all I'm trying to say. I need a part of my life for myself."

"Jon is right," Sean said in his calm, gentle voice. "He is very right, Sally. And you know it." Without waiting for her reply, he held out the sheet music to Jon. "Here, take a look. We've changed a couple of chords, and one rhyme seems a bit forced. Can we go over it together?"

They went to join the band. Jon could still feel the tension in his shoulders, and he shook them to loosen the stiffening muscles.

"Something has to change," he muttered, but so low that only Sean could hear him. "I can't stand this situation. I'm sorry, but it's distracting and not very much fun."

"You couldn't make your heart feel something for her?" Sean didn't look at him but ordered the sheets on top of his keyboard. "It would have been such a good match."

"Yeah." Sally was sitting in the same spot, her hands pushed under her legs, watching the conductor talk to the orchestra. "It would have been very convenient. But when I wanted her, she pushed me away; and when she wanted me, my feelings had turned cold. And I'm not in a mood to talk my heart into changing its mind." Jon picked up the rosewood. The strings sang softly when he touched them. "And now I have this strong feeling that…" He had to start again. "I don't know. It wouldn't be right. I can't settle. I want more than that, and I think I deserve more than that too."

"Everyone does, Jon," Sean replied.

"Yes." His pulse was calming down. "Everyone does. Only what happens if you fall in love with someone, I mean, *really* fall in love so deeply that you can't remember the time of day or where you are, or even your own name. When that one person is the only thing you can think of, when not having her near feels like a part of you has been cut out, when you can't even breathe if you're not whispering her name with every breath and she doesn't love you back? What do we do then, Sean?"

Sean grinned and pushed the sheets toward him. "Then, my friend, you're in deep trouble. That's what happens. And I hope that you'll never have to go through it, because your romantic heart would surely be ripped to shreds." Still shaking his head, he sat down on his piano bench and massaged his fingers. "You're a strange one, Jon Stone. I've never met a man like you before or heard anyone talk about love the way you do. It's as if you know some secrets about it that the rest of us don't, that we can't even see." He tilted his head to give Jon a measuring stare. "I'm curious what will happen to you. I can't wait to see the woman you'll marry someday who will have such a hold over your heart. I'm guessing she will be very special indeed."

"I haven't met her yet; that much I can tell you." Regret, and something that felt suspiciously like pain. "I wish it would happen soon though. That house is a mighty lonely place at night, and my bed feels much too big and cold for just me. I could use some company."

That made Sean laugh out loud. "Jon, it's not as if you don't have a choice. I bet when we leave tonight, there'll be more than enough pretty girls hanging around outside, waiting for a glimpse and an autograph. All you have to do is raise a finger!"

"I know." The rosewood pick Jones had given him felt familiar between his fingers. Jon gazed at it, remembering that night at Bob's when all this had begun. "Have you ever been down in the vault, Sean?"

Sean shook his head.

"They keep all the fan mail down there. I have my own shelf.

Some of them are interesting. I wonder if any of the girls who sent them are out there. Waiting for me to leave the building, waiting to be noticed." Jon let his fingers glide over the strings, trying out one of the chords Sean and Jones had added. They were right; the song sounded better this way.

"I wonder what they really feel for me. Sometimes I think I'd like to talk to them and find out. Then again, they scare me. Sally is right; there's a fine line between being a fan and a threat. I don't know. This is a weird life. So popular, so well-known, and yet so alone. Very weird."

The rosewood pick came down on the strings.

Chapter Thirty-seven

"I'M SORRY."

Busy with the lyrics of the new song, he hadn't heard Sally come up behind him. Something just didn't fit. Something was jarring, missing, and he couldn't figure out what it was. The band had taken a break, and they'd sent the orchestra home. There would be no recording today. Jon was too preoccupied with that rough verse.

"Yeah," he mumbled, his back to her, absentmindedly crossing out the irritating words.

"I didn't mean to intrude."

Suppressing a sigh, swallowing the curse that was hovering on his tongue, he dropped the pencil and turned. "I know you didn't mean to intrude, Sally. No need to apologize." He could feel the muscles in his shoulders draw together. "Seriously. Everything is fine." The rhymes were still dancing in his mind, weaving a tantalizing ribbon around him, teasing, giggling, but never getting close enough for him to catch them. "Give me a sec, will you. I need to straighten this out, and then we'll all go for dinner."

Her lips trembled. "Okay. But there's something I want to say to you. I was just offering to help. You're very busy, and, well, you're a man, and men generally don't know much about interior design. I only wanted to make you feel comfortable in your new house."

"Thanks. I'm sorry for being so brusque earlier. But I'm fine. Really." Jon could see the others waiting in the control room. They were smoking, drinking the last of the stale coffee from the urn, laughing, sharing jokes; only he was still in the studio, fighting with the lyrics.

"I want us to get along, Jon. Please don't let that scene in New York stand between us." She raised her hand to stop him when he opened his mouth. "Please. Don't say it. I know something between us has changed, and it can't be helped. But I want us to get along, and well. Tell me what to do."

"Sally." Rubbing his eyes, Jon slumped on the piano bench. "You don't have to do anything. Just please stop apologizing, will you? We're friends, and we're fine. And thank you for wanting to help." He took her hand in his. "Okay, I promise. I promise if I need help, you'll be the first one I ask. Good enough?"

She nodded, but her eyes were sad. "You don't want me there, right? You think if I decorate it for you it will reflect my taste, not yours. And you don't want that."

"No. Yes. I don't know." Again he rubbed his eyes. His brain was too tired to deal with her logic. "Maybe it's just that I want to do this on my own, so it feels like it's mine and not an extension of the studio."

"You said that before." She didn't pull her hand from his. "But I think the truth is closer to what I said. You don't want to see *my* touch in *your* home."

Something in him broke. It didn't feel like a hard, clean break, not like a stone shattering, but more like the crumble of sand under the assault of surf that had been eating away at it.

"Why is it so hard for you to accept that this is something I want to do on my own, without any ulterior motives? I don't question your love for polka dots or bright-red patent leather, do I, Sally? I tell you you're pretty anyway, even though I think bright-red patent leather is not the most elegant thing in the world. But who am I to criticize your taste? It's your taste, not mine. And the same goes for my house, my car, my clothes: They're mine, and I'm going to pick them. Simply put, it's none of your business. Or anyone else's. If I need advice, I'll ask."

Sally took a step away from him. Her hand slipped from his, and she hid it behind her back. "Okay. I get it. No more looking after you."

It was too much. The pencil flew across the room, hitting the glass panel separating studio from control room. "That's not what I said, damn it! Stop it, Sally!"

Curious faces were staring at them through the window. Sal was moving toward the door, ready to come to the rescue.

"I'm sorry." Jon reached out to catch her hand again. "Look, I'm sorry. I'm just frazzled and tired, and really…" He shook his head, trying to get rid of the annoying lyrics. "I'm trying so hard to get this stupid song right, and it just won't work. Come on. Let's go. I'll buy you a drink, and we'll talk about furniture and stuff. I know you don't want to take over. I'm being stupid, Sally. Forgive me." Exhaustion crept up his spine. "I need a break. Come on, let's go."

His arm around her shoulder, ready to walk out, his glance fell on the sheet with the wild scribbling and all the crossed-out words. Anger, disappointment, helpless rage churned in his chest.

"Words," he muttered. "Curse the need for lyrics. I should write movie sound tracks and leave the crap with the words to some other poor fool."

Sally stopped, her mouth open. "What a great idea, Jon! Do you think you want to do that? You'd be brilliant at it! I'll make some calls tomorrow. We have a few good friends in the movie business, you know."

Jon, his hand on the doorknob, grinned mirthlessly. "Why am I not surprised."

THEY piled out of the elevator, discussing where to go for dinner. The whole band was there, as well as Sally, Tom, Sal, and even Cole.

"It's too cold to sit outside," he was saying, glancing at his watch. "Let's go to my favorite Italian place. They always have room for me. We may have to sit in the kitchen, but who cares."

"Not Italian again, Daddy," Sally complained. "I want something exotic." Pushing open the front door, she stepped out into the mild breeze of a California January evening. Her short skirt blew up, revealing slim, muscular legs and red, polka-dotted panties that made Jon laugh out loud. He was on the point of putting his arms around her. She was smiling at him, her pale hair dancing around her face, the sun at her back, casting a halo around it.

There was a small group of fans hanging around near the curb, next to the van with the label logo on its doors. Most of them were girls and young women, giggling, calling his name, holding out magazines with his picture on the front. He was used to this by now and automatically held out his hand for someone to put a pen in it. This time it was Tom who handed him a ball point.

One of the young women was moving toward them, a pretty

blond with a mop of hair and a nice chest that was showing to its full advantage in a low-cut, tight shirt. Jon had an uneasy feeling that he'd seen her before and stopped.

"Jon." Her voice was nondescript, not really loud but not exactly soft and gentle either, the kind of voice you would expect to hear at a grocery store, calling down the aisle for a child or spouse to hurry up. "I've written you so many letters," she said, "and you've never responded. Why don't you respond? I've offered you my love, myself, and you never answer me."

"But—" Jon began, confused by the accusation. Behind him, the band stood, listening, waiting, and on the other side, the fans. "I didn't..."

Sally was reaching out to him, gesturing to ignore her and get into the van. That's when he remembered.

The vault, the pink pages, the photos. The scent of cheap perfume, the little hearts.

"I'm sorry," he said, "I am, but I'm so busy."

She gave him a smile that was a mix between a sneer and a voiceless scream. "I'll always love you. I know you sing just for me; your words, they're just for me. I understand you; I know what you're trying to say. I can't live without you though. Every day is a chore, and awfully lonely. Life doesn't mean a thing without you. But if I can't have you in this life, at least I know we'll be together in the next. We'll be together, forever."

A flash. It was no more than a flash in the sunset, the glint of metal moving fast toward him. Jon raised his hand to fend it off, stumbling back. There was no pain. Shocked, he looked down at his arm, at the cut and the warm flow of his blood.

He heard Sally cry out, felt Tom's grip on his shoulder, pulling him back toward the building, but he couldn't move.

Another slash. This time not aimed at him but at her own slender throat.

There was so much blood running from his hands, soaking his shirt, tasting of rank metal on his lips.

Someone was screaming, calling for an ambulance, for a doctor, and he couldn't move. Someone had ripped off their t-shirt, pressing it on his wounded arm.

The girl was lying at his feet, a sodden, crumpled heap of blond hair and twisted limbs, blood pulsing from her throat where she had cut it open, streaming out of her in ruby gushes onto his shoes.

"Inside, inside." It was Cole, his tone cool, collected. "Inside, and close the door, Jon. Sally. Take him. Tom. Call an ambulance. Go."

Jon shook them off. He watched as the others tried to stop the river of blood gushing from the girl's throat. Frozen in place by shock, he watched the girl die.

It took only moments. She was looking at him, her skin growing paler as the puddle around her spread, painting a map of blood on the sidewalk. Sirens were howling, coming closer. The other fans were staring from the edges, a few of them crying, entranced by the sight of death and violence.

"We have to do something." Jon's voice broke. "We can't just let her die there."

Tom held on to him when he tried to move forward. "We need to get you to the hospital. You're in shock. You're..." He fell silent, pointing at Jon's clothes.

He wondered, if he closed his eyes, if he returned to the studio and made up with Sally, if he found the right lyrics, if he could undo what had happened.

"It's not your fault." Cole, pushing back his gray hair, stood in front of Jon, forcing him to look away from the gruesome scene. "It is not your fault. Do you hear me, Jon? This didn't happen because of you. It happened because of her. Stay calm, and try to keep a cool head." His face was ashen, old. "I've never seen anything like this, not in all the years I've been in this business. But we have to be calm."

"You can't be serious," Jon said, but Cole nodded.

"I am, very much so," he replied.

Ambulances had arrived; the medics and police were rushing to the bloody scene. Blue and red lights flashed, drowning out the sunset. He wanted to explain to them what had happened, apologize for it, and somehow will her back to life.

"I'm serious, Jon, and very concerned about your safety."

Bitter laughter, mixed with bile and the taste of blood, stuck in his mouth. "Safe? How, safe? She's dead!"

"The media are here," Sally interrupted. "We need to go. Let's get you in an ambulance and let them look at your arm, Jon. Cole will take care of this."

Like a robot, like a man without a soul, he let her lead him away.

Chapter Thirty-eight

SALLY BROUGHT HIM wet paper towels, muttering all the while about the waste of his nice clothes. A medic arrived and ordered him to take off his sodden shirt. Sally held out a paper bag, and he dropped it in.

The stench of congealing blood was almost too much to bear, and it didn't get any better when it mingled with the odor of antiseptic the doctor applied to the cut on his arm before bandaging it. It didn't need stitches, he announced; the cut was shallow and would heal by itself.

Dazed, as if he was walking in a very bad dream, Jon let her take off his shoes and drop them into the bag with his ruined shirt.

"I love those shoes. They were one of the first things I bought with my advance. Those shoes, and the rosewood guitar. They're really nice shoes. I like to wear them on the stage too." He was babbling, and, realizing it, he bit down on his tongue.

"Well, you won't be wearing them anymore, I'm afraid." She had returned, carrying a pair of flip-flops. "Take these for now. It's better than walking barefoot."

The t-shirt she'd brought him was from their tour merchandise. He held it up to look at his image before putting it on, wondering if the nameless, dead girl out on the pavement had bought one at his concert, had maybe worn it to feel close to him at night, alone in her bed.

"Never thought I'd wear one of these," he said.

How carefully they skirted around the thing, avoiding any word that would force them to talk about it.

"Tea." Tom held out a mug to him. "With lots of sugar. My mom always used to say that in moments of distress, nothing helps like tea with sugar. Or chicken soup. She was a believer in the miracle of chicken soup." Leaning against the wall, he watched how Jon hugged it. "For the longest time I used to associate chicken soup with feeling sick. She always made it when one of us came down with something. Didn't matter what: flu, upset stomach, chicken pox. It would always be chicken soup."

"So did my mom," Jon replied. The hot, sweet liquid was warming his knotted stomach, relaxing the muscles out of their stasis, easing his breathing. "Always with the chicken soup. I couldn't eat it for a long time when I grew up without remembering how it felt to be sick as a child."

He wanted to be there right now. He wanted to lie on the couch in the family room, wrapped up in his mother's old quilt, mindlessly watching reruns of old movies, a bowl of steaming soup on his knees, dumplings swimming in it, and little bits of carrot. She'd be in the kitchen, his mom, and he would be able to hear her hum while she worked. He wanted it very much.

Instead, he closed his eyes and inhaled the aroma of the tea.

"I want to go home," Jon said.

"Are you sure?" Tom's tone sounded uncertain. "Are you sure it's a good idea to be in that house of yours, alone, now? Wouldn't it be better to stay with Sean, or..."

Jon opened his eyes to see a glance pass between Tom and Sally. She blushed and shook her head.

"Or a hotel?" Tom finished his sentence.

"Nah." Home, he had said, and he hadn't meant the Malibu house at all.

Sal and Cole came in, their faces drawn and exhausted.

"The police have left," Cole announced, "and we said a few words to the press. It couldn't be avoided. Jon, I want you out of town for a few weeks. I'm going to send you to a friend's place where you can rest and have some peace. If you stay here you'll be hunted by the press."

"I'm not going anywhere. I'm not going to run and hide. That would look as if I feel guilty for what happened." He shrugged. "I do feel guilty. I feel terrible. But I won't hide. I'm staying right here, and we go on with our work as always."

"Bad idea," Sal threw in. "Cole is right, Jon. Take a break."

"No." Jon put down the mug. "I'm not going anywhere except home. I'm tired, and I'm not in the mood for anymore talking."

Without waiting for them to react, he got up and, the flip-flops slapping the floor with every step, left.

THE sidewalk was empty.

Jon stared at the mess. Debris from the fruitless resuscitation attempts lay in the small red lake like islands with very white beaches: cotton swabs, bandage wrappings, broken vials, even a used and discarded syringe. No one had bothered to clean it up. Yellow police tape fluttered from a street lamppost, torn and useless.

Jon wondered where they'd taken her. He saw the lifeless, drained body outside a morgue, just like in those TV shows, waiting to be cut open and inspected. He'd never understood why someone would want to do that when the cause of death was as obvious as it was here.

His hand wandered to his own throat, to the spot where he could feel the blood pulsing. It wouldn't take a lot to cut into the soft skin. One flick of the blade had been enough.

To come here, to the doors of his record company, wait for him to show up, and then kill herself was more than Jon could grasp. He stood, stiff with a feeling he couldn't quite define. It was something dark, a silent, sinister bird sitting on his shoulder, listening to the rush of his pulse in his unharmed veins.

He didn't even know her name. She'd gone to her death and never told him her name, had suffered the indignity of lying on the sidewalk while the blood ran out of her, and no one had been there to keep her from killing herself.

"Jon." Sal had come up unnoticed and was standing behind him. "It's not your fault. You do realize that, don't you? You did nothing to invite this."

"Yeah, well." He felt so tired, so hollow and nauseated. "As it happens, I think I did; and yes, it's my fault. It's me. I'm the reason this happened. It's my fault all right, Sal."

"You know that's nonsense, Jon. You can't think clearly right now, that's all. You're upset and in shock. Hell, we all are. If you weren't, you'd know it's not your fault. You do what you have to do. You're a songwriter. You're a performer. You suffer the same restrictions and dangers as everyone else standing in the limelight. Crazy fans will do these things." Sal brought out his cigarettes and offered them to Jon, but he shook his head. His stomach was doing a merry dance as it was; he didn't want to upset it any more.

"Fans will do crazy things," he agreed, "but this, Sal, this is so extreme. I can't even think."

Guilt. That was the word that had been missing. Guilt was the thing resting so heavily on his neck and shoulders; it was the vise around his temples, the beast in his guts. Its name was guilt.

"I need a drink." Jon pushed his fingers through his hair. "A stiff drink. Want to come back to the house with me? I have a bottle of very nice single malt, a Christmas gift from Tom."

"Let's go."

They carefully maneuvered around the puddle to where their cars were parked.

"You know I may not be able to drive home." Sal stood, weighing the keys in his hand. "Maybe it would be wise to go together, and I can grab a cab later."

"You can sleep on the couch. I have some blankets you can use." Nothing mattered. Like someone in a stupor, as if he'd died himself, Jon drove them to the Malibu house.

THEIR steps echoed when they entered the large, empty mansion.

It was cool and dark inside, and very, very still. Sal went straight to the kitchen and opened the fridge.

"You're pathetic," he shouted. "Your fridge is empty! There's no food, no beer, not even ice cubes! Do you call this living, Jon? Why own a house like this if you don't make something out of it? This should be a mansion full of comfort and splendor, and yes, with a filled fridge! You need a housekeeper."

Jon didn't feel like arguing about his life again. Instead, he tossed a take-out menu from a pizza joint on the kitchen table and brought out two glasses to hold them up. "See? Glasses to drink from. And here's the booze." He poured, but his hand was shaking so badly that half the liquid missed the glass. Defeated, he put down the bottle and sank into a chair.

"It's my fault," Jon said, and he nearly choked on the words. "You can say what you want, but it's my fault."

"You know that's crap, Jon." Grabbing a towel from the rack near the sink, Sal wiped the table dry and filled their glasses. "I'm not even going to try and talk sense to you right now. It would be useless, wouldn't it?"

The ghost of a smile flew across Jon's face.

"Jon." Sal sat down, the bottle between his hands. "I admit it's probably one of the worst things that has ever happened to a celebrity, and will certainly go down in the Hollywood annals. But you can't stop because of this! We'll all need a few days to get over the shock, but life will go on."

"I wonder if she had any family. I wonder what her name was. She was pretty, such a pretty girl. Did someone inform her family, her parents? Will they have to go to the morgue to identify her?" The whiskey didn't taste half as good as he remembered.

"She can't have been more than what? Twenty? Maybe younger? And now she's dead. It's unbearable, Sal."

Shame and guilt, ugly sisters whispering their dirge into his ears.

Sal poured more whiskey into Jon's glass. "You need some sleep, and tomorrow we'll talk about all this. We'll discuss what needs to be done for the girl's family, and what your role in that should be. But first, sleep. God, I'm exhausted. Are you okay with that, Jon? Sleep, then talk? Everything will look different in the light of day."

It took Jon a while to reply. Then he said, "At the least I want to send flowers, and express my condolences."

Sal did not respond.

Chapter Thirty-nine

SHE WAS, COLE told them over coffee, just a farm girl from somewhere in Oklahoma who'd hitched a ride to LA, hoping to meet her idol. Barbara, that had been her name, and she'd been nineteen. It was all over the media. Her parents, drenched with tears, had been interviewed on all the networks.

Shrugging his shoulders, he added that she had a history of manic depression and had only recently switched her adoration to Jon. He hesitated when Jon asked who she had admired before.

"Neil Diamond," he then said. "I have no idea why she deserted him for your sake. Maybe she couldn't find him and decided you were easier prey."

There would be no flowers, no condolences from either Jon or the label, Cole informed them. In fact, his lawyers were debating whether to sue for assault.

"Who do you want to sue?" Jon asked, bitterness dripping from his voice. "Her family? That poor girl's family, you want to sue them after she killed herself? Haven't they suffered enough?"

Cole gave him a cool, level stare. "They may be, but so are we. Committing suicide on our doorstep is bad for business. That bloodstain will stay on the pavement for a while, even with all the scrubbing our cleaning crew did. Some would say it's bad karma."

"I feel guilty," Jon shot back. "I do! It's my job to make people happy, to make them enjoy my music, not to cut their throats over it. So yes, I do wonder why you'd want to bring more grief to that family."

Cole sat down, facing him. "It can go either way. It will either help turn you into a superstar, or it will ruin you. Right now, it's undecided." He gestured at Sally. "I know Sally has been lecturing you about security and being careful in public, and I know you've scoffed at that. It's a tough lesson to learn for a young man. But now more than ever, you'll draw attention."

Sal stirred in his chair but remained silent. They had gathered in the conference room. Sunlight was streaming in through the windows; the sky was a flawless blue.

"You'll have to lock up your feelings of guilt and shame, Jon, and be reasonable about this. Your career is at stake, and more importantly, your life." Cole pushed the tin of cookies Jon's way.

Two days had gone by since the gruesome scene, and Jon had avoided reading the newspapers or turning on the TV. Following Sal's advice, he hadn't even left the house so he wouldn't run into inquisitive reporters. He'd wandered through the house's empty rooms, listening to its quiet breathing., At night he'd lain awake in his bed, afraid of falling asleep and dreaming of blood and death. Sal and Russ had appeared, the van loaded with groceries, and filled up his fridge.

"If you don't want to leave town, at least lie low" had been Sal's advice. And Jon had learned to make scrambled eggs for himself.

HIS muscles stiff, a bitter taste in the back of his throat, Jon entered the studio where the rest of the band was waiting for the rehearsal to begin.

They were chatting, talking about the music, about lunch, the weather. Walter, sitting behind his drums, was leafing through a car magazine. Jones was chatting with the sound engineer about baseball.

Someone had set up his guitars for him in a neat row: his old one, the rosewood, the koa—all of them gleaming, ready, waiting for him.

Jon picked up the koa and played a chord, and then another, but the sound didn't resonate with his soul as it usually did.

It was just that: a chord played on a guitar. The mystical part, the part that made it all special for him, was gone. He was in a room full of noise, strange sounds coming from different sources, a carpet of voices talking about things that seemed so alien.

Jon sat on his stool, the guitar on his knee, the pick between his fingers, and his mind wandered back to the days in New York.

He'd played at Bob's, in parks, in subway stations, for birthday parties and even the occasional Bar Mitzvah, and the audience had always enjoyed his music, had clapped or sung along.

The music had been a happy place, an unsullied, safe, and joyful place where he could escape whenever life became too much. Now everything was gone. Someone had thrown open that door and let in the darkness.

Again he tried to ease into "The River," tried to make the well-known opening bars transport him into gladness and an easy heart, but his fingers struggled with the strings. It was as if the instrument was refusing him the escape of music.

Jon tried again, with a different song, but it was the same. His hands and the guitar had become strangers.

Russ and Sal had entered the recording room, joining the conversation, laughing at something Jones said. Walter had turned to one of the background singers and was busy chatting her up, asking her out for a drink after work; and she was smiling at him, nodding, blushing, accepting his invitation.

Jon put down the koa guitar to exchange it for the rosewood. A love song, maybe a love song would accomplish what "The River" couldn't. From his little bowl of picks he took the rosewood one that Jones had given him, his good luck charm.

"Forever" he'd called this song. Back then he'd believed in something like forever. Love had been good, had been the kind, sweet thing it was supposed to be. It had been his haven, his dream, the only truth.

He closed his eyes to listen to the melody inside him and tried to transport it to the guitar, but it didn't work. The rosewood did not respond. Like a dead soul, like rotten driftwood, it lay against his chest, gasping where it should have been singing.

His hand gripped the neck tightly until the strings cut into his fingers.

She flew well, his rosewood guitar. In a beautiful arch she slammed into the glass of the recording room, smashing it, creating a rainbow of glass slivers. He could see Russ and Sal duck, pulling the engineer down with them, and he could see the body of his beloved instrument crack open like a raw egg.

"Are you out of your freaking mind?" Sal regained his wits before any of the others. Brushing pieces of glass off his sleeve, he stood up to shout at Jon. "What's gotten into you? Get out of the studio, right now!"

It didn't matter. Jon, shrugging, got up and left the room, down the hall and through the doorway to the stairs, leaving the building.

He walked down the street, his hands in his pockets, his head bowed, and kept walking until the sun had set, and he had reached the beach. The sand was still warm from the sun. He took off his shoes and rolled up his jeans and kept walking, this time along the waterline, until it was dark. Then he sat where the surf couldn't touch him and pulled up his knees so he could rest his elbows on them. His head lowered on his folded arms, Jon sat and cried.

Chapter Forty

HE DIDN'T PICK up the phone, didn't answer the doorbell. Wrapped up in his misery, Jon spent the days sitting on the balcony of his bedroom, looking out at the changing colors of the sea and sky. At night he lay on his bed, his eyes on the moon while it wandered toward dawn. Only when the first rays of the sun fell on the trees would he allow his mind some rest, and sleep.

It took Sal nearly two weeks to get through to him, finally threatening to call the police if Jon didn't open up. He stared in dismay at Jon's unshaven face, the grimy jeans he'd lived in for weeks, the mess in the kitchen.

Jon watched how he dropped the pieces of the broken rosewood guitar on the kitchen table. In an eerie, ghostly way, it reminded him of the girl's dead body, and he looked away quickly.

"You're a disgrace," Sal said. "Look at you. You're letting yourself go, you don't show up for work, and we have to get ready for the European tour. Cole is mad because he wanted to release the new album before we leave, but with you wallowing in your pool of self-pity, I can't see that happening. That girl is dead, Jon, and no amount of punishing yourself will bring her back. No matter how much you drink or how long you don't sleep, it won't change the fact that you had nothing to do with her suicide. You have many fans. But she was the only one who thought killing herself would make you love her. It's sick, and very, very sad." He pointed at the destroyed guitar. "And you broke your wonderful rosewood. You should be ashamed of yourself."

"You're just not getting it, are you." There was no coffee. There wasn't any bread either. "I know she's dead and won't come back; I know she was unstable and a sad, sick young woman. But it's the reality that something like this might happen again. Don't you see, Sal?" Jon closed the fridge door. There was nothing inside that made him want to eat. "Don't you see that from now on this will be my cross to bear? I never thought about the impact my music might have on other people."

"No, *you* are the one who isn't getting it." Sal nudged the twisted neck of the guitar. "Yes, you carry a lot of responsibility. But it's not for you to worry about rabid fans; that's my job. All you have to do is worry about the music, write the songs, perform them on the stage. We'll take care of the rest. We'll tell you when you have to go public, and we'll very carefully pick those appearances, Jon." Stepping closer, Sal gripped Jon's shoulder and shook him. "You don't have to face fans, ever, except during a concert, and then security will keep them away. Everyone will understand if you refuse to give autographs after what happened. Just, please, don't throw away everything now. I beg you."

"You're the one who doesn't understand, Sal, and that makes me sad." Jon took a step away to free himself from Sal's grip. "I've had such an easy ride to get to where I am now. There was no struggle to become who I am. I never thought about the impact I'd have. I enjoyed seeing the desire in the girls' eyes. It made me feel good, important. There was never a dark side to it until that girl killed herself. Giving autographs, flirting with them, it was all a game, with no sinister side to it." Again he had the bitter taste of sorrow on his tongue. "But there is. There is a horrid, sinister side to this whole business that I wasn't prepared for."

He couldn't say it. It sounded whiny and accusing, like a child's excuse to run away. He couldn't say that he didn't want the responsibility, the burden of being adored and admired by so many.

"We sent a wreath." Sal poured himself a glass of orange juice from the canister on the counter and then, after sniffing it, poured the juice into the sink. "I know you wanted to do something. We didn't send it in your name though but in the company's. You need to be kept out of it."

"Yes." That much he'd understood and accepted.

"You know, of course…"

Jon looked up when Sal didn't go on, but he had his back turned, pretending to be busy washing his glass.

"You know that this entire sickening affair has driven your sales quite a bit. Your album made platinum, and it's still selling like hot cakes. Cole has the plague in his office. He said he wouldn't give it to you until you show up and pay for the smashed window. I don't think he wants an apology. They understand why you were upset. To be honest, I think they like you even more because of it."

When there was no response from Jon, he went on. "Are you planning on coming back? Or are you going to throw it all away? Because if that's what you want, you might as well tell me now."

Exhausted, tired of talking, Jon wandered into the living room, where he opened the door to his studio. It was empty except for a table, chair, and a few sheets of music. His dream of putting a Steinway here, of buying recording equipment and using the space to compose, and rehearse with Sean and Jones, seemed like something from a different life.

"I don't know," he said when Sal came to join him. "I just don't know. Right now I feel as if I'm dead. There's no music, no joy, no life. Give me a little more time, Sal."

He heard the entrance door shut, and the motor of the starting car, and once again he was all alone in the big house.

A whisper woke him, the memory of a word spoken in a dream. His eyes wide-open, listening to the echo of the voice, Jon watched the moon play hide-and-seek with the clouds. The surf was as loud as faraway thunder, and the palm trees just outside the bedroom window rustled in the lively breeze. It was raining. The drops falling on the marble tiles of the balcony sounded like small frogs hitting muddy ground. The scent of jasmine mingled with the aroma of wet earth, flower and green, blossom and dust, creating the richest, most soothing smell ever.

Something had changed. While he'd slept, something had changed for him, as if gentle, benevolent hands had lovingly put the jarring pieces of his puzzle back into order.

Carefully, not yet trusting this new feeling, Jon sat up.

He felt hungry, and very dirty. The stubble on his face had grown into a beard, his hair was now long enough to tie it back. Discarding his clothes, he went to stand on the balcony and let the rain wash down on his skin.

In his dream, he'd walked along the shore again. The deep, slow bell had tolled, and this time he'd heard it loud and clear. It was like a call, like the pulse of the universe, the place where all the songs lived; and it was talking to him, trying to breathe him back into life, and into loving it.

He drew a deep breath, inhaling the smells dancing around him through the night air, and let it go in a soft hum, in the flow of a melody. It resonated in his chest, tickled his heart, soothed his aching soul, and opened the claws of sorrow around his mind. Gently, gently, it pried at his lips until he let the hum become a slowly sung tone, nothing more than a low sound; but on it, carried by it, Jon could feel the burden slip away. Like the wisps of ghosts, the feelings of guilt and shame drifted from him, only to dissolve in the rain and wind.

Cold and wet, he walked into the bathroom and stood under the hot shower, eyes closed, until his muscles eased.

Shaved, clean, and in fresh clothes, he picked up the pieces of the rosewood guitar and carried them to his car.

His first stop was a coffee shop, where he bought the biggest cup of coffee available and a bagel with ham and egg on it, which he ate while waiting for his turn at the barbershop.

"Short," he said. "A neat, adult haircut, please." And watched as the black locks fell to the floor all around him while he sipped the coffee.

HIS next stop was harder.

Roy watched silently as Jon laid the ruins of the rosewood on his worktable.

"I'm sorry, Roy," he said. "I know you'll never forgive me for this. All I can say is that I regret it from the bottom of my heart. Is there any way you can repair her?"

The rain had stopped. Through the open door of the workshop Jon could hear birdsong, the cries of gulls, the sounds of life.

"You know I can't." Roy's hands touched the broken instrument in a sad caress. "She's dead. She'll never sing again. Why did you do this to her? I loved this guitar."

"So did I." He couldn't explain. He couldn't put into words how he'd needed to feel the pain, how he'd wanted to suffer at least a tiny part of what the girl had suffered, and destroying the guitar had been worse than hurting himself.

"I was angry," he said, "and I didn't think."

It was almost unbearable to watch how Roy placed the parts of the guitar in a carton and pushed them under the table.

"I'll see which parts I can use for other instruments, but she's gone forever." He wiped his hands on his trousers. "So what now? Are you here to order a new one?" When Jon didn't reply, Roy added, "I'm not sure I want to sell you another one though. I hate for my creations to be destroyed."

"I promise it won't happen again. I was so distressed, so helpless." There were no words good enough.

"Ah." Soft understanding crept into Roy's eyes. "The girl. Yes, that would make me flip too. You needed the pain. I see." He gestured for Jon to follow him into the back room, where he usually worked. "I don't have any guitar quite like yours at the moment. If you want one built, you'll have to wait a couple of months."

"I want another rosewood. But I want it to be different. Something stronger, with a more mature sound. A grown-up guitar." Jon's hand wandered over the sweet curve of a pale-blond instrument with beautiful mother-of-pearl inlay along her neck. "May I?"

With a nod, Roy handed it down to him. "It's maple," he said. "Nothing like your rosewood, and a lot lighter. It has a nice sound, but you're beyond it, really." He sighed. "I'll build you another rosewood, Jon. And I'll tell you something: I'll give you that maple. She's like a willful child, like a kitten, and it may be a good thing for you to try and tame her. But I'm also telling you this: I'll never make another guitar for you if you destroy one of them like that again. I understand your pain, and I commend you for feeling guilty about that poor, misguided girl." Shaking his head, he wiped the golden surface of the maple guitar. "But it's not your fault, much less my guitars'. You'll have to toughen up or the music business will eat you alive, hair, teeth, and bones. The path you chose, it's a hard one, Jon Stone. There aren't many roses strewn on it, and those that are have a lot of thorns."

"I'm beginning to learn that," Jon said.

The maple guitar giggled when he touched its strings.

Chapter Forty-one

THE GUITAR CASE on his back, Jon walked into Sally's office.

"I want to call a meeting. Could you please gather everyone together," he announced, and not waiting for her reply, he went into the studio, where he unpacked the maple guitar and sat on his stool. No one else was there; the big room belonged to him alone. It looked as always; the glass had been replaced, all the debris cleaned up. The place seemed to be waiting for what was to come.

One after another they filed in: Tom greeted him with a nod and the flicker of a smile, then Cole and Sally, and a few minutes later Sal, who looked a little harassed, as if he'd rushed in from some other meeting.

"I want," Jon began, without waiting for any of them to speak first, "to apologize for throwing a fit, and also for throwing my guitar through the window." He nodded toward the recording room. "It was uncalled for, and I put people in danger. Of course I'll pay for the damage. It was entirely my fault."

He could see how they relaxed, how the tension eased out of Cole's face. With a small sigh he pulled over a chair and sat, nearly knee to knee with Jon. For the first time since he had come here, Jon realized that Cole was in his sixties at least, if not older. Curiously he looked from him to Sally and back, wondering if there were older siblings, maybe a young, second wife, and that made him look at Tom and wonder why they'd never taken the time to talk about their families, their private lives. It was always about work, studio time, concerts, marketing, and money.

Even Sal. They'd been working together for more than a year now, and he'd never been to Sal's house yet.

"We'll be going on tour in a few months," he said, pushing those thoughts aside for now, "and I want to lay down some rules for that. And for how we're going to go on from here."

Sal shifted uncomfortably, and Tom threw a dark glance at Cole, but no one replied.

"Nothing like this should ever happen again," Jon went on, settling the guitar on his knee. He needed the security of its weight. "I'll not allow anything like this to happen again. One death for my sake is more than enough. So this is how it's going to be: At the hotels, I want maximum security. No one, and I mean no one, gets access to our rooms without a guard breathing down their necks. The same personnel all the time. I want Sal or one of you to check them out thoroughly before hiring them. I prefer men, but if that's not possible, then no young women. I want all our rooms on one floor, and that floor closed to anyone else."

Sally, her pen flying over her clipboard, interrupted. "We could have them set up a private hospitality room for us on the reserved floor. Also, it can't be on the first floor but must be higher up, which means we need a guard at the elevator to restrict access. Personnel will have to be cleared. I'll get it done."

Jon nodded and, when no one else had anything to add, went on. "No autographs before or after shows. Keep the fans back. No one from the audience gets closer than ten steps from the stage, ever. If someone asks why we do this, tell them we want to prevent anything like that suicide from ever happening again." He took a deep breath, wishing he'd brought some coffee with him. "And I want more security in the lobby of this building. Make them send away any fans hanging around on the sidewalk. No more. One was almost more than I could bear. Another one, and…"

Cole nodded slowly. "I agree with that, Jon, and with all you want done. I think your demands are not only sensible but in fact very clever. We should, however, allow a few representatives of fan clubs in before each show. Not more than half a dozen people, carefully vetted. It would be a well-regulated, official meeting, no longer than five minutes."

"Agreed. No more chance meetings. I want us traveling together at all times. A private plane, a bus, a wagon train, whatever. Now, the fan mail."

Sally stirred. "I know. We need to read it more carefully."

"I want to see all the mail that's not just a friendly pat on the back or request for a photo. I want to be forewarned," Jon said, ignoring her. "I want to know what's coming my way, and know about any potential danger."

"I'm sure we can do that, Jon, without you bothering about it." Tom nodded toward Sally. "I think we might have to hire an extra secretary, just for you."

"No." Again he surprised them. "I want my own office. That was the next thing I was getting to. Sal and Russ. I want them to work for me exclusively. We'll start out with that and add who we need as we move along. For now I'd like Sally to run it. If you don't have room for that, I'll ask Sal to find something nearby that we can use." Jon's hand ran over the guitar as if to glean security from it.

"That won't be necessary." Cole's voice sounded raspy, tired. "I 'm glad that you're back, and that you've overcome your sorrow, Jon. I agree with you; we need to start thinking, and acting, differently. But I hate that it had to happen like this." He rose from his chair, pulling at his shirt cuffs. "Everything will be done the way you want it. But before we do that, I want you to consider a new offer we are going to make you. It's time to discuss contracts."

They moved to the conference room where there was coffee, and sandwiches hastily provided by Sally, and talked well into the afternoon.

"YOU crazy man," Sal said when they left. "You got everything you wanted, including exclusivity with the band. I have no idea how you do it, but you always get your way."

"Yeah." Once it had been fun standing outside the building smoking a cigarette on the sidewalk and watching life go by. Now all he could see was the ugly shadow of the spilled blood and the menace in everyone walking past him. "I didn't go to business school for nothing, Sal." The cigarette tasted bitter. "Maybe I should have been the banker Jenny wanted me to be."

"Never!" It came out with such vehemence that Jon forgot the blood for a moment and smiled. "Jon, you're so talented, the angels would weep if you gave up music!"

"I've come to realize that I want to be in control," Jon said softly, watching a Ferrari thunder down the street, its shape a streak of red lightning. "I have to be in control of my life. If this career is going to be my future, then I need to take control of it." It felt like such a heavy burden. "After all is said and done, I'm your boss now. I run this company called Jon Stone. It's my responsibility to see to our safety, and success. I can't have others decide that. I can let them handle it, but all decisions must be my own." He tossed the butt into the gutter. "It's the only way this will work. I can't hide behind the music and hope for the best. I need to do both: be the songwriter and be the businessman." Tilting his head, he thought about what he had just said. "Yes, that's how it has to be. I think I'm in control of my life now."

With that he left Sal standing there and returned inside. He needed Sally.

"NOTHING fancy," Jon kept repeating, "and nothing that looks like it's straight out of a designer magazine. I want comfortable, unpretentious things."

She rolled her eyes at him in that expression he knew only too well and told him that he'd have to at least furnish the living room, his studio, the dining room, and a couple of bedrooms in case his parents or siblings decided to visit. And hey, his own bedroom wasn't inviting either, so he'd better do something about that too.

"My bedroom is mine," he growled, but she ignored him. A couch, she said, and maybe a painting on the wall? Something to make him feel at home in that huge house, something to make it look as if someone actually lived there.

"And tables and chairs for the porch and the terrace," she added.

"Fine." As if he would ever throw parties or have guests in that house. It was his refuge, his most private and beloved hideaway, and he'd never allow anyone to spoil it for him. Never.

"And you need a housekeeper."

"No." His blood wanted to curdle at the thought of having a stranger in his home day in, day out.

"Yes. Yes, you do, Jon. You need someone to keep the place clean and in order, someone who'll keep your fridge filled and your freezer too, and preferably with cooked meals you only need to heat when you get hungry. Yes, you do need a housekeeper in a house with seventeen rooms! Who do you think is going to clean your bathroom for you? Who's doing it now?" Her fists on her hips, she glared at him until Jon looked away and admitted that no, he hadn't thought of cleaning the bathroom quite yet, but he'd planned to get to it this weekend.

"Yeah, right." Shaking her head, Sally made another note in the little red book she was carrying around as they walked through the furniture store. "I'll ask our housekeeper to recommend someone. She's been with our family for ages, and she practically raised me. Do you like Mexican food? Maria is Mexican."

It didn't matter, he mumbled sourly; Mexican was fine. As long as no one expected him to get up early just because breakfast was ready—he'd had enough of that at home, thank you very much.

By the time they left the store the sun was setting. Jon's head was spinning. It felt to him as if he'd purchased enough furniture to fill a midsize hotel and not his home.

"You can afford it," Sally commented, seeing his face. "You can also afford to take me out to dinner now. You're stinking, filthy rich, Jon."

And it was true; he was. Cole and Tom had offered a new record deal. In return for the millions they were going to pay him, he had promised to deliver three new albums over the next five years and do at least two more world tours.

"I'll buy you dinner," Jon replied, his heart beating in his throat, "but first you'll come down to the Porsche dealership with me. It's time I got the car I've always wanted."

Black, it had to be black, and a convertible. The dream of his childhood, the one thing he'd always connected with being a star, and there it was, waiting for him.

Jon took in the new leather smell of the seats and ran his fingers over the gleaming walnut dashboard. The radio sounded almost as good as the speakers in the studio.

Sally looked on with a patient smirk as he accepted the keys in exchange for his signature on the credit card slip.

"You're a fast learner," she said and sighed when he held open the car door for her. "Not even Cole buys a car with that much panache. Very cool, Jon Stone. You're now the star you always wanted to be."

"I know," Jon replied, and turned the ignition key. The Porsche rumbled to life.

Chapter Forty-two

JON WATCHED SPRING arrive in California, thinking how the weather would be back home now, the weeks between the dismal cold and wet of winter and the steaming humidity of the summer months.

They'd often walked the two blocks to Union Square to spend their lunch break in the sunshine. Jenny would bring the sandwiches she'd made at home and unpack them, neatly placing a paper napkin on the bench so it looked like a set table. There'd always been something to watch, something going on: a street painter creating a piece of art with his chalks, a musician singing songs or playing an instrument, tourists conferring over maps of Manhattan. Pigeons, there had always been pigeons, and he liked them even though Jenny called them vermin and rats with wings. To him they looked romantic, something remembered from the Mary Poppins movie.

Jon wondered if Jenny still took her lunch there and if someone else was keeping her company now.

A couple of times he was close to calling her, just to chat, to find out how she was doing; but something had always held him back, a small, warning deep down inside his soul.

The second album had been recorded in just three weeks; work was all that mattered to him, all that he wanted to matter, and he drove the others to move along at the fast clip he was dictating.

He had a housekeeper. Amparo was her name, and she showed up every morning before he rose and made breakfast for him. Sometimes she packed him a container of cookies or cake or even tamales to take with him and share with the band. It made him feel as if he was a schoolboy again. Strangely, it wasn't as weird as he'd thought it would be to have another person in the house. In fact it was quite nice always having ironed shirts and fresh towels, and finding food in the fridge when he got home late at night.

Life settled into a comfortable, quiet rhythm centered around the music, just the way he wanted it, while the tour crept closer.

Intrigued by the way the company was working like a well-oiled machine, preparing for the overseas concerts, Jon spent a lot of time in the office, watching Sally and her assistants make endless phone calls, type out memos and letters; and he was there when the shirts and jackets for the tour crew arrived. Sally dug out one of the jackets and held it up for his inspection.

"Well?" she asked. "What do you think? It's your show, master."

Snorting, Sal turned away from his desk. "Master," he repeated, "I like that. Young Master Stone. Like Little Lord Fauntleroy. Don't let it go to your head, Jon."

But Jon waved him away and took the jacket from Sally.

His name and all the tour dates were printed on the back. London, he read, Frankfurt, Berlin and Geneva. Amsterdam, Paris and Brussels, and even Dublin. Jon whispered the names of those far-off places, places he'd only seen on TV or in an atlas. He'd be seeing a lot of Europe. He'd be able to walk under the Eiffel Tower and stand in front of Buckingham Palace. He'd visit Picadilly Circus and go shopping on Saville Row, walk down Bond Street and have tea at Claridge's.

Jon slipped into the jacket. "Can I keep this one?" he asked.

"Seriously, Jon." Sally held out her hand for it. "You don't need a souvenir from your own tour, do you? Give it back, please!"

She returned it to the box, neatly folded. "These aren't for you. They're for the stage crew, the light and sound people, the roadies. You know that."

Of course he did, but somehow, putting on that simple piece of clothing, the tour had become real for him.

"I still want one," he repeated. "I want to give it to Roy."

With a sigh, Sally handed it over.

"THIS one won't come cheaply," Roy said. "I put aside everything else to get it finished before you go on tour. But, Jon. No more smashing my guitars through windows. Do you promise?"

"Of course I do. It was an extreme moment. There won't be any more of those." Jon sat down, the empty case of the dead rosewood on his knees. "And I don't care what you're asking. I want it."

Roy gazed at him through narrowed eyes. "Something has changed in you. I can't put my finger on it, but you seem grown-up. So serious, focused. Some of the magic has gone from you. The young artist, the dreamer, that's gone. You have embraced reality."

"It was a brutal awakening." Through the dusty window Jon could see Rose coming toward them through the garden, a tray with tea and cookies in her hands. "I'm aware of who I am now. I've accepted my role and taken on the responsibility."

"Sad." Somehow Roy's shoulders seemed to slump. "Very sad, Jon. I only hope your creativity hasn't taken a beating too. That would be terrible, terrible beyond words."

"No. Don't worry. Sacrificing the rosewood was a high price, but it brought me back to my senses." The memory of terror and sorrow was trying to inundate him. "For a while I thought everything was over. The guilt was so hard to bear." His palms felt sweaty. "But it's part of who I am now. I'll carry that burden with me, but I can't allow anything like that to happen again, ever."

Rose, standing in the doorway, was listening to him. Putting down her tray, she softly said, "Jon, you can't hold life at arm's length. You can't cut love and joy and happiness out of your life just because there's the danger that someone will come to harm. You need friends, and you need someone to love you! You deserve someone who loves you! Pain is the price we pay when we open our hearts to people, but without that risk there's also no love. You can't live like this: contained, secluded, and solitary." Without looking at him, she poured the tea and handed him a mug. The familiar scent of rose and hibiscus was calming, soothing, and delicious.

"After all is said and done, you are still a young man, and as far as I can see, right now a very lonely one," she added, holding out the plate with cookies. "If you go on like this you'll be another one of those cynical, wealthy Hollywood guys who always hang around with women who seem to get younger the older the men get, and everyone knows those girls don't care for them at all but for their money. Don't become one of those, Jon, I beg you."

"I'm not ready to love anyone." Jon bit into the cookie. "And I don't need anyone right now either." He shrugged, blowing on his tea. "I don't want to fall in love just now. I don't know. All I'm thinking about right now is the tour, and the mountain of work that will be waiting for me when I get back."

Waving at Roy, Jon added, "I need the money so I can pay for your husband's extravagantly expensive instruments. Now, let's see what you've conjured up for me, Roy. I'm on a tight schedule and haven't the time in the world to sit and natter."

"Natter," Roy mumbled. "He calls it nattering. I call it wisdom." But he went into the workshop and returned with the new guitar.

"I did a little extra work on it," he said. "Maybe it will keep you from smashing this one."

Jon's heart turned over. Along the neck, spelled out in meticulous, curly letters, was his name. He ran the tips of his fingers along the shining inlay, the strings singing softly when he brushed them. They were eager to be touched, these strings, inviting him to play, vibrating with the need for a tune. Gently, ever so gently, Jon laid his hand on them, letting their joy melt into his skin.

"She is a needy little thing," he said, smiling. "I think she wants to sing love songs."

How clear her tone was, like a silver bell, like a brook in a summer meadow, frolicking over pebbles, like a girl smiling at her lover.

"Treat her well then." Roy dropped a handful of wooden picks into Jon's hand. "And pay me well too."

THE phone kept ringing, but he ignored it. The guitar had his attention. He loved it; he loved it more than the old rosewood, more than the koa. It almost seemed as if Roy had built the melodies right into it; they sprang that easily from the strings, faster than he could write them down.

He knew he was supposed to meet with Sean and Jones for some drinks and a round of pool, but he didn't feel like leaving the house. Not even the tamales Amparo had made for dinner could entice him away from the rosewood.

It had grown dark before he put it aside and went to the kitchen to grab a beer. Amparo had left long ago; the house was silent, curling up for the night. His dinner sat in the pan, cold and neglected, with a note from Amparo beside it telling him to pop it in the oven if he wanted to eat.

The phone rang again. Bottle in hand, Jon picked it up.

"What?" he asked, unwilling to be ripped from his music.

"Come to the studio, Jon." It was Sal.

Jon glanced at the clock on the counter. "Now? Are you still working? I was going to meet Sean and Jones for pool. Anyway–"

He didn't get any further than that. "Now, Jon. There's something you have to see. And I know you'll want to see it. Trust me."

Dread, his familiar friend, how it loved to play havoc with the cold beer in his stomach.

"What's happened? Has something happened, Sal?" He could hardly say it around the fear congealing on his tongue.

"Oh good grief, no. Nothing bad, Jon. Sorry, didn't mean to upset you." A heavy sigh, a slow clearing of his throat. "I just think you should see this. It's a good thing. At least I think so. Someone sent a batch of lyrics to you, and man, I know you'll love them. So please come have a look at them."

"Lyrics? You mean someone sent us poems or something?" It sounded so ridiculous that he almost hung up on Sal. "Seriously?"

Sal didn't answer, saying instead, "Okay, listen to this." He began reading, his voice raspy and halting, stumbling over the words describing a night in a hidden garden, words that were the call of someone lonely and in love, calling to his girl, asking her to join him.

"Stop," Jon said. He nearly missed the counter when he tried to set down the bottle. "Stop reading. I'm on my way."

"I told you!" Sal crowed with relief.

"I'll be right there."

He didn't even turn off the lights before leaving the house.

Chapter Forty-three

Come to my secret garden, in the middle of the night
Come to me, I will be your guiding light
Like fairies we will be in our secret garden
Dancing in the stardust, the moon our only warden
I am your lover, my heart wants only you
You are my keeper, you know me through and through.
Come to me, my love, the night is calling
Come to me, just come, while dusk is gently falling.

HE KEPT RETURNING to those rhymes, the envelope of typed pages on his knees.

The words pulled at his heart, resonated with him as if they were his own, as if he'd spoken them in another life and forgotten them; and now that they were returned to him the loss hurt all the more. Whispering them stirred a buried memory of things he'd said to someone, but he couldn't remember who or when.

The stamp on the envelope was foreign. He examined it closely until he could make out that it was from Switzerland. The sender's address was on the back, but it too had been typed and didn't tell him what he wanted to know. There was nothing handwritten at all, no letter, nothing, just a slip of paper with a terse message: "Sing this."

That was all. No declarations of love. No requests, demands. Nothing.

"It says Naomi Carlsson," Sal said, "and it's a Geneva address. But that's all."

Jon sniffed the pages, but there was no telltale scent. Nothing.

"I have to meet her." He knew he had to, and if necessary he'd fall to his knees and beg her to let him use her lyrics. He'd go all the way to Geneva, alone if he had to. He would do anything to own these words.

They were sitting in the large room that was now his tour office. The boxes of crew jackets still sat in the center of the floor, making it look as if it was a storage area of some retail store. Everyone else had left long ago, busy with their weekend plans.

Sal had found a bottle of bourbon somewhere and was pouring some into a paper cup for Jon.

"We'll be in Geneva in a few weeks; I'll set up a meeting. She can come to our hotel and talk to you there. But you know..." He pushed the cup at Jon. "If you agree to use her lyrics, you'll have to share your income for those songs with her or buy them from her. Whatever she'll agree to."

"I don't care. She can have her share, and more." Holding them up, Jon added, "She sent them to me. She wants me to sing them. So I guess she'll be okay with me using them. They are mine now. I must have them." His heart was beating so fast, it was hard for him to think, let alone talk. "There are enough lyrics here for an entire album, Sal. Maybe she has more that she's willing to part with. I want them."

"Yes, you said." Amused, Sal downed his drink. "I had a feeling you'd jump at these, but I didn't expect you to go totally round the bend." Critically, he gazed down at them. "They are good; I'll give you that. But really, Jon?"

"Yes, really." He couldn't put it into words. His lips moved, his tongue was willing to speak, but his mind was too excited to form sentences. "Yes, I want them. They must be mine."

It was as if she'd walked through the wild garden of his house, walked by his side along the trail down to the beach and sung those rhymes to him as they sat on the stone bench hidden in the arbor. Like the gentlest caress, like a kiss blown on a flower, like the first wisp of sunrise, her songs were like tendrils of love wrapping around his heart.

"I want to meet her," Jon repeated, his voice gravelly and low. "I want to know the woman who wrote these. Call her, set up a meeting."

Sal waved him away. "I bet she's a cat lady in her midfifties, swooning over strapping young you. You'll be so disappointed when you meet her in person. All the mystery and miracle will go out of those verses when you meet her. I bet she's a primary school teacher or something, hey, maybe a librarian! And you're the only rock star she adores. Normally she goes to the opera, by herself, and takes a bar of chocolate that she eats during the performance, annoying everyone around her. And then she'll return home to her small apartment where her cats are waiting, and she'll sit at her desk and stare out at the empty street and dream of her youth, and you." He paused.

"She isn't a cat lady." Jon tried to ignore the last part of Sal's description. "And anyway, even if this…Naomi is really like that, what does it matter. She'll get a nice, fat check, enough to buy a nice, little house somewhere outside the city, where her cats can run free."

"I bet she knits." Smirking, Sal refilled their cups and held his up in a toast to Jon. "And she'll present you with a scarf. Or hey, socks! I'll bet you five bucks she'll give you a pair of hand-knit socks!"

"Deal." Again he read through the verses. It seemed as if they carried their own melodies in them, and all he had to do was write them down.

"I'm going home." Jon rose. "I need to work."

"It's Friday," Sal called after him. "And you said Sean and Jones are waiting!"

Jon didn't respond. His mind was racing ahead of him, straight to his studio.

"TALK to me, Naomi Carlsson," he whispered, his fingers on the piano keys, the lyrics propped up in front of him. "Tell me your secrets."

She couldn't be an old spinster; he refused to believe that. No one who'd never known love could have written these; Jon was convinced of that.

He tried to imagine her: a young woman, a musician herself, maybe someone who played the cello or the violin in an orchestra and was having a torrid affair with the older, married conductor. She'd have wonderful, chestnut hair that shone in the sunlight.

Or maybe she was a writer, a novelist, a poet—someone who did this for a living—and her books were famous in Switzerland, maybe even all of Europe and just hadn't made their way across the Atlantic yet. She'd show up for their meeting with her manager, her lawyer, even her publisher in tow and present him with a folder full of legal documents while he was there alone, without even Sal, and totally at a loss what to do.

He wondered what she would look like, how her voice sounded, if he'd like her as a person, if he'd want to work with her in the future, maybe even entice her to move to California so working together would be easier.

Carlsson didn't sound like a Swiss name. It sounded Scandinavian. And Geneva, he knew nothing about Geneva. Somehow it made him think of politics and spy movies, of snow and music.

Chocolate, someone had told him they made the best chocolate there. Jon liked chocolate.

Sitting on his piano stool, watching dawn creep up across the sky to play with the treetops, he imagined being served hot chocolate for breakfast and chocolate cake for dessert at lunch.

His hands sank to his knees.

Just a few weeks from now they'd board the plane to Europe. He'd be performing on strange stages, traveling across the continent for two months, a new bed, a new hotel nearly every night. Sal had warned him that there wouldn't be a lot of time for sightseeing; their schedule was tight, they couldn't afford to do a leisurely trip yet. Next time though, he'd promised, next time they'd take it easy and do some fun stuff too.

THE key turned in the entrance door; Amparo called out a good morning.

Jon glanced at his watch. He'd spent all night composing, humming, dreaming of meeting that strange woman with the incredible words.

He realized that, for the first time, he'd gone an entire night without reliving those moments of blood and terror. He was tired, but in a good way.

"Can you make eggs and bacon for breakfast, Amparo?" Stretching, he made his way into the kitchen, where it smelled of coffee and toast. "And lots of it? I'm asking the guys over."

His hand on the phone, he smiled at her. "It's good to have you here. Thank you."

Amparo wiped her hands on her apron and assured him that it was no problem to prepare a breakfast for six, or ten, if that was what he wanted.

"Just my friends," Jon replied, "Sal, Sean, Russ, and Jones."

He had never done this before. No one had been invited to the house, not even Sally, even though she'd helped him pick out all the furniture. Only Sal had been here, but now Jon felt the urge to let others back into his life at last.

"Hey," he said to a sleepy Sean, "get your butt over here. I want you to hear something. Breakfast is on me."

Amparo was moving to the pantry, bringing out the things she needed.

"You? You're inviting me to your house?" Sean sounded more awake right away. "What happened? You sound as if you want to announce you're married!"

"Nah, nothing that drastic." He wanted to laugh and sing, his heart felt that light. "But something pretty great. Come on, hurry, and bring Sal, Russ, and Jones with you. Amparo is making breakfast."

Taking the key to the gate from its hook, Jon made his way out onto the terrace, where he stopped for a moment to inhale the tart scent of the cedars. He could hear the surf; the tide was high. Walking down the path, he hummed the sweet melody of "The Secret Garden," his favorite from the lyrics Naomi had sent.

"*Like fairies we will be,*" he sang softly. The jasmine bushes leaned toward him to listen, their green branches touching his hair. "*Dancing in the stardust...*" Like a sigh, a slow breeze went through the leaves and petals.

The beach was almost empty. High waves thundered onto the shore, their backs golden and sleek in the early-morning sun. They broke into copper foam that curled and danced over the wet sand like layers of lace.

Jon opened the gate and went out onto the beach. Debris lined the water's edge. He looked down and poked it with his toes. There were shells among the seaweed, some pieces of sea glass, pebbles, a few stones. One of them stood out. Picking it up, Jon rubbed away the sand. It was heart shaped, the size of his palm, a black stone with fine, white lines in it. It lay in his hand as if the sea had carried it for millennia, carving its shape for just this moment.

Jon closed his hand around it. For a second he considered tossing it into the sea, but he put it in his pocket and returned to the house and placed the stone on top of the Steinway where he could see it while he worked.

From the kitchen he could hear Sal and the others chatting with Amparo. The aroma of frying onions and garlic, of bacon and eggs, filled the air.

For the first time since he'd moved here, the house seemed wide-awake, alert, and having fun.

Jon stopped in the hallway, listening. "She's brought you to life, hasn't she," he said. "Her words, they've done their magic on both of us."

The house sighed.

Chapter Forty-four

"I CAN SEE why you love these," Sean said, pointing at the lyrics. "They sound like yours, only better."

"Thanks, I needed that," Jon growled from where he was lounging on the couch, a mug of coffee in his hand. "Don't mind me, Sean; please go ahead and say what you think!"

Sean smirked at him. "Hey, your music is fantastic. You can't have both, can you? You're either a genius composer or a genius writer."

As if he didn't know that. "I'm going to meet her when we're in Geneva." How preposterous that sounded. Geneva. He was going to Geneva, Switzerland, and he was going to meet a stranger, a European, a writer. "I want those lyrics, and I'll give her whatever she wants for them."

"Including yourself?" Sal asked, entering the room with a plate of nachos Amparo had given him.

Jon grinned. "Who knows? If she's pretty enough…and not as old as my grandmother?"

"So you want a great writer who's also a winsome maiden, one willing to fall for you. Right, Jon. Talk about being conceited!" Sean snatched a handful of nachos before Sal could put them on the table where he couldn't reach them.

"I figure she's fallen for him already." Opening a beer, Sal dropped down beside Jon. "Why would she write lyrics for him otherwise? Though I have to admit, it's a rather novel approach to winning a rock star, and, it seems, a very successful one too. You're quite smitten, Jon!"

"With the words, yes. I don't know anything about the person except for her name, and that she's in Geneva." Jon fell silent, thinking of how he'd walked along the garden path to the beach and how it had felt as if he wasn't alone, as if an unseen figure had walked beside him, singing those words he loved so much to him.

"Well, we can always draw a mental picture of her for you," Sean offered. "I bet she's a middle-aged librarian."

"That's what I said!" Sal raised his bottle in a friendly salute. "But Jon is certain she's the most beautiful girl who ever walked the earth, someone he'll fall in love with the instant he sees her. He believes she's a maid created just for him from mist and love songs. God's answer to his sleepless prayers."

"Oh, will you shut up." Disgusted, Jon waved them away. "I'm thinking nothing of the kind. Besides, it's best not to mix job and private life, ever. Look what happened with Sally! I don't want to lose good people over a brief tussle in the sack. Really, guys…" He took another sip of his coffee to loosen the knot in his chest. "What would I do with a girl in Europe? It would be a senseless one-night stand. Hearts would be broken. And I'd lose the source of some great lyrics."

"I'll be interested to see how this all works out. Heck, I'm curious to see this wonder woman." Sean returned his attention to the music Jon had penned, his first attempts at a melody for one of the song lyrics. "'The Secret Garden,'" he read out loud. "How very fitting, with your wilderness in the backyard. I have to admit it's just a teeny bit creepy how well your music and her words fit together. You do know that this is top-hit material, don't you?"

Jon shrugged. Of course he did. By now he'd developed a good instinct for what would work and what wouldn't.

"It's not creepy, more like a miracle, and why shouldn't there be miracles?" he replied. "My career is sort of a miracle. Look at me: Just over a year and I have a frigging mansion in Malibu, a Porsche, and a platinum album. I'm about to release a new record, and in a few weeks we're off to tour Europe. I call that miraculous, especially when I know how long and hard others have to work for this. Or how they never make it. I have to be one of the luckiest men in the business."

"That you are, indeed." Serious now, Sal set down his beer. "I've never seen anyone thunder to the top the way you did. But, my friend, I can tell you the secret of your success, and it has nothing to do with miracles at all. It's focus, and discipline." He raised his hand when Jon opened his mouth to interject and went on. "I've never seen anyone with the focus you have, or with the same level of work ethic. Most of the time, with young, creative types, it's the manager's job to kick their butts into doing their job. But you, you're kicking *my* butt instead. It's no wonder you're racing to the top of the charts."

"Yeah, yeah. It's not as if this is different from any other job. I signed contracts. I do my best to fulfill them. I'd do the same if I was a doctor or a lawyer or…whatever. It's nothing special; it's just the way I am."

"But you see, that's exactly the point. You're that rare breed: a disciplined, creative person. There aren't many of those." Leaning across Jon, Sal snatched the bowl of salsa. "Fame has this tendency to warp people. It's not about the person; it's about the art they create."

Jon leaned back into the cushions of the couch and mulled that over for a while. "If it's not about the person, then why do I have to wear such tight pants and hideous shirts onstage?"

Sean laughed, pointing at Sal. "Good one. I want to hear the answer to that too."

"You know what I mean, dammit!" Grumbling, Sal heaved himself off the couch. "I'm going home. We've spent an entire day with those lyrics, and trying to conjure up a dream girl for Jon. I need to get back to real work. The tour is looming before us like the Rocky Mountains. See you later."

They heard the door fall shut, and a moment later, the motor of Sal's car.

"I want," Jon said, coming over to Sean, who was sitting on the piano bench, "I want this song to be very gentle, lyrical. I want it to sound like the most enticing invitation. A harp, a piano, only two or three violins. I want it to sound like a morning breeze over a calm sea. I have this vision of performing it live, and it's just you on the piano and me singing. Something very personal, very intimate."

Sean began playing the melody, one note after another; and when he'd gone completely through what Jon had written, he started again, this time adding the chords. Jon, standing behind him, hummed along with the tune.

He could see himself singing it on the stage: the lighting blue and dim, the band silent, and him, standing beside Sean's piano, quietly, gently, sending out that invitation. It would be such a heartbreaker, it would make the girls swoon.

AMPARO had left them potato salad and steaks for dinner, and while Jon lit the grill on the terrace, he listened to Sean inside, playing the piano.

It had been a mistake to hide in this house for so long and keep his friends away. The house loved company; it basked in the music and the laughter; it loved hearing voices and feeling the presence of human beings. Jon wondered how it would react to children, to a female voice, to a family. He could see himself playing with his children, could see them running down the path to the beach ahead of him; and by his side, her hand in his, a girl, a woman, his wife.

The image was so overwhelming that he had to close his eyes for a moment and take a deep breath.

There was time. He was young. He'd find someone someday, and she'd be the right one. Jenny's face flitted through his mind, and Sally's, and a few of the girls he'd dated since he'd moved to LA.

"I'm not lucky with girls," he said when Sean joined him. "It's always as if when I like them they don't like me, and when they like me I lose interest. It's as if I live in a time bubble of my own, and I can't get it synced to theirs." That was a bitter thought, and he fell silent.

Sean didn't respond right away but pretended to poke at the glowing coals instead. After a few minutes he said, "I think it gets harder the more famous you are. Who can you trust? Who will love you for yourself and not for who you are? It's bad for us, your band, but it must be even harder for you."

Jon put the meat on the grill. "My former girlfriend, Jenny. You know, the one who came to that show in New York last fall?"

Sean nodded.

"She begged me to take her back. Before I came out to LA, she threw me out. Said I was a hopeless dreamer, that I was wasting my life, and hers. She wanted to me to live a normal life, as she called it, at all costs. But when I returned to New York a star, she suddenly had a change of heart. She apologized. Said she'd misjudged me."

Grinning, Sean lit a cigarette and sat down on one of the new lawn chairs. It was getting dark. The sky was a wonderful turquoise color, and Jon knew that if he went down to the beach now, he'd see a sunset in a riot of purple and orange. A cool breeze stirred the fronds of the palm trees, whispering words of love.

The tip of Sean's cigarette gleamed like a phosphorescent insect. "Me, I want a family, kids. Not right now, but someday soon. I want the stability of a wife and a home. I'm not made for a vagabond life, and Jon, I think neither are you. We can do this for a while, the partying and the one-night stands. But not forever. Life would become empty, meaningless, and one day we'd wake up and discover that we'd become lonely old men with a lot of money and empty hearts. I don't want that."

"No." The steaks were sizzling nicely. "I don't want that either. And yes, I want a wife and kids too, someday."

"But how will you be able to tell, Jon?" Sean took one of the plates from the table and came over to the grill. "How do you know that it's true and not just someone who wants a piece of your fame?"

"I'll know." He had no idea where that certainty came from. "I've said it before, remember. I'll know. Nothing has changed. I still believe that."

Jon took a deep breath. "I can't explain it. I'm just utterly certain. It will feel different. It will feel like coming home, like reaching a peaceful harbor, a distant shore where I can rest and be safe." He handed Sean the ketchup bottle. "I'll just know."

Chapter Forty-five

THEY ARRIVED IN Geneva just in time for lunch after a relatively short flight from Paris.

Jon, standing at the window of his hotel room, looked out at the lake and the snow-capped mountains in the distance. A fountain not too far from the shore was producing a huge plume that threw rainbows over the water like a veil of a million colors.

They'd flown in from the other side of the lake, gliding across the huge stretch of azure blue, the city growing before them. How different it was from New York or LA, how ancient and civilized in comparison. The bus had taken them along broad roads with massive stone houses, their façades more elaborate than even the older buildings in New York; and along the lakeshore, they seemed like sentinels that had stood here for centuries.

He was nervous.

The show in Berlin had gone well. He'd been a star in Germany. The enthusiasm had first surprised and then scared him; he'd wondered how people in Europe even knew about his music until Sal, rolling his eyes, had asked him if he really thought Europe was still stuck in the Middle Ages? They too had TVs, radios, and record players. And yes, he was also a centerfold in the German girls' magazines.

Brussels, he'd thought it was the most boring town until they went for dinner at a restaurant on a small, cobbled street behind the old city hall, where they'd sat at a table outside, right on the sidewalk, and had eaten the best steak and fries he'd ever tasted. They'd been served very thin pancakes for dessert, which had been doused in orange brandy and lit right beside their table. Later, walking along a busy street back to the hotel, Tom had made him buy a big box of chocolate to take home for his mother.

"Chocolates from Belgium," he'd lectured him, "are the best in the world. Don't let anyone fool you. Even the Swiss know it."

So now he was in Switzerland, and it seemed like the most peaceful place he'd ever seen. People were strolling on the promenade that ran along the lakefront; there were sailboats on the water. A little farther down he could make out a marina with some impressive yachts. It was warm, but neither as humid, nor as hot, as it got in New York in the summer. In fact, it was a perfect day for a walk along the water's edge, for coffee on the hotel terrace, or for sitting on one of the benches under the tall trees, eyes closed and the sun shining through the leaves warming his face.

He wanted to meet her alone. Sal had tried talking him out of it, but he insisted: Jon wanted an artist-to-artist meeting before they began talking about money and contracts. He wanted to make sure that he'd want to work with that woman.

It was almost time.

Once again he checked his appearance in the mirror: groomed and shaved, in a linen shirt and jeans, he didn't look like a rock star at all. He was himself, Jon Stone, not the star.

There was a knock on the door. Sal stood outside, nervously glancing at his watch. "Better you go down now," he said. "I want you to be there before she arrives so you have the advantage of picking the spot. Are you ready?"

"I am." Strangely, seeing Sal so fidgety, Jon calmed down. He breathed slowly, evenly, and squared his shoulders. "Come on, let's go." Patting Sal's shoulder, he added, "What can possibly go wrong. Either we can work something out, or we can't and move on."

Sal pushed the elevator button. "I don't know. You seem quite taken with her lyrics. I don't think it will be that easy. If I'm guessing correctly, we'll have to part with a lot of money if you decide to sign her."

"It'll be worth it." Jon checked his image in the elevator mirror again. "I'll pay her out of my own pocket if I have to."

He picked a couch at the rear of the lobby where he could watch the entrance but wouldn't be seen right away and ordered coffee from the waiter.

Sal was hovering. "How will you know her?" he asked, glancing at his watch. "How in the world will you know it's her?"

272

"She'll know me." There was a tiny bar of chocolate next to his cup, wrapped in paper with the Swiss flag on it. Jon opened it and popped it into his mouth. "You know, Tom was wrong. This tastes far better than the Belgian stuff. I need to get some of these for my mother!"

Exasperated, Sal threw up his hands and walked away.

Jon, alone with his coffee, settled back to wait.

A couple entered the lobby, followed by a bellboy with their luggage. The woman wore a smartly tailored suit and small, matching hat, a pair of kid gloves in her hand. Jon stared. He'd never seen anything like that before. She looked so elegant, so stylish that his heart skipped for a moment, and he had to overcome the urge to run and change into a suit.

Only, he realized, he hadn't brought a suit. Not a single one, and now he wondered if that had been a mistake.

Maybe she wouldn't even give him a second glance, the way he was dressed: American, informal.

What if she was like that, a coolly elegant European woman who for some reason had taken a fancy to American music, and to him? What if, after seeing him in real life, she'd turn away in disappointment, and all those wonderful songs would never be written?

Jon looked around, trying to find Sal, but he was nowhere to be seen. The lobby was almost empty; there was just that elegant couple standing at the desk checking in and a small group of businessmen sitting near the elevators talking about some documents they'd spread out on the table between them. A maid in a black dress rushed by, an empty tray in her hands, and vanished through a doorway behind him.

Light was streaming in through the open entrance doorway, bright-yellow sunlight that pooled on the red carpet and the shiny hardwood floor. It seemed almost liquid.

There was a movement in that light, a stirring as if it was a portal into a different dimension. A shape appeared, a girl. She took two steps into the lobby and gazed around, then looked straight at him. Her chin came up in a tiny movement.

Jon, jumping up, watched her walk toward him, watched how

she left that puddle of light and turned from a fairy tale vision into a real live person, and his heart beat so hard against his ribs that each pulse felt like a stab. His arms wanted to open and reach out for her. The impulse was so strong that he had to push his hands into his pockets, and that was how he stood there, waiting.

"I'M Naomi," she said.